GOOD WOMEN

by the same author

SEVERAL DECEPTIONS
LONDON BRIDGES
ASTRAEA
THE PRETENDER
THE EMPRESS OF THE LAST DAYS

GOOD WOMEN

Jane Stevenson

JONATHAN CAPE
LONDON

Published by Jonathan Cape 2005

2 4 6 8 10 9 7 5 3 1

Copyright © Jane Stevenson 2005

Jane Stevenson has asserted her right under the Copyright,
Designs and Patents Act 1988 to be identified as the author of this work

First published in Great Britain in 2005 by
Jonathan Cape
Random House, 20 Vauxhall Bridge Road,
London SW1V 2SA

Random House Australia (Pty) Limited
20 Alfred Street, Milsons Point, Sydney,
New South Wales 2061, Australia

Random House New Zealand Limited
18 Poland Road, Glenfield,
Auckland 10, New Zealand

Random House (Pty) Limited
Endulini, 5A Jubilee Road, Parktown, 2193, South Africa

The Random House Group Limited Reg. No. 954009
www.randomhouse.co.uk

A CIP catalogue record for this book is available from the British Library

ISBN 0-224-07351-6

Papers used by Random House are natural, recyclable products made from
wood grown in sustainable forests. The manufacturing processes conform
to the environmental regulations of the country of origin

Typeset in Dante MT by Palimpsest Book Production Limited,
Polmont, Stirlingshire

Printed and bound in Great Britain by
William Clowes Ltd, Beccles, Suffolk

For Pat, without whom it could not have
been started, and Alison and Allan, without whom it
could not have been finished

Contents

Light My Fire

I

The really ironic thing is, I hadn't been thinking about sex at all. I'd been thinking it would've been the perfect day to murder your wife, and I'd probably have got into less trouble if I had. You can get away with murder, if you keep your head, but stonking great errors of judgement don't get forgiven, ever.

When I got on the road that morning, I'd made the unwelcome discovery that every single policeman in Aberdeenshire was out clutching a hand-held speed camera. The place was crawling with them; there were pulled-over cars in every lay-by. You could only hope they'd rung round the criminal element and told them to take a day at the seaside. Thank God I'd decided to go down by train, I thought to myself; if the traffic on the Edinburgh road was observing the speed limit for the first time in human history, it must be adding forty minutes to the run, if not more. I'd had a site meeting in the morning, for which I had been twenty minutes late, and due to further buggering about from the polis, I caught my train by the skin of my teeth. I just chucked myself on as the doors were shutting, and fell into the first seat I saw.

But once I'd caught my breath a bit, I started to notice the woman sitting opposite. Her legs were crossed, and she was wearing brown velvet trousers, very tight round the thighs and hips, so that the straining seam emphasised that emphatic feminine curve from knee to waist. We were sitting across from each other in the 'disabled' space with no table sticking out between us, so it was a view well worth looking at if you're a man that likes hips, which I do, and I admired it for some time before my eye drifted upwards. She was wearing a suede jacket, expensive; and a linen shirt under it, just transparent enough to show the bra beneath, an elegant lacy affair of impressive capacity. Her hands were relaxed, resting loosely on her thighs, small and plumpish with short fingers; the left one was wearing a wedding ring, and a hefty diamond. Finally I flicked a glance up at her face. She was looking straight back at me, so I dropped my eyes at once. Not quite a beauty, but very attractive. She had dark eyes, wide set, under straightish, heavy brows, in a broad, fair-skinned face. Chin beginning to go a bit, she wasn't a girl, but a very confident fortyish and looking good on it, a bit younger than me, but not much. She had a greedy little red mouth, unsmiling; she put just the tip of her tongue out as I looked at it, and licked her lips deliberately.

So much has happened since then that it's hard to be sure I'm remembering exactly what I felt at that first meeting, but the absolutely key thing which stuck with me was the intensely feminine quality of her presence. She was the kind of woman who made herself into a challenge simply by existing in the same space. I risked another look up, and felt an electric shock as our gazes clashed. She was the first to look away, but it was for a long, ostentatious look-up-and-down; and as her eyes travelled slowly over my body, I have to say, I knew perfectly well I was starting to give her something to look at. I could see that the reaction was mutual; her nipples had popped up, and she was nibbling her lower lip. She had unusually small teeth, square and very white, they looked sharp.

Some time went by. The train pulled into Stonehaven, then out again. I could feel her looking at me, trying to provoke me, but I was determined not to get drawn into her wee game. I had plenty to think about, so I stared out of the window for fifteen minutes working out what I was going to say to my client; then something drew my attention back to her, willy-nilly. It was hard to think what it was that had caught me, at first, and then I realised that she was breathing a little more heavily – with a chest like that, of course, it was hard to overlook. She was also getting a tiny bit flushed, eyes and lips soft and shiny. The small, short-fingered hand resting on her leg tensed, and then suddenly the penny dropped, and I realised what she was doing. If you were observing really closely, you could see the slight rhythmic play of her thigh muscles, clenching, holding for a moment, releasing. I had a girlfriend once who confided to me that if she was on a train and she was wearing really right trousers, she could bring herself off like that, just by crossing her legs tightly and sitting forward a bit, due to the vibration. Diddly-dee, diddly-dum, diddly-dee, diddly dum . . . Bitch. Cow. Whore. I thought. She was doing it on purpose; she'd damn well made sure that I'd noticed, and she knew I couldn't do likewise without getting myself arrested. I could've killed her. She was starting to rock fractionally in her seat, her spine tense; she wasn't far off . . . I couldn't make myself move, or speak; I just stared at her as if I'd been hypnotised, knowing I was going scarlet, waiting for it to be over. She was staring through me blankly, seeing nothing at all. The wet red lips parted, she gave a little sigh. The end, and nobody else had noticed a thing.

There was an elderly couple sitting across from us: she was reading *Bella*, and he was reading the *Angling Times* and they were sharing a bag of smoky-bacon crisps. Not a rustle or a twitch suggested that they were aware of the drama going on across the aisle, but I could sense the animal heat coming off her in waves. I grabbed my raincoat to hold in front of me, and fled to the loo to get myself decent. As I'd pretty well expected, I came just about the moment I'd unzipped, though I stopped long enough to have a pee, just to be on the safe side.

I washed my hands, and went back to my seat, absolutely furious with her.

'Well, I think that's us introduced, don't you?' I said icily. 'I'm David Laurence.'

She smiled, slow and secret. 'I know.' We must have met; though for the life of me, I couldn't remember where, and I wasn't going to give her the satisfaction of asking. Fortunately, she couldn't resist telling me. 'My husband went to one of your maintenance workshops. He was dead impressed, and he showed me your brochure. My name's Freda Constantine.'

I couldn't recall the husband, not that it mattered. I'm an architect, part of a partnership in Inverurie, and several times a year I run weekend surgeries on how to keep an old house in good nick. Our webdesigner had talked us into putting out a snazzy brochure with pictures; there was a very good one of me on a roofing ladder in jeans and a tattersall shirt peering at a welded steel bracing on an old chimney stack. I'd always assumed it had been a total waste of money and effort, since we were a highly competent outfit and custom basically came by word of mouth, but it had just paid off in the most unexpected way. 'What were you thinking of doing in Edinburgh?' I asked her.

'Haircut at Charlie Miller's.'

I took my mobile out of my pocket, and tossed it into her lap. 'Cancel it.'

'Why?'

'Because I say so. I've got a meeting with a client. Only, just as soon as you're finished with the phone, I've been unavoidably detained. Railtrack's screwed up again, and I'm stuck in Montrose, so sorry, can we reschedule?'

'What makes you think I'm the sort of girl who obeys orders, David?'

'I don't. You look like my idea of an awkward bitch, to be frank. But I think you'll go along, because you owe me, and you want to see what's going to happen next.'

She picked up the phone and dialled the hairdresser's, and I knew I'd won. In some corner of my mind, I was crossing my fingers I could still rise to the occasion, but she moved me so strongly, it was worth risking it. In the event, I needn't have worried.

Look, you don't need the next bit. We got off the train and crossed the road to the Old Waverley Hotel, which is just the other side of Princes Street; passed through a blur of tartan and silk flowers, and went straight up to an absolutely null little room which I barely saw. I was still livid with her for what she'd put me through and determined to make her pay, and she was just as wonderful as I'd expected: avid and greedy, a perfectionist of pleasure. But she was more than that. I'd never had sex like it. For me, she was the inescapable woman, the goddess, the other half of my whole self as a man. It was enough to make you religious.

'You're very good,' she observed quite coldly, somewhere round four o'clock. I was flat on my back, absolutely drained, and she was sitting on top of me, her dark brown hair tumbling down round her shoulders. Her skin was very white, with just a dusting of freckles on the chest and upper arms like the chocolate on cappuccino, and she had the most wonderful thighs. Muscled like a horsewoman; you could feel the grip in them, but softly padded, sleek and smooth. Above the rounded hips, the waist nicked in sharply, then the ribcage came out again like a bolero. A figure like an Indian goddess. She was absolutely right to stay pale, I thought, a tan would've looked common on her, she'd just've looked as if there was too much top and bottom, though in her own way, she was perfect. 'You're better than Malc,' she went on. 'Better than anyone I've had, if I'm going to be honest.'

'You're fabulous.' I meant it, too. There was a sort of whole body communion, an instant rapport, which I still felt dazed by. She felt like the woman I was meant to have. 'I want more, I'm warning you. Lots and lots.' I shifted slightly, feeling her body sway as she adjusted automatically. 'But tell me. Do you make a habit of picking up total strangers?'

'I knew who you were,' she pointed out. 'I know people who know you.'

'Such as?' She was busily answering the wrong question, sure mark of a practised deceiver, but I was intrigued.

'Sheena Johnstone.'

Ah. Yes. I remembered her well. 'And what did she say about me?'

'Said you were a grade A, ocean-going shit, of course. What d'you expect?'

'On which basis you picked me up?'

She shrugged, an impressive manoeuvre in the circumstances which caused her breasts to lift and shift mysteriously. 'That wasn't all she said.'

She climbed off me then, and padded to the loo, leaving me thoughtful. I'd had a bit of fun on the side with the winsome Sheena a year or so back, which had started very well and ended in tears after she started getting the idea that I owed her something. It looked as if Foxy Freda had deduced that I would do nicely for her own purposes, which seemed on the whole like good news. I heard the flush, then she reappeared, standing unselfconsciously naked in the doorway with her hip thrust out and her arms folded, like a cross between Dürer's Eve and Andy Capp's Flo, and looked at me sombrely.

'It's so piss-awful boring in Newburgh, you start thinking your brain'll just rot one day and trickle out of your ears,' she said suddenly. 'We've got a very good lifestyle, of course. It's a lovely house.'

'Which one is it?' I was interested.

'Calicut Lodge, on Main Street.'

'Oh, I know.' Newburgh runs to retired shipmasters' houses, some of them very handsome, and it's dead handy for Cruden Bay where the pipelines come in, so naturally it's been taken over by the higher echelons of BP and Shell. I'd done a number on Shanghai House, a few doors down from Freda's place, back in the Nineties, so I knew the town well. It seemed a fair deduction that she was an oil wife. I'd seen something of the breed, and I knew from experience that her choice of hobbies was not absolutely unknown as a response to life in the corporate meatgrinder.

'We travel a lot. And when Malc's home, we do a lot of entertaining.'

'And when he's not, you make your own entertainment?' She couldn't resist a sly wee smirk, for all that she was preoccupied by her sense of grievance. 'I take it he's away?'

'He's in Nigeria. He's with Shell-Exxon,' she explained, confirming my initial leap to conclusions. 'They told me not to come along this time. Something sensitive's going down, and the advisers are worried about kidnapping or something. They never really tell you. I hate Nigeria anyway. They don't let you go anywhere.'

Suddenly a picture of Malcolm Constantine popped into my head. Tall, lean, deeply tanned, with a Tom Cruise smile which had to represent a fortune in orthodontics – no Briton ever had a mouth like that as nature's gift. But it'd been a total waste of money, because the eyes were still saying, 'Do you approve of me yet?' No wonder I'd forgotten him. The thing is, once you've had your teeth capped, you can't actually bite anything all that hard. I could see wee Freda taking dainty lumps out of him with those sharp little fangs till he fell over and bled to death. More fool him for letting her, and more fool him, too, for leaving her at home to get into mischief. She wasn't a woman to take your eyes off. But if I hadn't known she was going home to an empty house, I don't know how I'd've let her go that day.

Fast-forward. I thought about Freda nearly all the time, waking and sleeping. I'd never really been jealous before, at least not on this scale, but now I lay awake in the small hours, wondering if she ever played her game with anyone else. There were nights when for two pins, I'd've got out of bed and driven the thirty-odd miles to Newburgh just to see if she was there. She kept her answering machine on all the time, so I couldn't check on her that way, and the one thing I knew about her for sure was that she was a woman you couldn't trust if you couldn't see her. I was always on tenterhooks: she really wanted the sex, she liked the extra edge which came out of the risk involved, and the passion; but fundamentally, she was seriously pissed off that I'd fallen in love with her. That hadn't been part of her game-plan at all, so there was always that fear in the back of my mind that she'd drop me and find herself someone easier to manage. It all made for Olympic-standard rumpy-pumpy, but it was driving me insane.

Unsurprisingly, it wasn't long before my wife was certain I was seeing someone. She's no kind of a fool, and I must have been behaving as if I was absolutely demented. Unfortunately, after one of Freda the Bitch's magical mystery tours, it was hard to summon up much interest in Lilias. There were tearful scenes and tantrums, but I found I was caring less and less; I couldn't even lie with conviction after a while. My attention was somewhere else, and there was nothing I could do about it.

In the end, Lil threw me out, and I can't say that I blame her. Scots law being what it is, I fully expected to be taken to the cleaner's, so I simply went and lived in the office in the interim – the architectural partnership of which I am a third works out of a respectable Georgian house in the market square in Inverurie, so there were modest washing and cooking facilities on the premises: all I had to do was move a futon into the back attic among the filing cabinets of obsolete drawings, and there I was, cushy enough to be going on with, physically speaking. Just me and my guilt.

I saw Freda as often as I could. I never set foot in Newburgh – the place is full of oil execs and their bored and sharp-eyed wives, so it was far too risky. We met in Edinburgh sometimes, and there's a flat my brother owns in Stonehaven which I could get the use of once in a while, but it all took a bit of negotiation. When Freda left a message on my work email, pretending to be a client, and saying she wanted to meet urgently, there was nothing for it but to tell her to go to Tarlair, the last resort, in more senses than one.

Angry and anxious as I was, I found Tarlair, as always, inescapably touching. A disused Thirties swimming pool along the coast just west of Macduff; a great place for assignations. I turned right at the Inshore Fisheries, and drove out of the end of Macduff down a narrow winding road between dramatic rock-formations, black pillars of striated stone stacked up like plates, jagged pyramids, and even, at one point, a natural archway framing the sea. I pulled up in the scruffy little carpark, and was not wholly surprised to find someone else already there, a brittle-looking, thin-lipped blonde chainsmoking in a BMW with vanity plates. A fisherman's wife, at a guess, from one of those introverted wee villages on the north coast where the trawler-owners make huge money and the wifies spend it as fast as they can. Or did; they must be something of an endangered species now that the EEC's pulled the plug on Scottish fishing, but last year, their problems were of quite another order. Her eyes flicked over me without interest. I wasn't her man.

The swimming pool itself was a bit further along, in a natural amphitheatre carved into the cliff by some ancient cataclysm.

There was a boxy Modernist white concrete villa which had presumably once held a café and facilities, and the pools were so formally arranged that they extended in front of it precisely like an Italian terraced garden; a shallow pool in front of the house, a concrete retaining wall, a deep pool, another wall, and then the open sea; three textures of water and a stupendous view framed by cliffs. With just a couple of concrete obelisks where the cypresses should have been, the effect would have been complete. There were broad, shallow shelves curving out from the house and embracing the pools, conjuring up visions of pretty shingled girls in sagging stockinette bathing costumes, vanilla ice-cream and interwar optimism – the whole place ought to have been sparkling white and clean, or to be absolutely precise, hygienic.

But it was out of its time, nobody in the Noughties would even consider bathing in unheated seawater. The concrete was cracking and greying, the paddling pool an uneasy slough of kelp stems and decaying leaves; it was as sad as Cinderella. I loved the place, and wished it well; even with Freda on my mind, I could not but canvass for the umpteenth time whom I might persuade to rescue it.

As it was, in its neglect and isolation, it had its uses. I was mooching around the theatrical semicircle of shelves which girdled the pools when I saw Freda hurrying towards me with her dark hair lifting and wafting round her face. She looked a little preoccupied, but that wasn't unusual; she wasn't free with her smiles, and in any case, she took her pleasure seriously. I was severely pissed off with her, but as always, my heart started beating faster the moment she came into view. She was manifestly dressed for adultery, in a blouse which unbuttoned down the front; with, at a good guess, a front-opening bra underneath. Flippy skirt blowing round her lovely bare legs, pink kitten-heeled slingbacks. If she was mine, I thought, and I saw her leaving the house dressed like that, she'd be cruising for a bruising, as they say in Glasgow.

'I hope it's urgent', I said as she came up to me, looking as if she had something on her mind. 'I ought to be in Huntly.'

'It's urgent.' Without another word, Freda set off across the short grass, and I followed her. If you climbed out of the scoop in the cliffs where the swimming pool was, scrambled up the steep bit and went along the clifftop path for a hundred yards or so, there were various nooks and dells furred with short, seaside grass within reach of the pathway where you could be fairly sure of privacy. Since there was a right of way along the top, there was always a risk of free-range dogs and/or children, of course, but Freda seemed rather to enjoy it. She had an exhibitionist streak, as I'd known since day one.

We slid down into a dip we'd used before, well concealed from the cliff path by an overhanging granite outcrop. It was a nice wee spot, a dry oval bowl carpeted with grass and wiry little tufts of thrift and thyme. A fringe of harebells nodded against the horizon, and the sea carried away the sound of voices. We sat down, and then Freda put an arm round my neck and pressed me onto my back.

I was wondering, of course, what she had on her mind, but if she wanted to do things that way round, I was agreeable; I pushed my various worries out of my awareness, and let the mood of the moment take over. Snogging in the open with most of my clothes on always tickled me, the daft, teenage, retro feel of it, like being fifteen again. I got the impression that she was dead worried about something, but there was an undercurrent of excitement; once I got my hand up her skirt, she had an orgasm almost immediately. I had a sudden, dreadful thought: dear Christ, could she be pregnant? – which had the effect on my libido of a sudden bucket of cold water. But no, I thought, collecting my scattered wits, it couldn't be that. Her reactions were all wrong, and anyway, she'd had the curse just about a week ago, there'd been a chance of meeting and she'd passed it up because she was feeling like death. I didn't think she'd been lying. So, whatever it was, it could wait, while I returned my concentration to the task in, as it were, hand.

I always tried to keep actual sex to a minimum in these al fresco encounters. I hated the feeling of exposure; I wanted her on top, and not for too damned long either. Something about the thought of someone watching my naked bum bobbing up and down absolutely froze me. Fortunately, Freda likes fingers just so long as that's not all she gets, so it all worked out. I came; she rolled off me, and I made myself decent as rapidly as possible. I propped myself up on one elbow, and looked at her where she lay sprawled in the sun with her eyes shut, her dark hair tangled in the grass, round white breasts spilling magnificently out of her blouse. I was aware of a dry, warm herby tang in the air, a corrective to the primeval odour of hot woman and the too-sweet perfume which Freda favoured; there was a tuft of thyme under my hand, so I picked it and rubbed it between my fingers to intensify the smell. Then, on a sudden impulse, I flipped her skirt up and parted her knees so that I could look at the source of all the trouble. She was as shameless as a cat, and spraddled obligingly. I crumbled the flowers and scattered the tiny pink petals on the black, moist hair where they clung like confetti. I was vaguely imagining that she'd find the odd flower in her knickers later on, and think of me.

'What are you doing?' she asked, not bothering to sit up.

'Footering about. It's rosemary that's for remembrance – I don't know what thyme's for.'

'A reminder we haven't got all day,' she said tartly. She got to her feet, brushing herself off, did up some buttons, and went and tossed the condom over the cliff into the sea: she was neat about things like that. A dislike of leaving evidence, I suspected.

She came back and sat down sideways like the Little Mermaid, leaning on her arm, and looking down at me seriously.

'I wish I knew how you really felt about me,' she said.

'I love you to pieces, darling,' I replied automatically, but privately, I was struck by her shrewdness. I wished I knew how I felt about her, in fact; the only thing I wanted to know even more was how she felt about me.

'What would you do if I said it was over?' she asked. Her eyes never left my face.

'Christ.' I looked back at her, stricken, realising that I was completely unable to imagine life without her. I'd rather kill her than lose her. I'd rather die. 'What's going on?'

'They're sending Malc to Caracas. We're through with Scotland.'

'I see.' I was filled with a sort of despair, or was it anger? Whatever it was, it was rising in my throat, suffocating me. I wasn't sure what she was telling me. 'Freda, you're not going. I won't let you.'

'You can't stop me.'

'Oh, can't I?' I came up off the ground and grabbed her, pinning her down with my full weight. I didn't know myself what I meant to do. Her shoulders felt small and brittle under my hands.

'David!'

I'd really frightened her. Her eyes were quite black, the pupils huge, and I could feel her heart hammering.

'I'm sorry,' I said, letting go of her and starting to weep. 'I love you. I didn't mean to hurt you. Don't go. Divorce him. We belong together.'

'I don't know', she said, rubbing her neck and shoulder. 'How can I trust you? I'm going to have the most God-awful bruises.'

'Oh, Freda. There's more to life than lifestyle. You were bored out of your brain when you picked me up. Okay, you won't be as well off. But you're not bored, give me that.'

'No,' she conceded.

'Marry me, Freda.'

'I might.'

She slipped her knickers back on then, and I let her go, watching her walking away till she disappeared round a bend in the path. Twenty minutes ago, she'd been rutting like a weasel, and now she was just a pretty woman in the sun, neat and sweet. There was something appalling in the way nothing actually showed. You could meet any woman, any time, and under her dress, she'd be all hot and liquid, only you'd never know it. I leaned my back against the rock, and stood watching the sea for five minutes, arranging the facts in my mind like a row of bricks. I'd thrown away my marriage, my kids. Freda was absolutely necessary to me. She'd said she might marry me. The whole thing was a disaster. Except, except . . . just for those moments when I was inside her, life and the universe seemed to swing on that one pivot, and that never changed.

Once I was sure she was well on her way, I climbed up onto the cliff path, and walked back to the car. The Beemer had gone. When I was about halfway down the track, I passed the blonde's fancy-man, a smug-looking sod in a Vectra. You'll be looking a bloody sight less pleased when you get to Tarlair, I thought to myself. Serve you right for keeping her hanging around.

Meanwhile, of course, my divorce was rumbling through; I was deeply unhappy and guilty about it, but I wasn't contesting, of course. The house was Lil's anyway, morally speaking, her parents had gifted it to us, and of course she had custody of the kids. I had to contribute to maintenance, though her parents helped out with school fees. Losing Helen and Effie was a wrench; I was astonished how badly I felt about it. It had been an old-fashioned marriage where I earned the money and Lil stayed at home messing about with the garden and a couple of pampered nags, so the girls were basically Lil's project. I didn't see all that much of them, but all the same I knew I was going to miss them like hell. They were leggy and cheeky and pretty, and knew how to get round me; I was proud of them, and I'd found I was enjoying seeing them getting more confident, growing up. But there was nothing to be done; I'd blown it with Lilias, so I'd lost them.

I don't know how much the girls actually understood about what was going on – they did a bit of shouting and throwing things, but as far as I could see, they were more worried about keeping the ponies than anything else. I reckoned that, given time, the wounds would heal, and I'd see them again. Practically everyone's got a divorce behind them these days, it's not as if they'd be the only ones at St Margaret's with trouble at home. I felt pretty much of a shit when I thought about them, and I was desperately sorry to be losing them, but I wasn't all that worried about their future. There were grandparents, after all, and Lil's not any kind of helpless little princess. She's got plenty of gumption in her own way. She'd been running a mail-order hand-baked fruitcakes business for about five years at that point, and it was starting to do surprisingly well; she more or less covered the ponies' costs just treating it as a semi-hobby. She could build on that. She'd get on, and she'd make a good job of the girls, and she'd marry again, she's a heck of a good-looking woman.

At least there weren't any kids on the other side. I was so obsessed with Freda I'd've carried on regardless even if she'd been a mother of ten, but the Fredas of this world, thank God, are strictly ornamental, like those strange toys you're not supposed to give to children. A perfumed garden, not a fertile field. She'd never wanted kids, she told me, to my unspeakable relief. I've got a couple of pals who've settled into this grotesque pattern of finding someone new around the time that the current wife's just about got Number Two potty trained, and starting all over again. What a carry-on. There must be some kind of death wish involved – fifteen or twenty years of Pampers and sleepless nights, it's a thought to freeze the blood. Anyway, Freda's breasts were mine. I found the mere notion of them being used to feed an infant weirdly unpleasant.

Scottish law is quite good when it comes to swings and round-abouts: on the one hand, Lil and the girls did well out of me, which they deserved to, but Freda also did surprisingly well out of Malcolm, all things considered. And that, in short, is how Freda Constantine, née Hatchin, übercow and bitch from hell, became my lawful wedded wife, me being of sound mind and under no duress.

Once the dust had settled, financially speaking, I found that we had just about enough to make an offer on Kilmollich House. It was in the middle of nowhere, miles too far from Inverurie, let alone Aberdeen, and in the most terrible nick. But on the other hand, it had what estate agents call potential to no uncertain extent. It was a tower-house built in about 1580, standing in three or four acres of woodland and granite outcrop, and I could see just what to do with it. . . How to describe it? It was not quite a castle, though it was heading that way: a tall, high, intensely Scottish stone house with small, deepset windows, crowstep gables and a couple of wee conical turrets on the corners of the west face, beautifully positioned in a dell above a stream with a drift of silver birches around it. As picturesque as a whisky advertisement, and highly desirable in its peculiar way. I'd been deeply relieved when I heard about it on the grapevine. While I had no doubts that Freda had got bored with Malcolm, she hadn't got bored with his money, and she was a high-maintenance sort of girl. I had no illu-sions: in her ideal world, she'd have kept me as her bit on the side

indefinitely. If I'd moved her into a miserable wee farmhouse somewhere up the Gairie, there'd have been hell to pay. No amount of
good sex would've made up for it.

Of course, the downside was that Kilmollich was practically on
the point of collapse, or we wouldn't have been able to afford it.
The roof was dropping to bits, there was no central heating and,
as I had discovered, no septic tank – the household's ordure just
seeped into the ground, as it had done since the place was built.
It was when I got this last detail pieced together out of the Land
Registers and so forth that I knew I'd got the vendors on toast;
it's not everyone who thinks to worry about shite, but that's the
advantage of a professional training. The vendors had been, till
recently, farmers, in a somewhat Old Macdonaldish fashion by all
accounts, but they were well past it, fed up with living in a collection of weeny rooms up winding stairs, and anxious to retire to
somewhere more manageable. I pointed out to them that the place
was not, as it stood, legally habitable, and they had a spirited try
at bluffing, but not for long. They'd lied to the estate agent, of
course, and the letters after my name put the wind right up them.
They knew I knew all the right people, and that if I set the Public
Health onto them, they'd never get it shifted.

In a whole lot of ways, punning aside, it was as crappy a house
as the early seventeenth century has left us. Sizing it up, I reckoned it had originally been built on quite a modest scale as little
more than a defensible farmhouse, but in the second generation,
around 1600, there'd been a burst of prosperity, and a major refit.
The second lot had taken the kitchen out of the basement, where
there were still the remains of a mighty vaulted fireplace, and
resited it on the ground floor at the opposite end of the building,
with a vast new chimney stack which did wonders for the general
picturesqueness. Looking at the whole set-up professionally, I did
wonder if the unoptimistic attitude of the first generation had
been entirely misplaced. The new stack was on the side which got
the worst of the weather: you could tell quite easily, even in the
middle of the summer, because most of the harling had been
scoured off it over the centuries, exposing the bare grey stone
underneath. Four hundred years of Aberdeenshire winters had, I

strongly suspected, taken most of the strength out of the mortar. It might need pinning, and in an ideal world, the whole thing would be re-harled, preferably with crushed shell and quicklime, an unspeakably vile and expensive job, especially if you need to erect a fifty-foot scaffold to do it off, but, at the very least, it'd have to be repointed with lime mortar just as soon as I could find the money. We could pretend we had a septic tank for a while, and the roof would last another year, but lime was the top of the 'To Do' list, whatever Freda might think. I consoled myself, meanwhile, with the thought that anything that's been up for four hundred years tends to stay up out of sheer force of habit. The first hundred years are the worst, with any building.

One thing hugely in Kilmollich's favour was that it didn't really have a garden, just a bit of lawn round the house and a couple of rhododendrons. It's common for old Scottish houses to have a walled garden located purely pragmatically in order to catch every available photon of solar energy, regardless of the convenience of the laird and his lady wife, and, not unusually, Kilmollich's was the best part of a mile away. Another stroke of luck: due to the ridge of granite which protected all but the north-eastern corner of the house from the prevailing wind, the farm-buildings complex had similarly not been built absolutely on top of the house; they were well on the other side of a *cordon sanitaire* of woodland. The garden had long since become a separate property, a weird-looking place with a hideous modern breezeblock house dropped into a rectangular enclosure formed by ten-foot-high, sixteenth-century stone walls. If I knew who the planning officer was who'd let the builders get away with it, I would personally have taken out a contract on him, but the really important thing was, it was not my problem. The woodland wanted a bit of work, but it looked all right; it could wait till I got round to it. The farm buildings had been sold to a property developer and were even then in the process of becoming a cluster of foul little homes, but they had a separate access road, thank God, and because Kilmollich was in a dip in the hills, one couldn't even hear the work going on.

II

'It's absolutely fabulous', she said, when I took her to see it. 'It's practically a castle.'

'Hang on to that thought, darling. You haven't seen inside. You're going to need a lot of bottle.'

'I've got a lot of bottle,' she said at once.

'Good. Because unfortunately we don't have a team of Shell lackeys in boiler-suits to sort it all out for us. We're going to have to do it ourselves, a bit at a time, as and when we can afford it.'

I opened the door. The vendors had already moved out; they'd gone off to a hideous bungalow in Rhynie with double glazing and central heating, which represented their notion of absolute domestic felicity. The neighbouring hayseeds had been happy to buy the fields, but they hadn't wanted Kilmollich or the steadings, so Old Macdonald and his missus had put them on the market separately. According to trade gossip, the house'd netted them plenty of lookers, but no takers: most of the old-buildings-fanciers of Aberdeenshire and the North-East had been in for a good look round, but the consensus was, not with a bargepole: too far from anywhere, needs too much work. Which explains why the vendors had been glad enough to close with my very low offer in the end, even without the element of blackmail.

I had told Freda that the place had been owned by elderly and by all accounts, unsuccessful farmers, but clearly this statement had not held any overtones for her. Anyone more experienced would have known what to expect, but from the look of absolute horror which came over her face when I turned the light on, she hadn't understood what I meant.

'Oh, my godfathers.' One thing I'd learned about Freda, it was when she didn't quite swear that she was serious.

'EEC subsidy carpets,' I explained.

'What?'

'Farmers round here must've got this massive dose of Euro-money in the mid-seventies, because a lot of them redecorated round then. I've seen this squirly green Wilton all over Banff and Buchan, it must've been on special. The silver wallpaper with the special effects is a bit original, I have to say.'

As I led her from room to room, I had to admit it was almost unbelievable what they'd managed in the way of misplaced zeal. It was a sort of design-history lesson in the absolute worst that the Sixties and Seventies had achieved between them; after that, fortunately, they must've run out of money or energy, or both. Freda looked stunned. The master bedroom was papered in beige with geometric purple and orange flowers – I vividly remembered Mrs Old Macdonald showing me it on my first visit.

'. . . Now, I've aa-wyse thocht this een's awfie cheery. It's a wee bittie modron, but we like the modron style . . .' Another bedroom had a paper with Bridget-Rileyish psychedelic wave patterns in shades of green; while the drawing-room looked as if someone had spent a long dark winter throwing fried eggs at the wall. It was at the point when we got around to the one and only bath-room with its bubbling, mildewed walls and dark avocado suite that she finally cracked.

'Just get me out of here. It needs an effing flamethrower.'

I had anticipated this. For reasons very far from clear to me, you can buy a double gin and tonic in a sort of ring-pull jar in off-licences: I'd often wondered why, but when I was gearing up to show Freda the joys of Kilmollich it had crossed my mind that this was one occasion when a portable G&T might be just the thing to have on hand. I took one out of my Barbour pocket, and handed it to her. 'I thought you might need a drink.'

That made her laugh, fortunately. She ripped the top off the thing, and took a healthy swig. 'I prefer vodka-tonic,' she complained.

'I know, darling. It was a question of any port in a storm.' She's not generally a great drinker because booze tends to go straight to her head. In many ways, she's quite disciplined, the one fact in the whole situation which I thought represented a glimmer of hope.

'Show me the kitchen before I've finished this gin,' she said grimly.

The kitchen was ghastly, even by the standards of the house as a whole. The walls were covered in pine-panel-effect vinyl paper, and the floor with brown and white tile-effect vinyl. It was a melancholy thought that it was probably laid over good slate slabs. I wondered if I could get the concrete screeding off without cracking them; probably not.

Freda, clearly, was treating my jollying-along as a sort of challenge to demonstrate her much-vaunted bottle; it was the way to manage her, as I was beginning to realise. 'It'll start looking like home once we've got this crap off the walls and got the Aga going,' she declared bravely.

I looked at the Aga. Dismiss at once whatever cosy associations might have entered your mind. What I was contemplating was a lump of scarred, cream-enamelled metal approximately the size and shape of the Flying Scotsman, awesomely crusted and mephitic with the remains of innumerable farmhouse meals. A cold odour of cabbage, rabbit, pork fat, and imperfectly burned coal seemed still to hang about it. I opened the fuel hole and peered inside; an elven grotto of clinker met my gaze; I poked at it. It had roughly the texture of lava.

'Where does it turn on?'

I straightened up. 'It doesn't. It's solid fuel. I'm going to have to sort it out. I don't think it's been serviced since the Year Zed. I think they must've stopped using it – I noticed they had an electric cooker as well. Even Old Macdonald said it'd need "a wee bittie wurk" – this, mind you, from a man who was running electricity into his shed from a wire he'd spliced off an external power-line. I'd translate that as "deathtrap" and leave well alone for the time being.'

'But it'd clean up all right?'

'Oh, I'm sure it would. They're practically indestructible.' It had better; what it would take to get the thing out was beyond my imagination. You'd have to smash it to bits in situ with a heavy sledgehammer, I suspected, and take the shards out in barrowloads. It was probably full of asbestos into the bargain. 'It takes a lot to do in an Aga, but I think we'd better use a cooker for the time being.'

After we'd seen the kitchen, we went and sat in the car. There were stones still left unturned, but I thought she'd had about enough. It was one of those moments when I wished I still smoked. 'Don't panic, Freda,' I said after a while.

'I can't live in somewhere like that,' she said, a simple statement of fact.

'Fair enough.' I wasn't surprised; she'd been very insulated from that sort of thing. 'We haven't a lot of spare money, as you well know, but there's some, and when we get the place looking a bit better, we can remortgage and do the rest. What I've got in mind's a sort of bootstrapping operation.'

'How's that supposed to work?' she asked, with a little more animation.

'We need to start off with taking out. Those bloody awful kitchen units, the bathroom, that fireplace – this was a stomach-turning monstrosity in the future drawing-room, with reflective copper tiles – all the partition walls. Taking out's not expensive. All you need's a skip, a barrow, and a couple of strong laddies with wrecking bars. Then we've absolutely got to get the wiring checked out, it's lethal, and that'll cost, but I know someone who doesn't charge the earth, he's more or less retired but he knows what he's doing. There's been typical farmer-y putting stuff over other stuff, so you'll be surprised how much better it looks once the taking out's done. It doesn't take long, either. Then we paint it with neutrals, and it'll look twice the size, and we do whatever we can about the floors; if we're very lucky, there'll be decent pitch-pine boards under all that crap. Trust me on this. It'll be habitable in no time.'

She was looking a bit happier, but not convinced. 'The rooms are very good,' I argued. 'If it's severely plain, the worst it'll look is a bit arty, but that's okay for the time being.'

'So what's Phase Two?'

'I want to check out the main chimney in Phase One if I possibly can – we haven't talked about outside. I might be able to do it myself off a cherry-picker – one of those portable cranes – and save the cost of scaffolding. Phase Two's the rest of the outside, plus plumbing and heating. We'll have to manage with the storage heaters in the short term. You see, we'll have remortgaged by then, because it'll look so good it'll have doubled its value. After that, we can worry about making it beautiful, put in more bathrooms, etcetera, etcetera. Believe me, Freda. It'll be somewhere you could ask your rich friends to inside three years. Probably sooner.'

She shrugged. 'Well. Let's go for it, then.'

'That's my girl. You like a gamble, don't you, darling?'

She smiled her feline smile.

Unfortunately, getting the work done turned out to be the next serious hurdle. When I first came to the North-East, I'd been taken aback to find workmen yodelling at me like the Swedish chef in *The Muppets*, and it'd taken weeks of tuning in before I could make out so much as hallo (locally 'aye-aye?'). But things move on; after nearly fifteen years of working in and around Aberdeenshire, I'd learned the local words for building materials, techniques, and all the rest of the stuff I have to deal with. I could translate the so-called Doric without much effort, and say 'Aye, aye, fit like?' with the best of them. Lilias, having been brought up in Strathdon, had never had a problem. But Freda, of course, had. She'd never needed to deal with workmen before. The Huntly trades were a perfectly civil bunch, but since she couldn't understand a word they said, things kept slipping: I'd ring the joiner to ask why the hell he'd faked up a cornice around the top of a cupboard he knew damned well was supposed to be coming out, only to be told aye, wull, he'd gan an' uskit the wifie fit tae dee an' she'd said, just go ahead, ken? Uf 'ere was aa-hing she'd wantit duffrent, she'd only to usk, ken? No point in calling the man a liar, word gets around, and anyway, it was almost certainly true. It was also clear from things they didn't say that the trades thought she was a snotty bitch, and weren't laying themselves out to meet her halfway; most of them can turn down the Doric and speak something more like standard Scots if they really want to. But I couldn't exactly stay home all

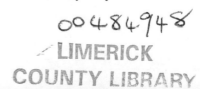

day; we needed every ha'penny I could earn. Things got better after a while; Freda started to find her feet a bit, and I took to ringing up on the mobile and talking the day's work over with the men myself. Anyway, it wasn't going to go on forever.

The next major hurdle was furniture. I was bringing almost nothing except my clothes, the car, and one wonderful painting, the only picture by my ancestor, Sir Thomas Laurence, that the family still owned – the Chevalier Macinnes in all the gold-encrusted glory of French military uniform: he was a hero of Waterloo, I believe, though unfortunately for him, on t'other side. The painting wasn't strictly speaking mine, in the sense that I couldn't sell it, it was the subject of a family trust, oldest child to oldest child: I was holding it for Helen, ultimately. Lil was letting me have it, on the grounds that it reminded her of me, which was good of her, since she could've kept it on Helen's behalf and stuck it in the attic. So we'd have to make do with Freda's furniture, and a rum go it was too, as I discovered when I went to help her with the removal.

Calicut Lodge was desolate, the way houses are when they're about to be dismantled – it's hard to put your finger on it, but you can feel it the moment you come in the door. It made me uneasy anyway, there was that sense of being on another man's turf, but beyond all that, the place was enough to make your heart sink. Freda let me in, dressed in businesslike fashion in jeans and a loose shirt, with her hair tied back in a ponytail, and she was the most beautiful thing I could see by a long mile. Once I'd kissed her, I stood looking over her shoulder and absorbing the full dreadfulness of the hall: there was a brand-new pseudo-Shiraz runner laid over celadon green carpet, a pair of suspiciously shiny-looking console tables, aiming at the eighteenth century, not very accurately, and an outsized Chinese vase in a corner, sort of famille rose. Ish. The ceiling was a particularly ghoulish touch: the dentils of the elaborate cornice were picked out in two shades of dusty pink.

After that, it could only get worse, and it did.

'Malcolm's notions, I trust?' I said acidly, when she showed me into the drawing-room.

'Shell. They send a design team, when you buy a house, to make sure it's all in keeping, because of the entertaining.'

It made a sort of sense. The mysteries of oil were a career open to talent of whatever origin, so Shell wives might be just about anybody. I had only to think of the stately pleasure domes furnished to the taste of trawler-owner's womenfolk in Gardenstown and Gamrie Bay to understand why oil's senior management might be unwilling to trust the unaided genius of their executives' wives. It also, in retrospect, explained a lot about the oil palazzi I'd encountered in the way of business.

'God,' I said, surveying the room. What it looked like, precisely, was the sort of hotel which makes most of its living out of middle-management conferences. A 'Georgian look' complete unto brass radiator grilles and a Hepplewhite-inspired TV cabinet, featuring wee tables covered with polyurethane varnish, Regency-striped uphol-stery, and hand-painted pictures of silver birches, lochs, and distant blue mountains. It struck me suddenly that it gave me not the faintest clue to what Freda's own taste might be like, or even whether she had any. 'No wonder you've been going out of your mind here.'

She seemed genuinely surprised, and I looked at her in horror. If she didn't actually mind this junk, then we had problems. 'I don't know why you're looking at it like it's crap from MFI,' she said. 'They won't *let* us have anything that isn't really good quality.'

'Well, we're going to have to live with it,' I said. 'The trouble is, this white-trash Regency shite costs about three times as much as the real thing, but it's got a resale value of zero.'

'Why? It's properly made. Most of it's Wesley-Barrell.'

'Because anyone dumb enough to want this kind of stuff wants it first hand. Don't be daft.' She opened her mouth, but I decided that whatever she might be meaning to say was just going to make things worse. 'Come on,' I said. 'Have you got the kitchen stuff packed up yet? Any chance of coffee?'

But she wasn't about to let go. 'You don't think I'm good enough for you. Well, you can – '

'Freda, Freda, Freda. I'm insane about you.' I reached out for her; she was as resistant as a plank of wood. I put my hands up under her shirt, and stroked up her smooth strong back till I reached the bra strap, and ran my fingers round underneath it. She began to soften in spite of herself.

'Stop it,' she said. I was nuzzling the side of her neck, and she bit my ear, hard enough to hurt. I let go of her.

'Darling. You've already told me this isn't you. It's something you've been handed as part of the kit. God, I'm not blaming you.'

She twisted out of my grip, to my regret; I was beginning to fancy the notion of a last leg-over in the old homestead. 'You want me to learn how to be a snob,' she said flatly.

Christ, what a way to put it, I thought, but she wasn't being deliberately sarky.

'How can I put this? "Snob" is my stock in trade. We don't have to look rich, but we've bloody well got to look adequately posh if I'm going to persuade the castle-owning classes to trust me with their renovations. Do you understand me?'

'Yes,' she said unexpectedly. 'I hadn't thought of it that way, but I see what you're getting at. I'm not thick, you know. I'll work it out.'

I looked at her with a sort of wondering admiration. She meant it, bless her cotton socks; she had a tremendous drive to succeed. 'Come on,' I said, 'we can spare twenty minutes.' I took the hem of her oversized shirt and whipped it up over her head. This time, she didn't try and stop me.

After that, we got back to work, and in the course of the day, the whole ghoulish collection, stripy sofas, nasty wee tables, Edinburgh crystal, Villeroy & Boch plates, over-engineered domestic machinery from Miele and Poggenpohl and all, was loaded into the van and carted up the A97 to Kilmollich. Driving along after the removal van, I could see storms ahead. If they let you have one wife for sex and another for everything else, I'd have been absolutely happy. I wanted Freda more than I'd ever wanted anything in my life, but there was no denying that she was a luxury item. I was already wondering how the heck I was going to afford her.

After Calicut Lodge, I'd expected to fight Freda every inch of the way over décor, but, to my astonishment, she'd taken the 'snob is our stock in trade' argument completely on board. You had to admire her. She bought herself a red notebook.

'What's this room going to have?' she asked, standing in the drawing-room, recently equipped with a brand-new fireplace copied from Robert Lorimer, and looking speculatively at the fried-egg wallpaper.

'Farrow & Ball Off-White, with their All-White in the ingoes to maximise natural light. Or, since we can't afford it, the best fake we can manage with Dulux, and maybe a skim of dilute F&B as a topcoat; it takes the light quite differently. The fireplace is supposed to've been there since about 1900, so in an ideal world, we'd have old-white panelling and a dado. I could maybe fake that up with picture-frame mouldings from a DIY shop, tacked on with panel pins. We might do that, actually.'

She was writing it all down as I spoke; she had perfectly work-able shorthand from distant days as a PA. 'Why?' she asked.

I had to think about it. 'Because you're trying to make it look as if you've just renovated something that'd been there for a long time. Because you're always better off with colours based on natural pigments.'

She not only wrote it all down, she absorbed it. It was being posh by numbers, but it was going in all right. I could see her starting to get interested.

'When we've got this place sorted out, I might start a business,' she said.

'You're not exactly an expert.'

'No? But I can talk to people like me,' she pointed out, 'which you can't without being bleeding offensive, and they're the ones with the money.'

She had a point. It struck me that she must have been like this when she first married Malcolm. The occasional Cockneyisms somehow suggested that she was reverting to an earlier self. She and Constantine were much of an age: she'd picked a man to fight her way up with, she hadn't gone the 'second wife' route, seduced some old fart and piggybacked off another woman's work. In some obscure fashion, she seemed to be enjoying it all; I suspected that she was using brain-cells she'd forgotten she had.

'You've not really got into that world,' she said. 'I've got some good contacts. With all your skills plus the people I know, we could really get somewhere.'

I looked at her in amazement.

'Why should I be the only one who's supposed to learn stuff?' she demanded. You're bloody good at what you do. We could be earning a lot more if we went into relocation consultancy, and we could offer the whole package.'

I could see what was in her mind: Crumbling Castle to Oil Palazzo in six months flat, with herself done up in ecru linen pretending to be Kelly Hoppen. It was, emphatically, not a future I wished to move towards, but I was interested to find her thinking that way. Freda as helpmeet was a phenomenon I had not even considered.

Meanwhile, none of our problems were going away by themselves. Her furniture looked even worse in Kilmollich than it had in Calicut Lodge. 'I'm going to have to start going round the farm roups', I said, looking at the sad items huddled against the walls of the future drawing-room.

'The what?'

'Farmer's auctions. A good way to pick up big, old pieces. Ever seen an eighteenth-century bureau that's done twenty years in a chicken-shed? I bought one once. Gave five quid for it, spent six hundred on French-polishing, and sold it for eight thousand at Phillip's.'

I spoke abstractedly, as a thought was beginning to form. The shapes of Freda's pieces were clumsy, for something which was aiming to look up-market; the effect was grisly. But quite a lot of it would pass as country-joiners' Georgian in the dusk with the light behind it, if it only stopped looking so new and shiny.

'Can you paint?' I asked her.

'I don't know,' she admitted. 'I don't see why not. I'm quite neat with my hands.'

'I'm going to try a high bluff with this shite,' I explained. 'Distress them, send 'em off to be dipped, then they'll get one coat of gesso and one coat of F&B's Old White oil eggshell. It might look a bit *Country Living*, but at least it won't look white-trash.'

There was a paved area behind the back door, meant for a drying green; it was revetted into the rising ground behind the house with a nice old drystone wall, and potentially an asset, but for now, it was simply a very useful outdoor workshop. I carried the tables and chairs outside and flogged them with a length of rusty chain I found in the shed, a job I found obscurely satisfying. Since Kilmollich had been a farmhouse, its limited amenities at least included a gun-safe in the cellar, so I hadn't been forced to leave my shotgun with the polis: to Freda's horror and amazement, I got it out and blasted her furniture with three cartridges' worth of Eley's no. 20 from forty yards or so; enough of a peppering to suggest a sufficient but not terminal case of woodworm. Fortunately she had not been misled, the stuff was, basically, quite well made, and nothing actually came apart. In the fulness of time, a van came and took it all away. When it all came back, pale, bruised and bald, I showed Freda how to make gesso, and we got the first batch painted up over a weekend.

'They look totally different,' Freda said, with a sort of clinical interest.

'Mmm. They'll pass.' Among the things I regretted having left behind me was a roll of antique grey toile de Jouy printed with philosophes admiring the tomb of Rousseau, which I'd snapped up the moment I saw it, because I'd known I was sure to want it some day. I wished fervently that I'd managed to hang onto it; I couldn't think what we could use for the seat-pads. 'A tiny touch of worn gilding here and there might help,' I went on, 'but it'd need an awfully steady hand. Maybe better not to risk it. I might line the tables – I've got a tube of Paynes Grey somewhere. Acrylic takes over oil eggshell. Look, darling. I saw you writing the formula for gesso in your book. Any chance you could paint up the rest?'

She nodded.

Meanwhile, all the squirly Wilton came up, together with its festering underlay, and went into a skip. There was crusted brown lino underneath that, and, thank God, good boards under the lino, though it took days and days of a man working full time to get them sanded down to clean. Outwith such purely practical matters, we were starting to get used to each other: I liked opera and lieder, she liked to wake up to Radio One; there was a certain amount of inevitable bickering, but in the end, we agreed to differ.

You can't spend your working life on building sites without hearing a lot of Radio One, so I was well used to tuning it out.

In a weird kind of way, we were both having fun by then, though I was running on empty: I was trying to ensure Freda wasn't left with jobs she couldn't handle, while at the same time, I was doing a full day's work, making sure she got enough sex to keep her happy and getting five hours' sleep a night, if that. But to my infinite relief, Freda showed signs of a certain taste for physical work, as long as it wasn't boring, and she made a good job of the furniture.

Since I couldn't be in more than one place at a time, I marked up various useful junk shops, scrap-yards, auctions and so forth on a map for her, and between us, we worked out a set of basic rules for recognising 'old and good' when you saw it: the agreement was that if she found something and it was more than fifty quid, she was to ring me on the mobile and describe it. I wasn't entirely enthusiastic about her stravaiging about the countryside on her own, but I could hardly stop her, especially when she was trying to help, and I comforted myself with the thought that she wasn't fed up yet, or anything like it.

She was learning fast, and she made one or two worthwhile finds quite early on, which encouraged her. She spotted a collection of big, old, weathered flowerpots, for instance, and got the lot for a fiver, Safeway's were selling off foot-high lavender and rosemary for £1.99 apiece at the time, so we made an instant garden for practically nothing. Then she came home in triumph with a real coup, a nineteenth-century cast-iron bench with fern-patterned ends; the wood was all rotted, but that didn't matter. I bought eight slats at the nearest woodyard and rubbed them down with the electric sander, Freda gave the metal a coat of dark green Hammerite, and with the pots grouped at either end of it, all of a sudden, there was the drying green dressed, and looking downright smart.

Another time, she went to the farm roup at Strichen. 'I found something, I think,' she said that evening. She looked uncharacteristically tentative.

'Show.'

She opened up the back of the car, and I saw a wicker laundry hamper big enough to hide Falstaff in. I lugged it inside, and when

I opened it, this dreadful mildewy stench wafted up; but what it turned out to contain was half a dozen pairs of hand-woven, thick, coarse linen sheets, a bit flecked with iron-rust and mildew, and a collection of tweedy old bothy-blankets in brown and soft-grey herringbone. Some farmer's wife had thankfully jettisoned the lot the minute poly-cotton and hollow-fibre duvets arrived in the North-East. The blankets were a wee bit holey here and there, but they were beautiful, and not at all bad for their age.

'I thought, "old and good"?' she said, watching my face.

'You were right. Absolutely brilliant. We'll cut them up for curtains. And can you use a staple gun?'

'What are you thinking of?'

'Upholstery. We desperately need something for the pads on the dining-room chairs; these sheets'd do the job. And we might even cover the sofa if we got really brave. You can just stretch the linen over what's there already, then it's a matter of bang bang with the staple gun and sticking a bit of expensive gimp on to cover the staples, one of the good greyish neutrals, stone or maybe mouse's back, and there you go.'

Freda was looking at the blankets with an expression I couldn't work out.

'Don't worry about the smell,' I said. 'It's just because they've been stored. Once we've run them through the washing-machine and hung them out to air, they'll be fine.'

'I can't understand people wanting this stuff,' she said suddenly. 'I think they're horrible. Filthy old things.'

'But darling – '

'Oh, I believe you. Thousands wouldn't,' she said with a flash of temper. 'But that's what I think.'

After a couple of months of intensive effort, we had achieved a sort of superficial order, at the expense of doing any of the real work. I hadn't managed to do anything at all about the exterior, as I'd half-feared from the start, because of keeping Freda happy – getting the inside to a state she could bear to live in had hoovered up all available liquidity for the time being.

All the same, there came, eventually, an autumnal Saturday

when all the most pressing jobs had been done, and we could walk round and look at it. It was still very sparse – under-furnished might be a better way to put it – but it had a sort of stark glamour.

'We've won,' I said, putting my arm round her shoulders. 'We can get married now, if you like.'

We traipsed down to the kitchen; it was coming on to lunchtime. The kitchen was transformed; the walls were warm white, and I'd laid clic-floor laminate in light oak; it depressed the hell out of me on principle, but, till I got around to getting a woodyard to carve up some railway sleepers and did the job properly (my long-term plan), it would do; I'd found a kind which had V-grooves between the pseudo-planks, which fooled the eye to a surprising extent. Everything that 'Astonish', elbow-grease and lashings of wire-wool could do for the Aga had been done. It had cleaned up nicely, and now, with an old stock-pot, a kettle and a wire egg-basket perched casually on what was supposed to be the cool end and a couple of French linen dishcloths hung over the rail, it passed muster, in purely visual terms, as the womb of the house, principal shrine of the feminine mysteries, and all that good stuff.

Beneath the surface, as with much else at Kilmollich, things looked rather different. I'd scraped the worst of the clinker out of the fuel-hole, but although I'd successfully dealt with most of the house's chimneys at an early stage of proceedings, dislodging an inconceivably large quantity of sooty twigs in the process, I'd damned nearly given myself a hernia trying to ram a set of rods up the kitchen flue, and for the time being, I had been forced to admit defeat.

I worried about the Aga every time it caught my eye. Trying to get a nineteenth-century heating device plumbed into a cavernous early-seventeenth-century chimney is not without its problems; in this case, I suspected that some major game of silly buggers had taken place. Perhaps the chimney-liner had ended up with a sharp angle in it, and the local rook community had bunged it up good and proper or – and at this point, a dreadful alternative always rose in my mind – surely nobody on God's earth would be dumb enough to vent an Aga into a capped chimney? It was a thought which kept coming back to me, as I recalled the vacant countenances of Old Macdonald and his missus. When we'd scaffolded and I was able to get up to the stack, which stood a good ten feet proud of the roof and therefore more than fifty feet above ground level, I'd know for sure once I was looking at the chimney. Whatever was blocking it would almost certainly be shiftable if I tackled it from the top, even if I had to fire the shotgun down it. But, for the time being, the Aga was out of bounds. In any case, I'd have to get it converted to electricity before it'd be any use to us; I couldn't see Freda lugging coal about. Or, indeed, making vast pots of stew and batches of crusty loaves. She might want to boil the odd kettle, but that'd be about it.

The Aga aside, the kitchen boasted a very decent old-fashioned walk-in larder with a meatsafe, and a double Belfast sink supported on tile-clad piers. There was plenty of room for Freda's brushed-steel cooker, dishwasher and fancy fridge. It had the makings of a nice room. I'd build a plate-rack over the sink when I got a minute.

I sat down at the table; a decent, scrubbed pine one which Freda had liberated from the Strichen roup, and she got some cheese and paté out of the fridge for me. She doesn't eat much at lunchtime herself; in fact, she seems able to keep going indefinitely on Cup a Soup and the odd finger of Kit Kat.

'Thanks, darling,' I said, cutting myself some bread.

'What are we going to do when we do it properly?' she asked.

'What?' It took a moment to see what she meant; I was still congratulating myself on fighting the house to a draw, but mentally, Freda was already onto the next round. 'Whatever you like. You can't do Baronial, the spaces are too small, and Country Clutter will just get messy, for the same reason. My guess is we'll probably end up with Arty-Eclectic.'

'Is anything ever allowed to look new?'

'Not a lot, unless you take up supporting Viscount Linley's home handicrafts. Hardly ever fabric, and never rugs. You could display modern paintings here, though. They might look wonderful, but you'd have to be very bold.'

'I don't know why you won't let me put my pictures up,' she complained. 'They'd at least be something, and they weren't cheap.' Fifteen hundred apiece was my guess, and a total waste of money. I had a sudden flash of evil inspiration.

'No. I'm sorry. Believe me, darling. They're never going to look right in here. But why not sell them? I'd've thought you could sell ice to Eskimos, if you put your mind to it, and then we could use the money to buy stuff we both liked. There's a dealer in Banchory and two or three up Deeside; it'd be a nice drive, if you fancied a day out. Just take a look in the *Yellow Pages*.'

As I'd guessed, she took this as a challenge; on the Monday following, she dressed with care, loaded half a dozen terminally kitsch oil-paintings into the back of her Renault, and zoomed off to prove me wrong. I went off to work, but from time to time during the day, I thought of her. In their own silky way, picture dealers are among the rudest people on the planet; it was a fair guess that she was getting something of an education.

She was in a very subdued frame of mind that evening; I asked no questions, but poured her a glass of wine, and was nice to her. In the days that followed, I started finding my art books lying around. Typical Freda; any major setback was treated as an advance in disguise. I heard no more about putting up her Walt Disney specials.

My parents refused to come up from Inveresk for the wedding. My mother was very upset about the whole thing, of course; she was absolutely on Lil and the girls' side, which was natural enough. My father sent me a brief note saying that he had no desire to attend more than one wedding per offspring and a cheque for a thousand quid, which was exceptionally decent of him. I was perfectly well aware that he thought I was being both a shit and a fool. I knew, and he knew I knew, that he was in no position to take the moral high ground on the topic of marital fidelity, but on the other hand, I'd offended against his code, which was straightforward: never let your mistress manoeuvre you into a position where she can embarrass your wife, and don't make children suffer for your misdeeds. He would see the point of Freda, if he ever consented to meet her, but not the point of marrying her. Of the two of them, I stood more chance of getting back on terms with Mummy; Daddy's letter, though scrupulously polite, had had a depressing note of finality.

Freda's parents were divorced, and she hadn't any siblings she was prepared to admit to. Her mother wrote from Australia saying, roughly, why must you make my life so difficult? – confirming my general impression that she was a woman I didn't want to meet. Her father, on the other hand, said he'd come to the wedding. I didn't get the impression that Freda was any too delighted by the prospect. My sister sent a curt note – I hadn't expected to see her anyway: she's married to a doctor in Cirencester and they've got three kids, so it takes a lot to get her shifted. But my brother Sandy said he'd come, which pleased me. He's a high-class scamster or, to put it more politely, a financial consultant, a couple of years younger than me, and we've always been pals. Of course, he's fond of Scotland, and likes having an excuse to come up. He's serving time in London, living in a flat the size of a cupboard in Crouch End, with plans to get back North when he can. Hence the bolt-hole in Stonehaven, of all places – that bit of the east coast's a great place for fossils, which he's been keen on since we were kids. He goes there when he can to footer about collecting significant bits of rock and generally to unwind, sometimes in female company; he's never married, but there's usually a woman around somewhere.

We went down to Dyce and met him off the plane. He gave me a hug, and kissed Freda, a bit more thoroughly than the occasion demanded; I'd known for certain he'd fancy her.

'Hello, Freda,' he said. 'Nice to have you in the family.'

'Nice to meet you,' she said demurely.

Then we had to hang around for four hours; infuriatingly, her dad was coming in on the next London flight. Freda said she needed some shopping, so we squabbled politely over whether two out of the three of us were going to go round Crathes Castle, the only marginally adjacent amenity, which Sandy and I had seen umpteen times and Freda wasn't interested in. We ended up all going to the big out-of-town Tesco, aimlessly pushing a trolley about and collecting odds and ends for the freezer while making desultory conversation.

Reg Hatchin turned out to be an odd little bloke in a bad suit with a secretive, heavy-lidded face; I could see the resemblance to Freda as he came towards us. He was about three inches shorter than she was; Sandy and I towered over him.

'You're looking good, doll,' he told his daughter, giving her a once-up-and-down after he'd kissed her. 'And this is your new fella? Pleased to meet you,' he said, turning to me and shaking hands scrupulously.

We were just having family, so the party was then complete in all its full and glorious awkwardness. Neither of us had friends we would have wanted to be there. You can't really ask couples to a second marriage, and my unattached pals by and large didn't see why anyone bothered marrying at all. Freda was different again. There were some women she went around with, they'd meet up and go shopping from time to time, but I suspected that these relationships were more in the way of temporary alliances than actual friendships. She was a man's woman through and through.

III

We had a most peculiar evening. Sandy and I drank too much, which is traditional. He liked the house, and understood it; I wasn't deceiving him for a moment, but I hadn't expected to. I don't pretend to understand his affairs, but I've known him have a vast wad of loose cash – the London and Stonehaven flats were both bought outright – and I've also known him be flat broke. Money's the tool of his trade to him, something you play with, not something you use for buying bog-rolls and whisky. He's completely un-scared of its absence, or presence, but he's also impossible to fool on the subject. There's nothing he doesn't know about putting on a good act. I suspected that once he'd had a proper look round, he could've made a guess on what we'd spent which would've been accurate to within a few hundreds.

'A good buy,' he said. 'It's got everything you can't fake. Once you've caught with yourself a bit, it'll be fabulous.' I saw his eye resting on Freda's wannabe Regency sofa, now a symphony of soft neutrals with a pile of Indian crewel-work cushions on it to provide much-needed distraction. 'You've done well, Davie. If I could afford to move North, I'd have it off you.' His glass was empty, and when I tilted the bottle of Rioja which stood between us, it turned out that was too. I got up and went to open another.

'A drop more, Mr Hatchin?' I asked. Reg was sitting with Freda on the other side of the fire.

'No, I don't think I will. Not just now.' He covered his glass with his hand protectively.

'Can I get you anything else? Whisky?'

'I could do with a cup of tea,' he said.

Freda got to her feet. 'I'll make us one. No, don't get up.' But when she left the room her father got up and followed her downstairs.

The atmosphere was easier once they'd gone. I was still completely unsure what he made of the place. When we brought them home and the car came round the corner, Sandy had wolf-whistled, and said 'Fabuloso!', while Reg's response had been 'Very nice. Romantic.' Since then, he had ventured remarkably little, except to say sedately that we'd done very well in the time we'd had, and that it was a pity we were having to make do with old stuff. Since when, every time he said anything at all, I could see his eyes sliding to Freda's face to check for her reaction.

I poured us each another glass. I'd found a set of nineteenth-century pressed-glass goblets, satisfying chunky things, in the junk shop in Old Rayne; full, one of them held about half a pint.

'God, what a woman,' my brother said. 'You've got some nerve, Davie. So's she.'

'Freda is very amazing. I wouldn't've left Lil for just anyone.' His reaction was making me feel better about myself than I had in a year.

'She's a sex bomb. But there's a hell of a lot to her. Pity you're a bit cash-strapped.'

'What're you thinking? She's tried designer lifestyle, she got bored. If I had squandering-type dosh she'd spend it good-style, but she chose me over money, don't forget.'

'Not what I had in mind. She ought to have some kids to take the edge off her.'

'God, no. And we're a bit old for that.'

'Hell, I was forgetting. And here's me, only two years younger. Funny how time passes.'

He was steaming, I realised. He's always held it well, but he must've been very tired. 'I've given her stuff to think about,' I said, 'not just a good going-over. And I don't think anyone's done that for a very long time. She's interested, and not just when I've got her on her back.'

'If she'd had any kind of an education, she'd be running something by now. She'll run you, if you're not bloody careful.'

'She'll try.'

The actual wedding went off without incident. Freda looked wonderful in a flirty Fendi skirt and jacket, no daughters, husbands or any such burst in to bring the proceedings to a halt, and we took everyone off to a charmingly 'traditional', though not unduly authentic, Highland hotel for lunch. Reg Hatchin and Sandy caught the same plane south in the afternoon, and there we were, married.

'Freda, we're going to have to start entertaining,' I said, a week or two later. 'We're going to have to manage social re-entry somehow or other, and for the time being, we can't afford to do it in restaurants.' I looked at her. I had no idea if she could cook; she didn't much, and what she did was erratic at best. We ate cartons of prefab soup from Tesco's, salady things. She Atkinsed, so there was quite a lot of flinging chicken breasts under the grill, and I took to buying my own bread on the way home since there never seemed to be any. 'Did you do dinner parties?'

'Sometimes. With big dos, you'd get caterers laid on, but I can do a party for six to eight.'

'Wonderful. We wouldn't be wanting to have any more.' The downside of a tower-house is that, though it looks enormous from the outside, the rooms are really quite small within the four-foot-thick walls. The room we had her dining table in would hold eight at the absolute maximum.

'You're not talking about astrononomic gastronomics, anyway.

The average posh girl can cook three party things – one of them's usually spinach roulade.' I was slandering Lilias when I said that; she's an excellent cook, but as a principle, I think it holds good. 'After that they fall back on lentil soup, fish pie, and overcooked roast chicken. Things you shove in the Aga and forget about, basically. I'm sure you can cook just as badly in a Poggenpohl oven, if you put your mind to it.'

Freda sniffed. 'I don't know how to make spinach roulade.'

'You don't have to. Everybody's sick of it anyway. I thought we'd maybe just have Robert and Mary for the first attempt, since you've met them.' My partners; I wanted people who knew a bit about the background and would make it easy for her. 'And their other halves, of course.'

Freda looked surprised. 'I thought they were married. To each other, I mean.'

'Absolutely not. Mary's not that sort of a girl. Robert's wife is a lovely Frenchwoman called Véronique, and Mary's as-it-were married to a lass called Sarah.'

'She's a dyke?'

'Oh, yes,' I said, surprised. 'I thought anyone could tell that a mile off.' I mean, she doesn't wear dungarees and a Hell's Angels jacket and shave her head, but she's pretty damn butch in a county sort of way, a sort of Caledonian Vita Sackville-West.

Freda was looking mulish; she hadn't much time for female company generally, and I think she was distinctly dis-chuffed by the thought that all that added up to a party of four women and two men. But there wasn't a lot I could do about it. I wanted our first party to be as straightforward as possible, with people I trusted, and eight in that room is two too many, we'd be elbow to elbow. Anyway, I like Sarah, she's large and jolly with a wicked sense of humour. I like them both, actually. The other two were no problem. Robert's just an ordinary decent bloke with nice manners; Freda could dazzle him, and with any luck that would keep her happy, and Véronique's a painter, vague, nice to look at, doesn't talk much. No competition, from Freda's point of view.

★

The following Friday, I got home from work and stuck my head round the kitchen door.

'Hello, darling. D'you need a hand with anything?'

'Bugger off.'

A number of cookery books were insecurely perched about the place, and every crock we possessed seemed to be piled in the sink. There was a discernible odour of burning, and Freda, looking a little wild-eyed, was ladling quails' eggs out of a frying-pan onto a pile of kitchen paper.

'Well, if you change your mind, just yell,' I said, buggering off thankfully in search of whisky and a nice hot bath.

There were a lot more clothes lying around than usual, I noticed. Freda's not indecisive in that way. I guessed she was conflicted between a desire to impress Robert, and some kind of primitive fear that if she made herself too attractive, Mary and Sarah would lose control, spring on her and rip her knickers off. I doubt very much if out-and-about lesbians form any statistically significant part of the Shell social scene, so God knows what was going on in her head.

When they all arrived, the two cars appearing almost simultaneously – trust a bunch of architects to know how long it takes to get from A to B across country virtually to the minute – there was the usual swirl of bodies; explanations, kisses, bottles of wine, flowers, marking off the fact that although I had seen Robert and Mary only a couple of hours before, this was different. I shepherded them through to the drawing-room, which they all exclaimed over in their different ways. While I was pouring drinks, Freda came in. She was wearing a fuchsia trouser-suit, tight, but with all the buttons done up for once, and, most uncharacteristically, with a camisole on under the jacket. And her spikiest Jimmy Choo shoes, the ones which looked like offensive weapons.

'David, this is for you both,' said Véronique. 'A little wedding present.' She was looking very charming in her own way; she's a Norman girl, with straight, light-brown hair, wide-set grey eyes and wonderful skin, and she was dressed as usual in several layers of shapeless greyish-brown garments, socks and clogs; in winter, one or more of the layers are wool, in summer, they're linen or cotton, and on unspeakably grand occasions, silk; beyond that, she never bothers herself. She was the least smart Frenchwoman I had ever met in my life, but not giving a toss worked for her, it suited her oval face and rangy figure. She'd brought us one of her engravings, a quietly elegant study of a corner of a room with an open window.

'Fantastic,' said Freda, coming up beside me while I was unwrapping it, 'thanks a million. It's brilliant it's black and white; it can go absolutely anywhere.'

Véronique looked at her as if she'd unexpectedly said something in Gujerati.

'It's beautiful, Véronique,' I said, giving her a kiss on the cheek. 'Thank you. We'll sort out the ideal place for it later on.'

'Can I see?' said Sarah, coming up behind us. Freda leaped hastily to one side and vanished, muttering about seeing to things in the kitchen.

'It's lovely,' Sarah said. 'There's almost a Gwen Johnnish feel? The way it's saying a lot with not very much. Your stuff just goes on getting better and better. How're you selling these days?'

'Not so bad. This year, Tolquhon are taking some engravings, and the paintings are in Fochabers and Banchory.'

'Have you thought of trying direct selling through the Net? I meant to say this last time I saw you. It might really be worth your while setting up a website.' Sarah is involved with computers. They wandered away together, and I propped the engraving up on a side-table where it could be generally admired.

For the next forty minutes or so, Bob, Mary and I talked solidly about Kilmollich and my plans for it; with Véronique and Sarah onto art, and Freda slaving in the kitchen, it was the perfect opportunity for serious shop. Then Freda called us through, and we all prepared in our various ways to start behaving ourselves.

There was a pile of pomegranates in the middle of the dining-room table; I could only hope that superglue had entered into the scheme of things somewhere, or we would all have to be very careful. There was also a pair of achingly genteel wee lollipop trees made out of dried flowers with pink ribbon spiralled round the stems, a forest of Edinburgh crystal, and lots and lots of

Villeroy & Boch. And, O God, coloured napkins in napkin rings. I thanked my lucky stars we'd only asked Bob and Mary.

'It looks wonderful, Freda,' said Sarah, who has address. 'Congratulations.'

'Thanks.' Freda said ungraciously.

For the first course, we found ourselves facing strange little stacks of edible items; the top and bottom layers were star-shaped pieces of tasteless puff pastry; in between, attacking the construction cautiously, I found pieces of Parma ham, halved cherry tomatoes, bits of fancy lettuce, and a quail's egg, the whole set-out glued together with Hellman's; the toughness of the ham, inevitably, ensured that the structure crashed in ruins at the first touch of a knife.

'How are the kids?' I asked, always a safe topic, as we all prodded the stuff about.

Robert rolled his eyes. 'Everyone in Philippe and Sam's class has got nits *again*. Someone's not doing it right, and we're up to our eyes in conditioner and permethrin for the third time this year. Véronique tried buying one of those electric combs, but it's completely useless.'

Freda was looking horrified. Once one's become a parent, it's easy to forget that headlice are not a universally acceptable topic of conversation. 'Have you got twins, then?' she asked bravely.

Mary smiled at her. 'No. Sam's ours, but he's the same age as Philippe.'

Freda opened her mouth and shut it again, flabbergasted. I could see the question 'how?' written all over her face.

'How's Rose?' I put in quickly.

'Blooming, as I can never resist saying,' said Robert. 'She got her Grade Eight violin, clever girl. I don't think you've had the privilege for a year or two, but when she's playing, it actually sounds like music now, and not like someone torturing a cat.'

'She's in the school orchestra, isn't she?'

'Yes. First violins. They're working on some Brahms, and she's having a lovely time. She's got her sights on auditioning for the National Youth Orchestra of Scotland next year. It'd be a nightmare, but if she really wants to do it, we'll have to sort it out somehow. It's a pity she's got into something so *collective*.'

'Well, if she took after Véronique and just sat upstairs drawing all day, you'd be worried she hadn't any friends,' said Mary.

'That's true enough. One can't actually win.'

I sat there smiling and drinking, feeling like someone who's gone swimming off Torquay and suddenly had their leg removed at the knee by a passing shark. I had engaged in variations on the Mobius Nit Conversation with Bob and Mary ever since Rose, who's two years older than Helen, first went to nursery school, and if I had any sense at all, I should've realised what I was setting up for myself. But I hadn't thought about that aspect at all, so I'd landed myself in it, slightly drunk and aghast, mugged by my own past in a way that I had absolutely failed to anticipate. I was agonisingly conscious of the absence of Helen and Effie from my life, the fact that I no longer shared in small triumphs with the blasted ponies or knew if Effie had written a poem which her teacher had put up on the wall. Véronique was looking at me as if she felt sorry for me, and I went round with the bottle again by way of changing the subject.

The bacon and egg towers were succeeded by a pale khaki dish of braised pheasant with celery and a most peculiar salad which seemed to have been dressed with chopped apple and melted Camembert. Freda herself ate almost nothing. The dykes cleared their plates manfully, if that's quite the word I want, and congratulated her on everything with immense conscientiousness, getting precious little response for their pains; Véronique, after her first encounter with the salad, lapsed into an abstracted silence.

Fortunately Robert, once adequately stiffened by Chianti, realised that his social duty was to flirt with his hostess, and set to; he'd been at university in London about the time that Freda was growing up, so he started fishing for common memories, and found some, bless him. She started to look more animated, and I even heard her laugh once. In any case, now the worst of the food had safely got to the table, she was beginning to relax.

Véronique seemed to be happy staring into space, so Mary and Sarah started telling me about their plans to introduce Sam to climbing, which they used to do quite seriously pre-parenthood. I'd climbed a bit myself, and indeed, I'd even gone off for a weekend in the Cairngorms with them once, so mountains was one of the points where we connected. You can't do our sort of work without occasional episodes of clambering about on roofs, so it helps to know how to handle heights. I was interested by their approach, though I had my doubts about actually encouraging a little head-banger like Sam to risk his neck, given that he's worryingly fearless – Sarah thought that if he was taught how to manage himself, he'd actually be safer. I wouldn't have done if he'd been mine, given what I could remember of my own asinine conduct at the age of nine or so, but it was a point of view, and in any case, it was something to talk about.

After the tasteless pheasant, there was a choice of chocolate mascarpone cheesecake or port wine jelly with frosted cranberries; typically, Freda hadn't thought about providing anything starchy by way of blotting-paper, and Robert and I were both showing symptoms of wear by then. I had some of both of the puddings, to keep Freda in countenance, and began to wonder if I ought to put out a bowl of Rennies alongside the mint chocolates which would doubtless make their appearance in due course. Once it had all been dealt with to the best of our ability, we went back to the drawing-room for coffee, and at quarter to twelve, they went away, thank God, amid the usual sociable hallooing.

'I thought that all went very well,' I said to Freda. There was a grease-stain of some kind on the front of her jacket. 'Lovely food, darling.'

'Liar.' She kicked her shoes off, and we went to do some clearing up. I stacked the dishwasher and got it started. When I was still loading it up, she came in carrying the remaining four-fifths of the cheesecake, and tipped it straight into the bin.

'You're throwing it away?'

'Why the hell not?'

Why not, indeed. The thought of seeing any of it coming round again made me feel quite ill. It was just that I had never in my life seen a woman simply throw edible food away. In my experience, everything, however unloved, went in the fridge or the larder, where it remained until it was no longer edible. And then it was thrown away, of course. Not very logical perhaps, but all the same, there was a principle involved. Lil wasted almost nothing; surplus meat became stock or the dog's dinner, rejected vegetation became compost, bread and so forth fed the hens; and of course surplus puddings tend to be a bit of a non-concept in a household containing two horsey daughters and a retriever. Meanwhile, back in the present moment, Freda was methodically throwing away the salad, hideously draggled with spermatic lumps of congealed Camembert, the rest of the pheasant, the jelly . . . Out it all went, and I found myself in one corner of my mind recalling the poor starving people in Africa who, in my long-ago childhood, used to be evoked every time I refused to finish my tea, and in another, wondering meanly what it had all cost me. Seventy quid? Eighty? More?

Freda was looking depressed and angry, which was roughly how I felt myself. I gave myself another glass of wine; I was pretty plastered by then, but it beat making conversation when I knew she'd just bite my head off. I did the worst of the sinkful while the dishwasher sloshed and churned beside me and my thoughts sloshed and churned in my head, and Freda collected glasses and put them on the table to be dealt with in the morning. I couldn't think what to say. Before we could conceivably entertain anyone in the acquaintance/potential client bracket, absolutely everything would have to be different, but how I was going to put this across without enraging her was a question I couldn't begin to answer. The repellent little trees I could, and would, impound the following morning and painlessly destroy, regardless of the fact that they had probably cost forty quid each in John Lewis's; if she asked about them it might provide an opening, but she probably wouldn't. Defeated, I stacked the last saucepan in the draining rack, and started up to bed, knackered, plastered, and infinitely sorry for myself.

The subject of dinner parties was avoided for some time. It's always possible to give people soup, cheese, smoked salmon, good olives, and crusty bread for a casual lunch, provided that I remembered to stock the freezer with bread, and this became our mainstay. We were asked out a few times, and I could see Freda making mental notes; before long we would try again, I told myself. After it occurred to her to acquire plain white linen napkins, perhaps; that would be a useful diagnostic. We'd crack it yet.

We settled into an uneasy routine. Freda made herself a small workroom on the top floor, installed a ghetto-blaster, bought a few picture frames and ruinous items of furniture at farm roups, and took to spending a lot of time up there listening to Blondie, Oasis and Linda Ronstadt at high volume while practising the higher fakery: I could only be thankful for Kilmollich's thick stone walls. She found out about bole and papier-mâché, and since she had a good steady hand, she got expert at lining and at applying gold leaf, and worked out quite a good line in pseudo-Chinese lacquer using dead flat oil and yacht-varnish. She also spent quite a bit of time reading about art and interiors, and the results of her labours came to look increasingly like the product of an educated taste.

Meanwhile, the next major challenge to our way of life materialised in November, as the winter party season appeared on the horizon, for the time being, as a cloud no bigger than a man's hand. When the stiffie fell out of its thick, expensive envelope, I looked at it with mixed feelings. There's always that question after a parting of the ways: which of you is going to get the invitations? Most of what passed for society hereabouts had probably sided with Lilias, but I'd done a lot of work at Pittullie and I'd been on lunching terms with them . . . a conundrum for poor Lady Pitsligo which even Ms Manners would've been pushed to find an answer for.

'What's that?' Freda asked, eyeing the gold-edged card in my hand.

'We've been asked to the Christmas do at Pittullie Castle.'

'Oh, yes?' She was a bit more interested that she was trying to sound. 'That's Lord Pitsligo, isn't it? How many people do they have usually?'

'Fifty to sixty? It's a big do. They've got a sodding great ball-room, which they put in out of sycophancy when Queen Vicky was a young married, so they've the space for major entertaining. I sorted out the roof for them after they started spending.'

'I thought they were filthy rich?'

'Oh, they are now. The family was just about wiped out by the agricultural depression after World War I, only the thing is, they owned a lot of miserable farmland around Cruden Bay, so when your old pals in the oil world needed a terminal all of a sudden back in the seventies, the present lord's father sold it for an absolute fortune, which was sheer dumb luck. But once they were in the money, they were intelligent about it, sent a son or two off to the City, and made some clever investments. Then the current Lord Pitsligo got interested in politics, so he started doing some putting-right at Pittullie, and took up hospitality in a big way. I mean, it's not quite the Aboyne Ball, but it's definitely a social landmark.' A sudden horrible thought struck me. 'Freda, can you dance?'

'I'm not bad. It runs in the family. You wouldn't think it to look at him now, but Dad was once the jive champion of Hammersmith Palais.'

'Oh, God.' I'd have been tempted to laugh if it hadn't been so bloody serious. 'Scottish dancing, I mean.'

She looked at me over her coffee cup. 'What the hell'd I know that for?' she asked simply. I stared at her across a vast gulf of mutually unexamined assumptions.

'Oops,' I said, when I could speak again. 'Sorry, darling, but "Strip the Willow" is in your future.'

'Can't you just say you don't do it?'

'I'm afraid that if you don't actually walk with a stick, you'll find it's quite difficult. I'm sorry, Freda. One's supposed to.'

'Whenever you say "one" it's always about something effing ridiculous,' she spat.

'Oh, darling. It's not difficult. You might even enjoy it.'

Her face was blankly and absolutely sceptical.

Actually, she picked up the basic steps very quickly. If it was at all difficult, after all, half-drunk posh Scots wouldn't be able to do it. Like her respected Dad, she was a lovely little mover. What she wasn't, unfortunately, was interested.

'It's all right', I insisted, while she glared at me, after an idiotic episode in which I had put a CD of traditional Scottish dance-music on the player so that we could spin each other around in the drawing-room with all the furniture pushed back against the walls. Hamish MacHoot and the Sporrans were still going a-yumpity yump in the background; I switched them off. 'Just walk through a couple of reels, and that's honour satisfied, and you can go and vamp Lord Pitsligo.' I didn't want it to sound as if I was actually pleading with her; it was always a mistake with Freda to admit weakness.

A couple of weeks later, I was up at six because I needed to be at a site meeting in Kirkcaldy before ten, and I was very surprised to find her stirring as well. 'How come?' I asked, when she sat up at the sound of my alarm.

'I wasn't asleep, so I might as well,' she said casually, like the lying bitch she was. 'I'm going shopping.' Then she just disappeared while I was in the shower. I'm not at my brightest at that hour, so at first I vaguely assumed that she was bound for Turriff, where there's a shop she likes, though on second thoughts, I couldn't think why she'd want to be there shortly after seven o'clock in the morning – but there's a swimming pool in Turriff which opens early, so it was a possibility. Or, perhaps more likely, she'd already canvassed the local shops, so she was heading for Edinburgh, hoping that if she got there early enough she might be able to find a parking place. I was disturbed, though, to find that she wasn't at home when I got in a bit after six, so I rang her mobile.

'Darling, where are you?' I yelled. It was a very bad line.

'About to head back,' I heard faintly. 'Don't wait for me.'

She turned up at twenty to midnight, just when I was thinking of ringing the police; I heard the car, and raced out.

'Where the hell have you been?' She straightened up, pulling armfuls of huge, expensive-looking bags from the back seat. 'Christ. What's all that?'

'I haven't been shopping for ages,' she said, slamming the car door. 'There was a lot I wanted. How was your day?'

'Have you been to Edinburgh?' I asked.

'London.' She brushed past, while it sank in that she'd gone and bought herself a ticket for the eight-fifteen plane and not even bothered to tell me.

'For heaven's sake! We haven't that kind of money!'

'I put it on the plastic.'

'You have to pay off cards, you imbecilic bitch!'

She tossed the bags into the closet under the stairs. 'David, I've got to have some fun. I've been climbing the walls.'

I'd had just about enough. I was ready to strangle her. But she came swiftly towards me when I'd expected her to back away or stand her ground, and letting her coat slip to the ground, pressed herself up against me.

'Hit me,' she said intensely. 'Do what you like. I've been very, very bad.'

'How bad?' I dug my fingertips into her bottom, hard enough to leave bruises, grinding her against me. I have strong fingers. It must've hurt quite a lot.

'Really bad.' She was pulling my shirt out, running her nails up my back, digging them in. 'Hit me till I scream and cry.'

It worked. I am ashamed to admit it, but it did, because she wasn't afraid at all. I took her shirt at the neck and tore it off her, the buttons ricocheting all round the hall, and by the time it was in shreds on the floor I'd forgotten all about strangling her; we clawed each other's clothes off, and ended up having very rough sex halfway up the stairs; she had bruises in the most unlikely places the next day, and I had to dig splinters out of my knees with her eyebrow tweezers before we went to bed. There was that brinkmanship in her always. She liked life on the edge, but I was appalled by the rage she'd unleashed in me – she assumed she'd always be able to control me, to deflect me, and I could only hope to God that she was right.

That was the last I heard of her shopping trip. She must've squirrelled her loot away discreetly in the course of the next day. When I thought about it, I presumed she'd had a sudden lurch of social confidence and rushed off to buy a ball dress. In the fullness of time, I was bound to find out.

I had a separate dressing-room at Kilmollich – the rooms were not large, but there was no shortage of them, and Freda's stuff took up a lot of space. And also, if I had an early start, it was handy to be able to dress and sort myself out without disturbing her. For the Pittullie Ball, my own dressing was, for once, quite a business;

the kilt and its accoutrements present one set of difficulties, white tie (I always ruin at least two before I get one to sit right) another. At last, thoroughly upset, I was successfully assembled from dancing brogues and socks in the same tartan as my kilt, i.e. Macleod (an arcanum: you need to go on your knees to an absolutely top, black-belt knitter to get a socially acceptable pair of socks; mine had been made ten years previously by a friend of my ex-wife's old nanny) all the way up to the deeply pansy Bonny Prince Charlie jacket with the silver buttons, and the white tie. I glanced uneasily at my watch, and went through to see how Freda was getting on.

I walked into the bedroom, and stopped dead. Freda was standing in the middle of the room in her new dress, contemplating the effect in the wardrobe mirror. The outfit in question was bright red, sewn with red crystals, skin tight, and asymmetric, with a slit up one side practically to waist level. Some kind of ghoulish infrastructure was shoving her mammaries up so high they sprouted from just under her collarbones like a pair of Cruise missiles. The bloody thing was quite patently designed to give the illusion of Marilyn Monroe curves to a woman with a figure like a lamp-post. Since Freda actually did have curves in the first place, she looked absolutely dreadful, and although looking dreadful is quite permissible in the context of a Scottish Christmas ball, she also looked as common as muck, which effing well isn't. God, I thought, I can't be seen with her.

'Christ Almighty, you can't go in that!' I said, before I could stop myself.

'It's Versace.'

'I don't care what it is. Get it off.' I was appalled. 'You look like something out of *Hello*. Actually, you look like two somethings out of *Hello*. Have you any idea?'

'I'll wear what I sodding well like,' she snarled, but I thought the last point had gone home, so I followed up while the going was good.

'Look, darling, have a bit of sense. That dress was designed for Liz Hurley. It's guaranteed to make an actual woman look like a hippo.' I saw her eyes straying towards the mirror with a hint of doubt in them, and I thought I'd probably won.

'The *Caledonia* happy snappers will be there,' I said. 'They always do Pittullie. The way your hips look in that, you could tell them you'd just landed the lead in *Moby Dick*, and they'd believe you.'

'Piss on you, David.' She was looking dangerous, and the impulse to rip the thing off her was rising unstoppably, but I knew what'd happen if I did, and it was vital we actually get to Pittullie. I'd got about three months' work out of the last ball, what with picking my conversations carefully.

'Freda. Wear that green dress you bought when we went to the Patons. You look fantastic in it.'

'I'll wear the Alaïa,' she said.

Fine. Just as long as she made her mind up. The Alaïa was obscene, but not actively ridiculous. I'd nothing against her showing off her assets, just as long as she didn't actually hang out a 'for sale' sign.

'I'll undo you,' I said. I wanted her in a better mood; she was angry and sulky with defeat, and would doubtless be thinking up ways to take it out on me. If she got plastered, which she probably would, I could see storms ahead.

Freda got changed, re-sorted out her hair and her make-up, and changed her shoes three times. I watched her, chafing, made appreciative noises at random, and otherwise said nothing, with immense self-control. We were going to be late; I could feel a clock ticking away in the back of my mind, but there was nothing I could do about it; if I said anything, she'd only punish me by taking off half her make-up and starting again, or stop to bicker. After an unconscionable time she finally decided she was dressed. There was an evening coat on the bed, heavy black velvet with gold embroidery here and there, and I put her into it, with a tweak and a squeeze and a kiss on the back of the neck to put her in better countenance with herself.

Actually, looked at objectively, things didn't go that badly. But by the time we arrived I was in such a state of nerves I was imagining one fearful scene after another. Freda looked a bit out of place, but not wildly so, there was a goodly sprinkling of wide taffeta skirts and tartan sashes, but a lot of the younger set were fashionably dressed. What was more, she neither talked nor drank to excess. The dancing was certainly not her finest hour. Her shoes, inevitably, were delicate pumps with smooth leather soles and heels like needles, so it took her all her time to stay upright; she didn't so much dance as get flung from one kilted buffoon to another like a pinball bouncing from flipper to flipper; I remember birling her in passing and catching a look of controlled desperation.

Things went a bit better at supper; with a cleavage practically down to her navel, she didn't lack for admirers. But I could see people I knew glancing at her and then at me. Cool, amused glances. My stomach was knotting up; one word out of place, and I'd end up belting someone in the mouth.

The trouble was, even apart from being on tenterhooks about Freda, I was miserable on my own account. I should've been enjoying it, which always makes unhappiness so much worse. I like Scottish dancing once in a while, the communality and the physicality. I knew a good many of the people there, and since the ball-aching correctness of my kit defined me as (in the modern sense) a member of the clan, I was already beyond the 'pass, friend, and be recognised' point with anyone I chose to address. But I began to realise with secret dismay, as I drifted about social-ising, trying not to lose track of Freda meanwhile, that not having Lilias's genealogy to fall back on was a significant handicap. When I was married to a Skene, I could always open the conversation with a reassuring ten minutes or so on family history, establishing precisely how my wife was related to the individual I was talking to or one of their immediate connections; the platitudes that followed segued very naturally into old buildings and from thence to chatting knowledgeably about their care, with my professional status mentioned only as we were parting, or not at all. Under the new dispensation, the problem was twofold: avoiding being identified as 'that bastard who walked out on poor Lilias', and, without county connections to fall back on, avoiding sounding as if I was blatantly touting for custom. I put my foot wrong more than once.

It all went on and on, but at last, we were able to make our escape. We got ourselves home without incident, and headed straight for the kitchen, Freda kicking off her shoes as she went. She was gagging for a cup of tea, and I was dying for a proper drink; it's not that the Pitsligos are mean, but I knew I'd have to drive us home.

When we got to the kitchen, Freda plopped into a chair, looking as defeated as I'd ever seen her. 'I've had it up to here with Aberdeenshire,' she said explosively. 'I can't stand it. I want to go back to London. Just let's go. When I went down that time, I felt like I was alive again. It wasn't just the shopping. I don't belong up here in Fit-Like-Land. I'm bored of trying to fit in, and seeing your posh mates sneering.'

'Yes, well, you married it, didn't you?'

'You don't belong here either,' she snapped. 'You came here because of Lilias.'

That was true; in fact, it was a very good point. I was born and bred in the Lowlands, it'd taken me long enough to get used to the North-East. She followed up her advantage swiftly. 'You could go anywhere. What's keeping you?'

I opened my mouth to object, and shut it again. The girls, was the response which came to my mind; they didn't actually want to see me at the moment, but they'd come round eventually, and I wanted to be there for them when they did. But Freda had a point, loath though I was to acknowledge it, though perhaps not the one she thought she was making. Since practically every big house in the North-East belonged to some member of my ex-wife's kith and kin, the divorce had damaged my long-term financial viability to an extent which I was only just beginning to realise. I was still doing good work, there were no complaints from the customers, but with Lil doing the Aberdeenshire wronged wives' circuit, I wasn't picking up new trade off my social contacts the way I used to. Freda's unspeakable cronies weren't much help: they were oil wives or near offer, and their husbands, like Freda's quondam Malcolm, weren't high enough up their respective hierarchies to be in the more prestigious types of house – and even if they had been, they wouldn't have had much say.

'It's not actually the land that time forgot,' I said defensively. 'You can buy fresh pesto and lemon-grass in the Huntly Somerfield's.'

'Who cares? You can't go and see a film. It's the land of the friggin' dead. And if the sort of do we've just been to's the pinnacle of the social calendar, I tell you, I'm leaving.'

Then we quarrelled, of course. Same old stuff: if you didn't think I was good enough why did you marry me, yada, yada, yada, shut up you stupid bitch, no I won't shut up, you can't make me, oh, can't I, and so to bed.

We talked a bit more reasonably the next day.

'Okay. Let's pretend I'm hanging my tile out somewhere else. What about Edinburgh?' I'd been thinking about Edinburgh over breakfast. I had a lot of contacts down there, and I was fond of the place: Daddy had been, in his day, one of the few demonstrably heterosexual members of the Scottish Bar other than Nicky Fairbairn, so Sandy, Caroline and I had enjoyed a privileged child-hood among the Edinburgh haute-bourgeoisie, in a beautiful three-storey 1800s house in Heriot Row (which my parents, alas, had contrived to sell just before Edinburgh prices went through the ceiling). 'There's a lot going on there. Don't forget the Festival.' And art-galleries, concerts . . . Scottish National Opera grudgingly tours a camper van with one piano and three singers around the boondocks, which it sees fit to describe as 'outreach', but I hadn't seen a proper production for fifteen years.

She just looked at me blankly. 'What the hell for? I've told you, I've had it with smug bastard Scots. I want to go home.'

Oh, well. It'd been worth trying, but I'd been pretty sure that was what she'd say. 'But where d'you actually want to be? Sloane Square?' Over my dead body, I thought privately; Freda within popping-in range of Harvey Nicks was not a prospect that pleased.

'No,' she said decidedly. 'It's full of snotty bitches, just like here. I want to live in the Barbican, where nobody knows anyone.'

Actually, I could see the attraction, though it offered a diametrically opposite combination of isolation with claustrophobia to the one we currently enjoyed. Since our social life in the North-East had gone definitively pear-shaped, physical claustrophobia plus social isolation was coming to hold a new sort of appeal. And Freda really wanted it. Habitual liar that she was, there was a particular timbre in her voice which indicated complete sincerity, not often heard. How long, I wondered, had she lain beside me at night, listening to the rooks squabbling in the birches and ettling for the rushing traffic of the City? Poor little bitch. Then Helen and Effie came back into my mind: they were Lil's babies for now, and their notion of bliss still centred on gymkhanas and making lumpy scones in the Aga, but in just a few short years, five at the most, London would be a magnet. It always was. And if Freda and I were in the Barbican, I'd have an alternative lifestyle to offer them, something really sickeningly cool, not just a variation on what they were used to.

Professionally, the move was far from impossible, in fact, I could see distinct advantages. I had a very good record – don't imagine from what I'm admitting about my nefarious doings at Kilmollich that they represented my ordinary professional standards. If it had been a question of a client, I'd've advised him not to touch the place unless he had £50k to spend on it, and I'd've insisted that he start with structural work. But then, I wouldn't've been the one living with the client's winsome wife, and that makes a difference. London is full of old buildings needing work, few places fuller, and there's an educated, wealthy clientèle wanting things done properly. The main difficulty would be getting decent workmen, given that no respectable tradesman could afford to live any nearer the Smoke than Chelmsford – working out of Inverurie, I was absolutely spoilt for reliable, competent people. I already drove for hours every day; a different sort of driving, but at least I was used to spending the time behind the wheel. And I'd rather liked the Barbican, when I went to look at it one time, the way it was a mightily bizarre combination of moats, modern flats, Roman walls, skyscrapers, and some species of medieval Fishflogger's Hall marooned in the middle of it all — more like Rome than London, really. It might be interesting living there, and working there too.

Trying to make Freda's dream come true, on the other hand, was insanely depressing.

'The Barbican?' said Sandy. 'You'd be struggling.'

I had rung him, in his capacity as Real World Consultant, and put the problem to him.

'What's the going rate for a two-bedroom flat?'

'Oh . . . four-fifty, four-eighty?'

'*What?*'

'Effing ridiculous, but true. What's Kilmollich worth, d'you think?'

There was no alcohol within reach, I wished there was. 'Three-forty.'

'Mmmmm. If you're lucky, Davie. You've not got around to the big work yet, and there isn't a garden.'

'Four acres of grounds.'

'But not very useful, except for protecting you from pin-headed farmers. It's mostly rock or shelter-belt. You haven't got stabling or grazing, and there isn't a staff cottage.'

'There could be. The woodshed round the back's actually the remains of the men's bothy. It'd fake up a treat.'

Sandy sucked his teeth reflectively. 'The trouble is, how long'd it take you? You haven't got loose cash, so you'd have to do most of it yourself. But by the time you'd added thirty or forty to the value of Kilmollich, there'd be another fifty on the price of the hypothetical flat. I'm not being a bastard for the sake of it, Davie, but them's the facts. Time's not on your side, and I can't see the crash coming yet awhile. Your best bet'd be to put it on at offers above two-nine-five, hoping to be bid up to three-twenty, maybe three-forty. You might get more, but you'd have to wait, and time's your problem.'

Lilias and the girls had a dog; an opinionated retriever bitch, as spoiled as hell. Bella loved the car, and if Lil was going somewhere where she didn't want to take her, and the dog hadn't been shut in properly, you'd find her hurtling down the drive after the Volvo – I timed her once, and she had a sprinting speed of around twenty-two mph. For the first hundred yards, she'd keep pace, level with the driver's door, then when Lil hit thirty or so, you'd see her falling behind, straining for some kind of miraculous gift of extra swiftness, till eventually she was forced to stop, panting and discon-solate, and watch the car out of sight. Listening to Sandy, I knew exactly how she felt.

'Does it have to be the Barbican?' he asked.

'It can't be the burbs. And the Barbican's what she's set her heart on.'

'Tricky. What you need's an idiot who falls in love with your place. Fortunately, there's no world shortage of idiots that I know of. Keep your pecker up, pal. Let me know if I can help.'

There was the briefest of pauses; I was trying to formulate the unaskable question, when he put me out of my misery.

'No can do, Davie. I haven't anything to spare at the moment. No hard feelings?'

'Course not. I know with you it's up and down like the proverbial whore's drawers. Thanks for the support . . .'

'. . . And you'll wear it always?' An old joke, we'd punted it back and forth for twenty-five years. 'Good man. Look after yourself.'

IV

First catch your idiot, as Mrs Beeton nearly said. I explained the whole thing to Freda, and I think she understood.

'We're going to have to abandon Phase Two,' I said. 'I doubt very much if anyone'll think of asking about the septic tank; they'll assume that since the house was bought and sold fairly recently all that sort of stuff was cleared up last time. I'm going for a sort of double bluff. Because I'm an architect, people are going to assume I haven't just papered over the cracks, but we don't actually have time to do anything properly. I'll start on the exterior work the minute the weather'll let me. The inside'll pass muster as the sort of temporary job you do while you're getting the place habitable, and I'll have to do the same by the outside. I'll colourwash it, by hook or by crook, and it'll look surprisingly good. If I nail the loose slates back and put one coat of paint on the outside windows, it'll pass. The goal is to get it looking wonderful by the end of April, and get it flogged before the schools go back. Received wisdom is that you can't shift a big house after that.'

There is simply no point even thinking about exterior work with sleety winds howling round the house. I was looking up the long-range weather forecasts twice a day, but there was nothing I could do to make them any different. I was able to exploit a patch of unseasonably mild weather in February, but after that, I couldn't do anything more until the end of March. The problem was, we had a queue of clients needing outside work, so I had a very limited capacity to take time off and work on my own place. All that spring, I endured agonies of frustration clambering about on other people's roofs and wishing they were my own. But, the minute Kilmollich looked like something, we got Saville's in.

I must say, the photograph they produced was a winner. You could've used it on a box of Christmas shortbread. They'd come on a sunny spring day with very blue skies, and used Ektachrome to sharpen up the contrast; the newly creamy-white walls rose tall and graceful like a fairy castle among the fresh, lime green leaves of the silver birches, the wee turrets adding an agreeable touch of fantasy. No loose slates were visible. It looked trim, cared-for, and charming, with a little ruff of daffodils around the base of the walls. The interior shots were good too, taken with a sufficiently wide-angle lens that the rooms looked quite spacious; they were full of flowers and so on, we'd done our absolute best.

We then proceeded to have a major row with Saville's: their view of what the place was worth was almost identical to my brother's, which came as no surprise, but I insisted that they put it on at offers over three-four-five which got me a lot of sniffing and 'on your own head be it'. I was therefore not expecting an awful lot from them, which is just as well. There was a healthy-looking list of 'interest' after the first couple of weeks, which deceived Freda momentarily, but alas, they were the usual suspects to a man and woman. I looked down the list of names.

'Hugh's a spectator . . . Peter's not going to want it, it's the wrong end of the county . . . oh, God, *he*'s coming . . .'

'You can't know all of them,' said Freda.

'Oh, can't I? Small Society Syndrome. It's not that everyone knows everyone else, it's that everyone can get to everyone else in one move, d'you see? This is the usual old-buildings mob coming out of curiosity, Georgian Society spies, undercover agents from SPAB, and the provisional wing of the Saltire Society. They're practically all of them living in old houses already, and they're none of them thinking of moving, because if they were, they'd've been putting the word around and I'd've heard it. None of them punted on Kilmollich when it was cheap, and they know perfectly well I haven't had time to do much. They just want to see what I've been up to. The only bloke on this list who might actually want it is Cosmo; they're in a wee tower-house just outside Buckie and they're as Catholic as all-get-out – I think Isabel's just had their seventh, and it must be straining at the seams. But I know for a fact he looked at it last time, and he didn't make an offer, so I doubt if he wants it at £350k.'

'So it's all useless? None of this is going to work?'

'I hope not, darling. But we can't fool the local castle crowd. They know how long I've had it, and they know I've not had money to chuck at it. We're after a foreigner. Someone from the South, who'll think it sounds cheap at the price.'

The showings were purgatory. I had no option but to be agreeable, everyone who looked over the place was interested in old buildings, and any North-Eastern old-building-fancier was either someone who had employed me in the past or someone who might employ me in the future. The thing is, there isn't a lot to do up here at weekends. I knew that anyone who needed to get into Aberdeen on a regular basis was a timewaster by definition, but I could hardly say so; by the end of a day's breezy civility, my piss was boiling, as a low friend of mine puts it.

But it was hard to keep my temper when I saw Glenlochie's old Bentley sliding up the drive. He lives in Edinburgh, for Christ's sake. He made no secret of the fact that he was just there out of interest. He was off to a Scottish Georgian Society meeting at Inverness and it was on his way. I wanted to throw him out, but he knows everybody, and what's worse, he's got very sharp eyes. I walked him round, chatting about various mutual acquaintances, and he was full of praise; he hadn't looked at it last time round, but he knew people who had. As he left, he touched my arm.

'David. It's looking marvellous. Go on. Tell us what's wrong? Subsidence, dry rot, dodgy access?'

'None of the above, Finlay,' I parried. 'Freda's keen to move South, so we're just trying to cut loose from it a-s-a-p.'

I wasn't at all sure he believed me. 'Well, I wish you the best of British luck. London prices're still ratcheting up like a taxi meter. D'you know anyone who actually wants it?'

I wished, how I wished, I had been able to say yes, but once the local antiquarians had seen all they wanted to, things languished.

What we really needed was someone with more money than sense who was ready, willing and able to live in rural Aberdeenshire. Put that way, it sounded like a tall order, but there, of course, *Country Life* was poised to do its very best for us; I hadn't thought that Saville's would sort us out unaided; it was when we appeared in the *Death*, or so I fervently hoped, we'd find our punter. Somewhere out there, there must be asset-strippers who'd stripped their last asset, and longed for blue remembered hills. My brother, twenty years on. Surely the Square Mile was full of burnt-out Scots and politicians with Northern connections who'd decided to spend more time with their families? It was a bit like dry-fly fishing; you sized up your river, worked out likely lurking-places, and dropped your lure delicately over the spot, but there was always the fundamental question: would anything rise to the bait?

We had a quarter-page in the *Death*, and even I, who knew better, thought that words like 'unspoiled gem' were the ones which rose naturally to the lips. It looked like a dream. Saville's were hard at work. Particulars were flying out of the door, they told us, they had to reprint twice. None of which seemed to be getting us anywhere much: there was a great deal of footering about, invariably concluding with 'lovely house, but too far'. Too far from the airport, from Aberdeen, from anywhere, really. I was going through a pack of Rennies a day. But at long last, there was a definite nibble. Some species of retiring senior civil servant, Sir Archibald Leithen – obviously a Scot, from the name – who wanted a house in the North. Even after he'd worked out where it was, he was not deterred; we'd become inured to losing people at that point, but Sir Archibald came back. There were phone calls and emails, and then he asked if I could send some more photographs; no hurry, he and his lady wife were off to Tuscany for their holidays. Another three weeks' delay, God damn it; though looking on the bright side, there was always the remote possibility another punter would break cover in the interim. It was a sweltering thirty to thirty-four degrees in the Med that July, I could only hope that they were having an absolutely vile time, and the whole experience had the effect of enhancing the charm of northern Scotland.

Meanwhile, I got a phone call from one of the joiners who worked for me; a nice, steady bloke. Decoded out of the Doric, it amounted to saying that his father-in-law, who was a farmer, had turned up an interesting stone on his farm in New Deer – so if a hud a mintie, dud a want a wee lookie?

I happened to be passing that way a couple of days later, so I gave the old man a ring on the mobile to see if he was there, which he was, and when I got there, I realised he was probably very seldom anywhere else. It was very remote, at the end of a series of winding, inconclusive roads ending halfway up a hill. A Marshall Plan tractor was standing in the muddy yard of a totally unimproved farmhouse, with the curtains faded to whitish, the pattern bleached off them by fifty or more summers. An old lady in a nylon wrapper was peeking out of the door and, otherwise, there were two frail, shy, spry, elderly men, unmistakably brothers, and a friendly collie, the four of them living a life which already looked like industrial archaeology. I felt as if I were looking at them down the wrong end of a telescope. The old chaps were very courteous, and after a ritual offer of tea, which I refused – I'd had all I could stand of unimproved farmhouse kitchens, and the water supply was probably shared with the pigs – we went and picked our way through the slurry to look at what they had to show me.

It was not a pretty sight, a lump of greyish limestone, with some almost unrecognisably weathered raised-sunk letters – i.e., the letters standing proud of the surface, not carved down into it, the giveaway marker of really crap stone. Even raised-sunk, they seemed to be melting back in as if the stone were made of sugar; I read them rather tentatively as I.K., W.F., with a date, 1681, or 1661, maybe. A typical sort of thing for that part of the country, it would have been made for a wedding – James Kerr with Wilhelmina Forbes, let's say. It was doing no good where it was; it didn't look like much. When I left, the farmer was twenty quid richer, the stone was in the boot of the car, and both of us were pretty pleased with ourselves.

I showed it to Freda at the weekend. She was understandably unimpressed.

'What d'you want that for?' she said, peering at it.

'I've had an idea. A major high bluff. I'm going to re-cut it.'

'I didn't know you could do that.'

'I wouldn't try it with marble or proper limestone, but this stuff is practically sand. I've got a couple of old stone-chisels and a mallet in my toolbox. I've sometimes needed just to tidy up the odd detail here and there. This is in such bad nick, you could get away with murder. By the time it's finished, it's going to say I.R., and then there'll be a blobby thistle with two leaves, and a rose, and 1601.'

'Why?'

'I.R. for James the sixth. Thistle and Rose, because those were his badges. 1601, because he was still in Scotland then. Let's say, in some parallel universe, he just happened to pay Kilmollich a royal visit. He was a notorious woofter, you know. Maybe the son of the house had long legs and yellow hair, and his loving parents were keen to catapult him into the royal bed, stranger things have happened. So surely, if they'd been honoured by a royal visit, or even a royal leg-over, they'd have got the local stonemason onto the job.'

I could see light beginning to dawn. 'The history of the house,' she said.

'Absolutely. Like my fake Lorimer fireplaces. We're giving the place more interesting antecedents than it actually had, don't you see? Though by the time you get that far back, it's debatable anyway. I'm not going to go claiming that there was a royal visit, there'll just be evidence, casually, that there might've been one. They'll do the rest themselves.'

She liked it; I don't think I ever got a compliment out of her, except about sex, but I was beginning to feel that I could tell when she was actually amused.

Then there was the question of photographs for the Leithens. I surveyed the scene, with a sudden access of despair. It wasn't anything like good enough. If we were going to bluff them to a ridiculous offer, then we were simply going to have to look a lot richer. Any hint of desperation on our side and the whole perilous scam would evaporate. It was pleasant, you could give it that. Neutral painted furniture against off-white walls, varnished plank floors, *très* Swedish Manor House, mutedly classy and inoffensive. There was the Chevalier Macinnes over the fireplace, of course, but he wasn't enough all by himself . . .

'What's wrong?' Freda asked, watching my face.

'It's all background and no foreground,' I said. 'You can get a long way with fakes, but you've got to have a few really grand pieces to lift them if it's really going to look *signorile*, and there's nothing we can do about it unless we burgle Leith Hall.' I cast a glance of loathing round the Ikea light-fittings. 'See? You don't notice them, but what we need's a bloody great oversized Venetian chandelier.' As I was speaking, I had a sudden and wonderful idea. 'Hang on. My brother.'

'Sandy? I liked him. He's nice.'

He *is* nice, and what is more, he is generous, and we had bailed one another out a good few times over the years. I thought he might respond to a call to the colours. 'The thing is,' I explained, 'he's got some very good furniture in store up here, waiting for when he comes back to Scotland properly. He's got an excellent eye, so he's picked antiques up as and when he's found them, but his London place is the size of a phone-box and he doesn't like leaving much in Stonehaven because he lets it from time to time, or lends it to friends.'

'D'you think he'd lend us them?'

'He might.'

I rang him after dinner – he's not often home before nine.

'Sandy Laurence.'

'It's David.'

'Oh hi. Don't make it too long, pal, the footie's on in half an hour.'

'Okay, short and simple. Can I borrow some of your stuff to

dress the set? Just while we're trying to get Kilmollich shifted? We need one great big fuck-off thing for each room, then it'll pass.'

There was a thoughtful silence at the other end. He saw the point at once. 'I don't see why not, Davie,' he said after a while. 'You know what you're doing, and it wouldn't hurt for it to get an airing. It's a shame you lost everything with Lilias, you had some nice pieces. Things going well up there?'

'Not too bad.'

'I'll give you a tinkle after I've spoken to the storage people. Oh – and Davie. You will insure it, won't you?'

''Course.'

'Best to Freda. I'll be in touch.'

He rang off leaving me breathless with relief.

Meanwhile, I went into overdrive. If we were photographing in detail, then there were things which would have to go. We were still using Old Macdonald's storage heaters, on account of the non-functional Aga, and it was essential that they vanish. They spoke only too eloquently of poverty. At the same time, in the unspeakable eventuality that we didn't shift Kilmollich, we couldn't do without them. There was a hugely strong laddie called Dod I knew of who had a job on the rigs, but was available for casual work when he was onshore, and he and I wrestled the damned things down the stairs and hid them in the back of the woodshed. Have you ever tried to shift a storage heater? They're literally full of bricks, and they weigh several hundredweight apiece. Even with Dod doing his share or more of the lifting, getting a round dozen of the things out of the house nearly killed me.

As it happened, I was working on a manse over by New Pitsligo around then, and as part of the refit, they were replumbing, and chucking out old radiators. They were the sort that are a nice, chubby, old-fashioned shape, so rather than putting them in the skip, I nicked them. They were covered with that odd rather dusty-looking bronze paint you used to get, so I stripped them off and sprayed them with white car-enamel. I could site them, at least; who was to know they weren't plumbed in? The partics said 'benefits from partial central heating', which referred to the revolting objects I'd removed. It's not the kind of thing people generally think to look into, and with any luck at all, we'd be over the hills and far away before the Leithens started telling everyone in Scotland.

Sandy nipped up about ten days later, and we hired ourselves a Ford Transit and went to meet him off the plane and carry him off to lunch at the Silver Darlings. I'd just about recovered the use of my stomach muscles by then. Mellow with expensive food, he took us out to an industrial estate on the periphery of Aberdeen, and we got his storage container opened up. He'd evidently been spending money to some purpose over the years: I admired his taste. He let us borrow two Bokhara rugs, a really good Biedermeier sofa with mellow old upholstery and gilt caryatids supporting the arms, a couple of Queen Anne chairs with petit-point embroidery, an inlaid bureau, and a stupendous Delft tile-picture of a sea-battle.

'That's a fabulous thing,' I said when he pulled it out. 'I've not seen it.'

'Good, isn't it? Admiral de Ruyter gubbing the English off Sole Bay, I believe. I haven't had it all that long – I picked it up in a closing-down sale in Fochabers for five hundred.'

I whistled. 'Lucky sod. It'd be worth a fortune if you sold it in Holland.'

'I could get £6k for it in Bond Street, easily. But I like it.'

'So do I. If we hang it over the Aga,' I said, 'nobody's going to look at anything else in the kitchen at all. Sandy, you're a star.'

'It's really great of you,' said Freda. She was wearing one of her linen shirts, and looking at him with an open admiration which was clearly reciprocated. He gave her a somewhat unbrotherly kiss and squeeze, and then we all got into the van together; we were dropping him at Dyce station so he could take the train to Stonehaven to play with his fossils. Then we hauled the loot back home to Kilmollich, where it transformed the place. It looked absolutely wonderful. Freda generally needed to have seen something for herself before she quite believed in it; I'm not sure she'd actually envisaged what a difference a few really good pieces could make. But once everything was in situ, she was delighted, as enthusiastic as I'd ever seen her.

'Can we get it into a style mag?' she asked, looking at the beautiful drawing-room with immense satisfaction.

'Takes too long, darling,' I said with regret. 'We might talk ourselves into the *Press & Journal* Homes pull-out, but I doubt if it'd help. I'm not saying posh people don't read the *P&J*, but it's only the local paper. It wouldn't bring in anyone who hasn't seen the place already.'

Then it was just a matter of waiting for a nice day. Like all restoring architects I'd ever encountered, I had a fair range of high-wattage portable lighting at my disposal – you never know when you're going to need it. Since all the windows are by definition at the end of a four-foot tunnel through an immensely thick stone wall, tower-houses are gloomy inside, and Kilmollich was no exception. I needed maximum natural light, plus all the back-up I could muster. I had Maglites taped to the walls, and Freda up a stepladder aiming a two-million-candlepower portable searchlight; I took about six of each shot, then we moved all the kit around, and started rearranging the lights for the next, taking good care that Sandy's lendings were well to the fore.

When we got the films developed and selected out the best photographs, they looked wonderful. What a place. I wished I lived there. They were also a vast success. When the Leithens got back from Italy, which I was delighted to hear they had not enjoyed, there was no inconsiderable amount of gush out of St John's Wood. I was getting a distinct impression that Lady Leithen had fallen in love with the house. Initially, we'd seemed to be dealing with Sir Archbald, but now, 'my wife thinks . . .' was coming up in every other sentence. Excellent; he was a clear-minded old sod; once sentimentality entered into the picture, our chances of success exponentially increased. After all, there wasn't the vestige of a rational reason for buying a place like that. You'd have to be buying a dream to want it at all. Freda, meanwhile, got herself some particulars, and started dreaming about the Barbican.

It was a very good summer work-wise – essential from the financial point of view, disastrous from the personal angle. I had a great big Scottish Heritage job on; the Kirkcaldy thing had suddenly got clearance, to my immense surprise. I was disinterring a fabulous Renaissance painted ceiling from underneath the remains of eighteenth-century decorated plaster in a building which was itself neglected, structurally dodgy and needing work, and the whole thing had to be done to an inflexible deadline and limited budget. It was a huge, delicate project, and a high-profile one: the Society for the Protection of Ancient Buildings, caught between fascination and disapproval, were paying a lot of attention, and it was, of course, intrinsically both demanding and absorbing. Absolutely not the kind of thing you can do on eighty-five per cent, it needed a hundred per cent commitment, dawn to dusk, because if I screwed up, everyone who mattered would know, and if I didn't, it would be the best advertisement for myself that I could contrive. The partnership hadn't done much government work up to that point, but there was plenty more out there. Moral: Don't screw up. Now, Kirkcaldy is a town much in need of more and better heritage, but the most crucially relevant fact is that it is nearly three hours' drive from Kilmollich. I had no time for my own house, other than weekends, and there was absolutely nothing to be done about it.

Time was crawling on; flats in the Barbican came and went, Freda's temper was on a shorter and shorter fuse. At last, the Leithens made positive arrangements to come up and see for themselves; they were starting to talk money with Saville's, who were bluffing them as best they could: unfortunately, even though we were into August by then, I hadn't finished all the outside work I had meant to do before they came. There was absolutely no way I could skip out on Kirkcaldy, so there was no hope for it: I'd have to get it done that Saturday morning.

The other problem which we faced was the weather. To my horror, the temperature dropped, as it can in August in Aberdeenshire; we were starting to see frost on the grass first thing in the morning. The day the Leithens were due, wouldn't you know it, was definitely cold. At six-thirty, when we got up, it was freezing.

'Freda, we're going to have to have fires all through the house, or they'll stay five minutes and that'll be it.' She nodded, shivering and wrapping herself up in a pashmina. 'You're going to have to do it. I'll have to finish the exterior painting somehow.'

'Okay. I can lay a fire. I'll hide the space-heaters.'

'You can lay anything you've got a mind to, I don't doubt,' I said vulgarly.

One corner of her mouth twitched in a half-smile. 'Leave the inside to me. I'll put all the lights on and make it look good,' she said. 'I'll nip down to Huntly and buy some flowers.'

A sudden thought struck me. 'Darling. Needs must. You're going to have to look like the kind of girl who footers about with open fires by choice, or they'll wonder why the radiators aren't on.'

I dragged on my jeans, a thick sweater and two pairs of socks, and went down to make breakfast; Freda never wanted anything much, but I had a morning's heavy work in front of me.

While I was stuffing some bacon between two slices of bread, she appeared with an air of conscious virtue, wearing a navy turtle-neck and a checked shirt tucked into a pair of boot-cut fine wool trousers, not too tight, hair pulled back into a tortoiseshell clip, pearls and her driving loafers. I had to hand it to her.

'Wonderful. Marvellous. That's fantastic. You almost don't look sexy. It's just what we need.' I gave her a kiss and a cuddle. 'Do your damnedest. Now, I must get this down me and get myself up that sodding ladder or they'll have turned up before I'm finished.'

I'd done all the first and second floor windows, most of the third floor, and the most accessible ones on the fourth floor. Accessibility more or less equals visibility, so it wasn't so much the windows which were the problem, I reckoned, as the gutters. I'd got the roof patched up before Saville's saw it, but the gutters were not well in themselves. There had been a certain amount of rain over the summer, and at the junction points, there were already visible rusty streaks on the new colourwash. Ideally, one does not paint either walls or gutters off a forty-foot ladder, it's incredibly tiring and dangerous, but there was no alternative; I'd hoped to be able to borrow a cherry-picker, which was why they'd got left till last. For the time being, the gutters were getting a scanty coat of black-board paint, the matte black would smooth out their deficiencies unless the sodding Leithens had actually brought a telescope, and I was also painting over the damage to the colourwash. It was an anxious business; on the one hand, I was leaning as far as I dared to either side so as to minimise the number of times I had to move the ladder, but I was also trying to not actually break my neck, and just to make it all that bit more difficult, I was having to paint neatly enough that there would be no tell-tale blobs of wet paint at ground level. My hands were freezing cold, they were also beginning to shake with stress and temper.

One fact I was able to hang onto: the Leithens were coming up by plane and hiring a car. It was therefore unlikely in the extreme that they would turn up an hour ahead of schedule. Up and down I went, laboriously moving the huge, heavy ladder along and going up again with my tins and brushes, working as fast as I dared, which was terrifyingly slowly. I got round at last, and hid the painting paraphernalia along with the storage heaters at the back of the woodshed. I wasn't, thankfully, covered in paint myself, and I'd had the sense to wear surgical gloves, so my hands were clean and not stinking of white spirits either. Then I collapsed the ladder and put it away, at just about the last minute of the eleventh hour; I thought I could hear a motor.

As I came round the side of the house, I saw them getting out of their hire car. Sir Archibald turned out to be one of those inter-changeable late-middle-aged Scottish aristos with a complexion of old red sandstone and eyes like frozen oysters of whom I had seen all too many, while Lady Leithen, with her pearls, puffa-jacket and green woolly tights, was also a familiar enough type, roughly what I thought Lilias would turn into in twenty years or so. Good legs, and still attractive for her age; I mean, you could imagine her getting up to mischief at the Perth Ball while her lord and master was drinking himself pallid in the dining-room.

'Hello, Mrs Laurence,' he said, as she came down the front steps to greet them. 'My wife, Hope.' He shook hands with her, and then with me as I came up to join them. 'Quite a place you've got here. We've been looking forward to this.'

'Did you have a pleasant drive?' I asked them.

'Idyllic. Communications are better than I'd expected. I hadn't realised it was almost all dual carriageway from Aberdeen to Huntly. And a pretty road, too. D'you know, I noticed that the first of the leaves are just starting to turn? Of course, you're a lot further north here.'

O God, remind me about it, I thought, and smiled as best I could. Having come from the airport, that is to say, out of rather than through the city, he had yet to find out about the Aberdeen ring road, I thought viciously. Hah. And you'll see how pretty the high bit of the A97 looks on a snowy morning ... They were Lowlanders, at a good guess, they obviously hadn't realised you can actually get cut off up here. We walked them into the drawing-room. Flowers here and there, a hint of old-fashioned beeswax polish and peat-smoke in the air, the fire was blazing merrily. There was a mellow Bokhara rug on the floor, and the Biedermeier sofa was drawn up convenient to the blaze. Freda had done wonders; if the rest of the house was as good as this, we stood an excellent chance of getting away with it.

'I say, what a picture,' said Lady Leithen. 'It can't be a Raeburn.'

'Just a bit later, it's Sir Thomas Laurence,' I said, delighted that she'd fastened on it.

'Any connection?' he asked.

'He's a direct ancestor, in fact. It's always been in the family. The Chevalier was from one of the old Jacobite families, and got himself killed at Waterloo, you see, so there was poor old Sir Thomas, three hundred guineas out of pocket. It never left the studio.'

'Not so very poor, if that was what he was charging in 1815,' said Sir Archibald dryly.

'He was very successful,' I agreed. 'It was the early commission to paint Queen Caroline that made his fortune. That and great competence, of course.'

'Stunning,' murmured Lady Leithen. Things were off to a good start.

Predictably, Sir Archibald felt the need to assert himself at this point, and started telling us all about himself, confirming my guess.

'The family's from the Borders, but I wouldn't go back there now. The thing about up here is it's still very unspoilt. It's like going back in time, as it were.'

'It is, round here,' said Freda. 'They got as far as the Seventies, then they stopped.'

'The last of the free, eh? Nice to know someone's holding out. We took a look around Deeside – you know, people always used to say, there's Deeside, Donside and Outside . . .'

'But Deeside's got awfully touristy,' said the wife. 'It was quite a shock to us, the last time we came up by car. Donside's much more like the Scotland we remember.'

'That's right. It's still what one comes here for. Mind you, there's some excellent fishing on Deeside.'

'The fishing rights to the burn go with the house,' I pointed out.

'Yes. I noticed that. Anything there? We'll have a proper look-see later on, but when we were coming in, I thought it looked like a good spot for trout.'

If there had ever been trout there, they had presumably been poisoned by Kilmollich sewage, not a thought I proposed to share with the old fool. I shrugged. 'Don't actually know, sir. To be honest, I've been so busy working in the house since we got it, I haven't ever had the time. But the farmers who were here before us won't've bothered themselves.'

'You had a lot to do, did you?'

Freda gave him the benefit of a megawatt smile. 'It was in the most terrible decorative order,' she said. 'I simply couldn't stand it.'

'Gosh, I know what you mean,' said Lady Leithen. 'Farmers' taste!'

Freda simpered at her. 'We should've taken pictures, but at the time it was just incredibly depressing, you know? It looked like a murder scene, I mean, House of Horror, and I couldn't wait to get rid of all the crap – the thing is, now, you just can't believe it was ever like that, and I wish I had. David's been wonderful. It makes such a difference, him being a professional.'

Cool it, darling, I prayed silently. I strongly suspected that Freda had taken against the old bat on sight, and I hoped to God she wouldn't overdo the gush by way of camouflage.

'So it's not been a case of "the cobbler's bairns"?' Sir Archibald asked. The bastard.

'I'm sorry?' Freda said blankly.

'Ah. I was forgetting you weren't a Scot, my dear. It's an old saying. "The cobbler's bairns go barefoot."'

'Do they?'

'Meaning, a chap never gets around to bringing his work home. A joiner never puts up a shelf for the wife, d'you see?' He was floundering, looking very uncomfortable; having been forced to spell it out, he was feeling he'd been a lot ruder than he'd meant to be. Freda always knew when she'd wrong-footed a man; it was like a shark tasting blood in the water.

'David's not like that,' she said, with idiot sincerity. 'He's worked and worked on this place.'

'A tribute to your powers of persuasion, if I may say so.' He looked relieved, obviously reckoning he'd got his foot out of his mouth with reasonable credit.

'I have to admit that my darling wife can be exceedingly persuasive,' I said, 'but you also have to bear in mind the purely technical interest of a sixteenth-century house, from my point of view. It's not as if this is just a pile of breezeblocks and a couple of A-frames. Every house of this age is different, and in a case like this, where it's been a question of just stripping out rubbish after a place has been in ignorant hands, one wants to get on with it to see what turns up.'

'Have you found anything interesting?' he asked.

'There's a stone,' I admitted. 'I'm not sure what it's off, or even what it is. I'd expect it to be recording a marriage, but I'm not quite sure in this case. I read the date as 1601, and there was some significant renovation around the 1600 mark. I wonder if there was a royal visit? It's got I.R. on it, and I think the two things after that might just be a thistle and a rose. It maybe came down when they remodelled the doorcase in the eighteenth century, because it'd got so worn. I'll show you when we go outside, it's by the back door.'

'Gosh, how exciting,' said Lady Leithen. 'I.R. would be Jacobus Rex, wouldn't it? They used I for J for some reason, I remember that from Jacobite glasses.'

'Right enough. Clever old you,' I said, beaming at her.

'He didn't leave Scotland till – when was it?' Sir Archibald chipped in. 'About sixteen-three? sixteen-five? Darling, when did Queen Elizabeth die?'

Lady Leithen glanced at her watch. 'This is frightfully interesting,' she said, 'but we'd better get back to thinking about the house, Archie. I'm afraid we're going to run out of time.'

'Another rather wonderful thing we found,' I said hastily. 'The doors are mostly original, and they're Baltic pine – it's as hard as teak by now. Look at this one. You'd never be able to replace them, they're made from single panels of timber. The trees must've been a hundred feet high or more. They just don't let them grow like that now.'

'Oh, yes, just like the doors at the Steels'. Lovely.'

'Hope's right to be reminding us about the time,' said Sir Archibald. 'I'm afraid we have a tiny problem – some very old friends heard we were coming up, and they've asked us to lunch; I'm afraid we felt we could hardly refuse. I wonder if we could trespass on your patience, take the quickest of looks now, and come back this afternoon?'

'Oh, absolutely', I said pleasantly. 'I'm glad to hear you've got friends in the county. We aren't going anywhere.'

'Super. It's a lovely place, and a lovely spot.'

'We were rather wondering why on earth you wanted to move?' said Lady Leithen, clearly a question she'd been intending to ask.

I was ready for this one. 'Combination of factors. I've had a very thought-provoking offer from a firm in London. I've been working on Scottish stone-built houses for a long time, and it'd give me the chance to extend my knowledge of other building-types. There's a lot about brick and stucco I don't know yet. And of course, Freda's people are in London, and her father's not getting any younger. It's an anxious time for us, I'm afraid.'

'Oh, I'm sorry to hear it,' said Lady Leithen automatically, though her tone faintly suggested that she hadn't got Freda tagged as one of nature's ministering angels.

'We've all got parents,' said Freda. I wanted to cheer; once more, she'd managed a virtually perfect wrong-footing of the opposition. She'd not sounded injured, but almost meek: I have the wrong accent and big tits, so you assume I haven't any feelings. But I'm used to it, and don't hold it against you.

'I hope there's nothing badly wrong?' the old trout asked, anxious to make amends. Freda looked at her, woman to woman.

'He's on his own, and he's started forgetting things. He gets lost on the Underground, and then he gets upset, and the police ring us up. If you're trying to get to London in a hurry, it takes four hours if you're lucky.'

Oh, Freda, I thought. Rub their noses in it. Let's hope they don't expect to pop down to the London Library every other blasted week. But she was right and I was wrong. Lady Leithen was quite melted.

'You poor thing. No, I quite see. I had that with my own father, and the trouble is, they just will not admit they can't cope.'

Sir Archibald was getting impatient, this wasn't his idea of good time-management. 'I wonder if we might divide forces?' he said. 'Perhaps Mrs Laurence could take Hope around the rest of the house, while you and I take a look at the exterior?'

'Good idea,' I said. Freda and Lady Leithen disappeared up the stairs, while Sir Archibald and I went back out into the garden, my fingers crossed in my pocket.

He had brought binoculars, not a trusting soul. Expensive, but not that high-powered; I was certain that he would not pick up anything that I hadn't been able to see through my own Zeiss lenses: the matte black paint on the guttering had done its job to perfection, and from ground level, the windows looked fine.

'You're actually an architect, I believe?' he asked.

'Yes, indeed.'

'Funny how none of you chaps ever live in your own buildings,' he said, as if it was an original observation.

'I'm a restoring architect,' I pointed out, a fraction tartly. 'If I saw the need of using my home as an advertisement, this'd be the way to do it.'

'Oh. I see.' He sounded quite impressed, despite himself.

We had worked our way round the side of the house as far as the drying green by that point, and very nice it looked too, with the flagstones swept and scoured, the lavender flourishing in its pots, the dodgy datestone casually propped by the back door. I couldn't spot any obvious splashes of paint.

'I'd like to take a photograph, if you don't mind,' said Sir Archibald. 'We haven't got the view from this side.'

He backed off to the far end of the green, which still wasn't far enough for him to get the whole place in; I vaulted up onto the braeside into which it was carved, and gave him a hand-up.

'Thanks.' Just then, Freda and Lady Leithen came out of the back door. 'Don't they make a picture,' he said. 'Charming.' They seemed to be coming towards us; I thought Freda was looking rather uncharacteristically perplexed. 'Could you just stay there a minute, girls?' he called, and they stopped obligingly while he focused the camera and took a shot of them standing framed by the door. There was a curious, heavy thumping in the air, I wasn't quite sure if I could hear it or feel it, but I could see that Leithen had noticed it as well.

He frowned, lowering his camera. 'Helicopter?' he enquired. 'It'd have to be a bloody great big one.'

'We're not far from RAF Kinloss,' I conceded, 'but we don't get much military traffic as a general rule. They mostly go out over the sea. It's maybe one of those vast troop-carriers, Chinooks, aren't they? They must exercise some time, I suppose, especially now that they might find themselves sent to Iraq. I've not heard one before.'

'Could well be.' Automatically, he was peering up into the sky. Given what a pretentious git the man was, I laid a small bet with myself what he'd say next. 'It's dreadful how suggestion works on one, isn't it?' he went on, confirming my worst prejudices. 'One can't help thinking of "The Ride of the Valkyries".'

If he started singing 'Hi-jo-to', I thought to myself, I might just kill him. I opened my mouth to make some kind of random response, but just then the house exploded.

In front of our appalled gaze, as all four of us stood rooted to the spot, quite slowly, or so it seemed, the chimney unzipped itself from the back of the house in a cloud of black dust, the keystones grabbing impotently at their sockets. For a long moment it seemed to stand proud like a giant erection, leaning away from the body

of the house, then it collapsed into a pile of rubble, with a miscel-
laneous collection of chimney-liners spilling from it like metal guts.

Once it had settled, I looked across to where Freda was standing
with Lady Leithen clinging to her arm, both of them now covered
in black, sooty fallout. Freda's eyes were patches of white in her
black face, like a panda only the other way round; she must've
screwed them up like a child, or put a hand over them.

'Freda, so help me God, I am going to kill you,' I said, quite
conversationally.

'You've got witnesses,' barked Sir Archibald. The habit of
command. I noted with vague surprise that I actually heard him
through the roaring in my ears, and even paid attention. 'You could've
killed the lot of us, you bloody maniac! What the hell is going on?'

'What happened?' asked Lady Leithen faintly. I could see her
shaking and so could Sir A.; he clambered down and hurried across
to detach her from Freda, put an arm round her and guide her
tenderly to the garden bench. She tried to smile, and said, 'My
ears are still ringing.'

'If my wife has sustained permanent damage to her hearing, I'll
sue you to buggery,' he threatened.

I ignored them, jumped down after him, and stalked towards
my wife. 'Freda, did you light the Aga?'

'Of course I friggin' did,' she snarled, bristling like a cat facing
down a dog. 'I thought it'd look so weird if I didn't on a day like
this. I opened the dampers and got it started with a lot of firelighters.'

I stopped abruptly. 'Oh, God,' I said.

'I still don't see –' said Sir Archibald.

'We don't use it. The chimney's blocked at the top, and there
must've been a hell of a build-up of soot and tar on the inside,' I
told him. There was no point in keeping up the pretence any more.
'All I can think is, with the sudden heat, a whole lot of this muck
fell down on the register plate. You left it for a while after you'd
got it started?' I asked Freda.

She nodded. 'Yes. I'd plenty of other stuff to do, and I wanted
to be sure it was going. Then I put in a bucket of those round
things in the shed. I did think about it, for Christ's sake! They're
the clean sort, so I didn't think they could do any harm. We had

fires when I was a kid and even after the Clean Air Act, they let you go on using them.'

Anthracite. Gets lovely and hot. I saw Sir Archibald put his free hand over his eyes. 'When the anthracite took hold, all the loose soot and stuff on the register plate ignited,' he explained to her, not unkindly. 'Then you got a flash fireball.'

'That's got to be it,' I agreed. 'A freak accident. It'll have gone up and gone on expanding, fuelling itself off the rest of the soot as it went. Because the chimney's a later addition and it was blocked at the top, it was the joint that gave way.'

Freda looked at me. I couldn't read her expression under the mask of soot. Without another word, she turned and went into the house. I didn't know if she'd gone to inspect the damage or if she just couldn't stand the sight of me. I was in such a state of shock, I felt as if she'd blown off my dick, not my chimney. The pain would come later; for now, I was completely numb, quite happy to babble on, making conversation, trying to get it all worked out.

'Darling,' said Lady Leithen, 'remind me to ring the Aga man and get it serviced. And the chimney-sweep.'

'Absolutely.' He looked at his wife carefully. The colour was coming back into her face, so he got up and pottered across to inspect the ruin. I suppose it's the Civil Service mentality, he seemed abstractly pleased to have worked out how it had happened. 'Extraordinary,' he said. 'I never heard of such a thing. It's a bit of a lesson, eh?'

Drearily, I had visions of him boring the Aga-owning classes with the story of Kilmollich's exploding chimney for the next twenty years. His cheerfulness was quite understandable; his lady wife seemed to have sustained no permanent damage, and though he could see perfectly well that I'd tried to pull a fast one, since it hadn't actually worked, he didn't seem disposed to hold a grudge.

'Now, I wonder if we might avail ourselves of your bathroom? And perhaps a clothes-brush?' he enquired. 'I presume it's safe to enter? The whole force of the bang seems to've gone upward, and the walls are sound enough.'

This was, by and large, true. The walls had, after all, been designed to withstand cannon fire. The actual top stack, the bit where the chimney stood proud of the house, had exploded, and some sizeable lumps of stone had gone through the roof, but mostly, it had been pushed away from its wall, leaving a long, horrible scar of raw stone with the odd gaping hole where a fireplace had been vented through to it.

The three of us were processing towards the back door when we were distracted by the sound of a car starting up: Freda's little silver Renault flashed into view at high speed from round the other side of the house, and shot off down the drive.

'Ah,' said Sir Archibald, thoughtfully. 'Poor girl. What a shock for her.' The malicious old sod.

I'd turned when I heard the car, and I was looking down the drive after her. I realised I must've been standing in the same spot for quite some time, because after a while he said, 'Don't trouble to show us up, my wife knows the geography of the house.' He went inside, but Lady Leithen paused to touch my arm. 'I'm so sorry,' she said. 'But you know, you will recover. One does.'

It was kind of her, but it seemed so very beside the point, when I knew that Freda would not come back to me. We could no longer get ourselves from where we were to where she wanted to be in a single move; we'd have to settle for a lot less, or even stay where we were. That was one thing. But the essential fact about Freda was the competitiveness. I knew in my bones that she'd feel that a screw-up on this scale was something you couldn't live down. I doubted very much if there was a single thing in Kilmollich she'd miss for its own sake – I had come to realise that she was not in any sense a sentimental woman, she valued objects principally as trophies or aids to self-presentation. She'd be on her way to London, that was almost certain. She would stay with some friend or other, and perhaps in time, she would blag herself into some kind of career as a designer, or a relocation consultant, or something of the kind, even if she had to invent it, and she'd probably be quite successful. Perhaps she'd even be able to afford a flat in the Barbican some day. I suspected the only things she'd bothered to take along were her jewellery and her little red notebook.

The Leithens went upstairs and washed; I found the marks on the new white towels, much later. Then they got in their car and went away. I don't know how long I stayed out there, utterly desolate and alone on the cold hillside, but after some time had passed, I went in and noted without particular surprise that my brother's tile-picture was lying in shards on the ground in front of the soot-blackened Aga; that was six thousand odd quid I owed him, then. I'd never got round to ringing up my insurers. And he was going to be dancing mad; he'd liked it. There was most of a bottle of Glenfiddich on the dresser; I picked it up and went back out to the bench in the courtyard.

I just couldn't've foreseen it, I thought. My mind seemed to be processing stuff very, very slowly. The proverbial bloody lightning out of a clear sky. I mean, yes, she'd picked up a few basic manual skills, but in the course of eighteen months' cohabitation, I'd never seen the silly bint try and work anything more complicated than a credit card. Perhaps I ought to be blaming Joanna Trollope for giving her the notion that Agas weren't something you needed to understand. It had never even crossed my mind that she'd meddle with the thing.

She'd turned lights on all over the place before the Leithens arrived, and in the fulness of time, the sun began to go down behind the silver birches. I sat on the bench drinking whisky, and looking at my house, the little warm, yellow squares of light gradually strengthening as the cold grey evening light faded away, thinking of the empty rooms beyond in which the fires had long since burned to ash.

Walking with Angels

I

There was an angel standing by the fridge again. He had a nice sort of goldy sheen, but it wasn't a good moment for that sort of caper. Mornings are always hectic, and I'd just mashed another pot of tea, so I walked right past him to get the milk. When I came up to him, he sort of smeared in the air and vanished, and by the time I opened the fridge door, he was gone. It made me smile to myself, though. I remembered how put about I was the first time I saw one. I mean, nobody likes to think they're going daft, but now it'd happened a few times and it was always just the angels I kept seeing. I was starting to wonder if it was some kind of communication from the Other World. I mean, an angel's supposed to be a messenger, isn't he?

Then I thought on: everything happens for a reason; there must be something about the fridge I was supposed to notice. I opened the door and put my hand in to see if there was anything gave me a funny feeling; there was nothing off the kippers or the custard tarts but when I touched the Walnut Whips I got a definite response.

'We are guided from On High', I said to Derek.

'Oh, aye?' he replied, which is typical, actually. He's not a talk-ative person. 'Anything in that pot?'

I poured out for him. He was getting stuck into his bacon and eggs, chasing the bits of egg round the plate with his toast. The yolk was all in streaks, sliding about on the fat. I can't be doing with grease first thing in the morning, but he sticks out for a proper breakfast. It's not nice to watch. He got the last of it shov-elled down, and reached for his tea. I bit the top off my Walnut Whip, and licked out a bit of the cream.

'Thanks, pet,' he said, drinking off his tea and standing up. 'Home about seven? I've a job out at Tinsley, it'll take me a while to get back.' He gave me a peck on the cheek, and he was off.

'Angel, can you hear me?' I asked aloud, once I'd heard the car start. It was just to see what happened. It's not a draughty house, but the minute after I said it, I saw something floating down from somewhere, a tiny white feather, and I felt a presence.

I thought about it all the time I was doing my little jobs, washing up Derek's breakfast and tidying out the bedroom. Why me? was my first thought, but then, it started coming back to me. I'd been sensitive from a child. I remember Mam saying she didn't know what to do with me. 'You always had too much imagination,' she used to say. She was a no-nonsense sort of woman, and both my sisters took after her. I was the odd one out.

When I'd got everything straight, I spritzed round with the air freshener to get shot of the smell of frying. Even with the extractor on, it gets into the lounge, and you can't be spiritual in a bacony room, it stands to reason. Atmosphere's very important. I'd a scented candle which my friend Jean gave me last Christmas, so I lit that, 'muguet' it was, sort of light and flowery, which seemed just about the ticket. It looked funny burning in the daylight, so I shut the curtains, kicked my shoes off, and lay down on the settee to see if I could find out what he wanted.

I was really straining myself to relax. 'Let your mind be a calm pool', I was telling myself, and I did my best, taking long deep breaths and all that, but of course, because I'd spoken out loud, I found I'd got some ruddy carol or other jangling in my head – the one with a bit about 'angels bending near the earth' – and there was something about 'angels from the realms of glory', but when I started puzzling if it was the same one, I sort of drifted off onto remembering Christmas, and I ended up deciding I'd definitely have a roast next time, I'd got us one of those little turkeys from M&S, but it still lasted till Old Year's Night, and it's not as if we even liked it that much . . . After that, I started to get the impression I was blanking out nicely, but actually, I was just dropping off. 'Wenda my girl, you're going about this all the wrong way,' I told myself, waking up suddenly when my head slipped off the cushion. 'Just pop down to the Public Library and see if you can get a bit of help.'

There's the main library in the middle of town, of course, but we've got a very good branch here at Woodseats. I knew I was doing the right thing, because when I pushed open the door, there was my angel again, just for a moment. As if he was playing with me, but in a nice way, like playing Hunt the Thimble, just saying, sort of, 'You're warm'. I went up to the desk and talked to one of the librarians, and she said they didn't have a book but she very kindly showed me how to use the computer. I tried to feel the angel's presence once the lass had gone away and I was looking at Google on the screen, hoping he'd help me to guess what to ask for. There was so much when I tried 'angel' in the little box thing, I didn't know where to start, I felt really discouraged. Help me, I thought at him; I wasn't getting anything at all. Was he telling me I was 'cold'? Anyway, I started typing in 'spirit communication', and before I even clicked the thingy to send it off, I knew he was pleased. I don't mean I could literally hear him in actual words, but all the same, I knew he was saying 'You're hot! you're boiling!'

Well, all I can say is, it turned out to be a proper eye-opener. I was there for ages, even though I always do Marks and Spencer's on Wednesdays. I printed out loads of pages to take away, and I realised I'd better get myself a binder and some kind of notebook. I'd ended up with pages and pages with just the odd nugget of information here and there, and it'd cost me a small fortune. I'd be far better writing things down.

One thing which'd come up quite a few times in the stuff I was looking at was the idea of guardian angels. I found myself thinking about that a lot, or being guided to it, maybe. We've each got two special angels of our own, apparently. I'd only ever seen one at a time, but now I thought about it, was it always the same one? I'd not thought about it that way, so it was hard to be sure, and I told myself that next time an angel turns up, I'll try and see if there's any way I can sort out who's who. One of the people on the Net said she could tell you your angels' names – for a price, mark you – but I reckoned if I could see them for myself, I ought to be able to find that out, now I'd thought about it.

I left all my stuff from the library at home, and got the bus into town. I'd a lot to get through, and there wasn't a minute to think about my angels. Only I popped into the remainder bookshop, because Derek asked me if I could try and get him a new road atlas, the one he had was coming to bits, and while I was looking round, I saw they had some really lovely books with leatherette covers and that old-fashioned gilt decoration all round, blank books, I mean. It seemed like another sign – they weren't even very dear. So I bought myself one, to start writing down my visions in. I fancied keeping a record. And I bought an ordinary notebook for jotting down things from the Net, and a binder – and Derek's atlas, of course.

By the time I'd done all my shopping, I was absolutely laden, and my feet were killing me. I staggered off to the bus stop, and the right bus came within seconds: I knew it was the angels helping me. There was even a seat, and I could see one of them standing guard – then it just came to me in a flash. He was called Itheriel. 'Thank you, Itheriel,' I said, and plopped myself down. And I knew that the other one was called Ariel, and they were sort of heavenly twins, though I reckoned I'd always know which was which. When I got home, that was the first thing I wrote in my new book. I left the first page blank, because I didn't know what I was going to call it yet.

I had my job to go to the day after that – I do three days a week at the chemist's – but the next day that I had a bit of time to myself I went back to the library with my notebook and dug a bit deeper. There were all sorts of people who were talking to angels, but I began to realise I must be highly unusual, because hardly anyone else seemed to be actually seeing them. There was a lady called Aryella who was a clairvoyant tuned into the higher celestial spheres, and she saw them all right, but people don't generally see their own guardian angels in the flesh, as it were. I felt very special.

There were some places I found on the computer where you could write about your own experiences and people would write back – I was quite keen to talk to some of them, actually, and I was wondering how I was going to fit in running back and forth to the library, when it dawned on me I didn't have to. Derek's got a home office in the little spare bedroom. He spends a lot of time there in the evenings, but it suddenly struck me there was nothing stopping me using it when he wasn't there; I wouldn't be disturbing any of his stuff, and I could get Google from there just the same as from the library, without paying out a pound an hour. We looked at the computer together once, when we were thinking of buying a new fridge-freezer and he thought we could get a better price for the one I was after, so I was pretty sure I knew where to switch it on.

So anyway, I popped up to Derek's study with my notebook, and pressed the button – but of course the first thing the wretched thing did was ask me for a password, and I was stumped. I sat there and thought about it. Then I tried 'Derek', and 'Wenda', and 'Marion', which was Derek's mum's name. Nothing. I had a go with 'Owls' and 'Wednesday' after that – he used to follow Sheffield Wednesday, but after Hillsborough, I put my foot down. I don't think he was too keen himself, actually, after that. I mean, it could just as well've been him crushed to death. He'd had a ticket for that game, only he'd had to pass it on because he was needed at work, providentially.

It was funny to be thinking about Derek like that, wondering what'd come into his mind. Now, if I ever wanted a password for anything, I'd pick Ariel or Itheriel, which'd take him long enough to guess! It was probably thinking of the angels that did it; they'll help you if you let them, because I suddenly knew what it'd be: I typed 'Skipper', and the computer said 'Welcome, Derek', and let me in. How funny. He was Derek's old dog – I never understood what Derek saw in him. Skipper drove me absolutely wild; he left his hairs everywhere, he smelt and if he didn't fancy the weather, he was dirty in the house. With Derek being so busy, it was me that wiped up after him and me that walked him half the time, but all the same, you could see he was just polite with me, he never bothered himself. He was one of those exclusive animals.

Anyway, I could see where you clicked on the screen to get it to go onto the Net, so I clicked it. It's all very straightforward once you get the hang of it. I'd written down how to get Google in the library, so I started putting it in, you know, one-fingered, 'h-t-t-p, colon, forward slash, forward slash, w-w-w', but when I typed the first 'G' for Google, the machine just filled in the rest of the line all by itself like magic, only it wasn't Google at all, it was gradeachicks.com, which got me properly flustered. I wanted it to give me Google, but I got in a muddle clicking about trying to make it go away, and suddenly there I was on this ruddy porno site.

I mean, you can't help but look, once you're there. Some of the stuff was just plain disgusting. Not anything involving kiddies, thank God, but just horrible – things you can't imagine anyone doing who'd an ounce of self-respect. I felt really sick and shaky inside, looking at those pictures. I thought our sex-life was all right. I mean, let's face it, it's a long time since we were young marrieds, but he's always seemed contented. Only you've got to remember there's that nasty, childish side to men, as if they never get over playing Doctors and Nurses. Some of those poor girls were practically deformed, I mean, they were so pumped up with silicone their bosoms were like a pair of prize marrows. I was in such a pother by then, there was no point in thinking about doing my research, so I just turned it all off and went back downstairs.

You always feel better once you've had a cup of tea. I put the kettle on, and while it was boiling, I had a bit of a think what I was going to give Derek that evening. There was a nice steak pie in the freezer, we could have that, and I'd bought a new bag of chips, so we'd have some of those, and some peas. Oven chips are a great boon. I remember when they came in; the day after we'd tried them, I threw away my chip-pan, and good riddance. Derek loves chips, so we've got to have them two or three times in the week, but I can't bear the house stinking of stale fat. When I was a little girl, and Dad was in the steelworks at Attercliffe, we lived above a chippie for a year and the smell was everywhere. It came up through the floorboards, and all our clothes were saturated, there was nothing you could do about it. They all laughed at us at school because we smelt, and when they took to calling me Greasebomb, I started getting tummy-aches, I was that upset. It's not a thing to do to a sensitive child. Mam'd put me into my coat and drag me off to school even if I was crying all the way; 'Rise above it,' she'd say, 'stop that grizzling.' Easy for her. She never felt things the way I did.

I made my cup of tea and took it back to the lounge with a packet of chocolate Hobnobs. I was thinking about Derek. Men are much of a muchness, I reckon he's no worse than the rest of them. But there's that coarseness in them. I've never heard of a woman liking dirty pictures. I mean, if you had a photo of a man with his thingy sticking out, what good'd it do you? They look bloody silly, frankly. But they can't help themselves. It starts with the lasses on page three, and then they get a taste for stronger and stronger meat, till they're just wallowing in muck. You can see it from the way that the minute you get two or three of them together, they start telling filthy jokes. It's their lower nature. They're sort of animals, really. When I stopped to think about it, practically all of the people who'd heard angels or seen them that I'd found on the Net were women, and I thought, it just goes to show. Basically, women are more attuned to the spiritual, because we just don't have that streak of filthiness in our natures – you can try all you like to raise men to your level, but it's bound to pull them down. I mean, I've been telling him and telling him to put the seat up for twenty-one years, and he still doesn't bother himself half the time.

I never wanted a son. My sister Lynne's got boys; they've turned out all right, but how she put up with them when they were little I just do not know. Voices like jackhammers, the pair of them. And the energy! They were never still, not for a minute. I'd've liked a daughter. She'd've been called Crystal, and she could've had everything she fancied. I'll say this for Derek, he makes good money. I remember what a little girl feels like when she sets her heart on something. My little fairy princess. I was thinking about all that, upsetting myself, when I sort of heard a voice. It was Ariel, and he was saying, 'But Wenda, dearest one. We are Crystal, in a body of light. We have always been with you. Do not grieve. We love you. How beautiful you are, how courageous; how creative; how perfect, just as you are. Thank you for all the work you do each day in just being and bringing your loving energy to the world. You are a beautiful radiant being of goodness and the light of love. You cannot hide your light.' I just filled up with tears, I could feel them around me, all that golden energy. I couldn't see them, but I knew I was under the shadow of their wings.

By the time Derek came home, I'd calmed myself down; I'd finished my tea and washed my face, and been round tidying up. Everything was looking just the way I wanted it, all quiet and clean, with the cushions plumped up, and everything straight. I put a lot of effort into my lounge. I heard his key in the door, and his feet; he hung his coat up and went straight into the kitchen as usual to fetch himself a beer. I heard the fridge door going. He came through with the can in one hand and a glass in the other – I don't let him drink out of the can – and plopped himself down in his chair.

'It's been a long day,' he said. 'The traffic's atrocious, and the lights on Hanover Way are out again. They're going to have to do something about 'em before there's an accident – one silly bugger chancing his arm, and you'd have a six-car pile-up. I'm absolutely knackered. Would you get the tea on, pet?' He knows I don't usually start cooking till he gets in. He's a worker, I'll say that for him, and he gets home at all hours. I got sick of sitting about waiting with his dinner drying up in the oven, and when it's just stuff you're hotting up, it doesn't take long.

He poured his beer, and started clicking about with the remote control. I'd had a game-show on, and he doesn't like them much. It was a stupid sort of thing, I have to admit, I wasn't really looking at it. I got up and went through to the kitchen. 'Could you bring us a packet of crisps?' he called. I popped the oven on, and put a packet of salt-and-vinegar in a bowl for him, and took them back through. 'Ta, pet.' He'd found himself some kind of cookery programme. It's not as if he can boil an egg, but I reckoned he fancied the presenter, she looked sort of his type. It's pathetic, really. Like the gardening; he can't be bothered with it, in reality, so we've a patio at the back and we concreted the front to make hard standing for the car, but whenever that Charlie Dimmock's on, he insists we watch.

We don't generally use the table on a week-night, I just set a couple of trays and bring it all through. I wasn't really hungry, so I gave him the lion's share of the pie, and watched him eating it. There was one of the pictures I'd found on his computer which stuck in my mind; one where the girl was tied up with barbed wire with her bum sticking up. I looked at Derek wolfing his tea, and thought to myself, so that's the sort of thing you like, my lad.

'Is there a sweet?' he asked, when he'd finished.

'I haven't made anything. There's some chocolate mousses in the fridge, or you could have a bit of cake. There's still some Battenberg.'

'I'll just have a cup of tea,' he said.

'Suit yourself.' I carried the trays through, and mashed the tea.

'Derek,' I said, once I was sat down, 'I want a computer of my own.'

'Eh? But there's a computer upstairs, Wenda. What the heck do we need another one for? I didn't think you could type.'

'It depends what you mean. Everyone can type a bit these days. I've got to do a bit at work. I can't do hundreds of words per minute, but I can use a computer! Not that it's any of your business, but there's things I want to look up on the Internet, and I can't go running to the library every five minutes. And I don't want to be bombarded with filth. I went on your computer today, and it made me absolutely sick. It's demeaning. I'd never've thought it of you.' Well, I've never seen him looking more shamed. 'It's not that I was prying. I was just trying to get Google, and all this porno stuff appeared out of nowhere. If that's what you want to look at, on your own head be it, but I'm not going to sully myself.'

'How did you know my password?' he demanded.

'Oh, come on, Derek. We've been married a long time. It was about the second thing I tried.' He looked quite worried, and I wondered if he was thinking whether he knew me that well; he doesn't, of course. 'It could go in here, on the phone-table. You can get those little ones now, they don't take up much room.'

I thought he was going to argue the toss for a while longer, but he gave in. 'All right. Have it your own way. Remember, we're not made of money. I'll look up Morgan, and find you a laptop. It's just a basic connection you need, isn't it?'

'That's right. I'm not after anything fancy.'

He was quiet for a bit. 'Wenda, it's just normal, you know,' he said after a while. 'I mean, wanting to look at women.'

'If it's normal, why are you looking so ashamed of yourself?'

He didn't seem to have anything to say. He looked away from me, and switched on the telly.

II

Derek was as good as his word. I got my laptop a couple of weeks later, it was about the same size as the phonebook, so you couldn't even say it cluttered the place up. He connected it up for me, and then I started going into the astral world properly. I found out all sorts of stuff, but I soon realised it's spiritual this and spiritual that, but you've got to be on the *qui vive*, there's all these come-ons and oh we'll just tell you a little bit and then all of a sudden you've got to subscribe when you don't even know if it'll be any use. Of course, I couldn't do that; I hadn't got a credit card, and even if I had, I wouldn't have wanted to pass the number out to all and sundry, after everything you hear, but it was easy enough to see a person could end up spending a fortune if they weren't careful. Some of these so-called spiritual guides must be making good money, I thought. I was a bit wary about subscribing to things as well; I'd joined up at a couple of sites when I first got started, and the amount of rubbish I got sent, you wouldn't credit. They must pass your name around, the way the catalogue people sell their address lists, and after I'd burnt my fingers like that, it made me very wary of joining anything more. But I did get myself into some chat rooms, and I picked up a lot, one way and another.

Anyroad, from everything I read, I reckoned the key thing was to start living a more spiritual life, and make myself responsive to the higher celestial spheres. One of the things I'd looked at on the Net was very interesting: it said that Chi energy forces are all around us, basically they're what holds the world together. And it'd make sense, surely, if angels like Itheriel and Ariel were sort of manifestations of that energy. After all, we know now that the physical world's just sort of solidified energy. It was actually Einstein who showed that it's actually the same stuff as the highest spiritual expression, so you can't say that's not scientific. Only the thing is, apparently, the mortal sphere's all happening at a very low vibration, which is why it looks solid to our eyes; so if you can get your vibrations up, then obviously it's easier for high-energy beings like the angels to make contact. I found out somewhere else Feng Shui's all about harnessing Chi energy, so that looked like a good start – I'd marked down a useful little book about Feng Shui in the remainder shop.

And another thing, there'd be no more kippers and bacon. I was positive they played merry hell with my Chi. Derek could have scrambled eggs, and like it. Some of the discussions had a fair bit to say about the kinds of food which'd help you tune into higher vibrations, and it had me properly puzzled. Half the time I didn't know what they were on about. Most of the people were Americans, and all I can say is, they eat some very funny things over there. I thought it was all hamburgers, but it's not. Derek's very conservative in his tastes, and I don't really fancy foreign food myself. Pasta's fine, I've got a nice recipe you do with macaroni and tuna and a bit of white sauce, but neither of us likes rice much, we tend to stick with chips and potatoes. He likes a decent bit of fish, but you can't go to Harry Ramsden's all the time, and I won't cook the stuff myself because it stinks the place out. They all seemed to think you shouldn't eat red meat, but how are you supposed to have a proper Sunday dinner without a roast? Chicken's for weekdays. And you've got to have ham, it stands to reason. Well, I ended up giving up on that one. The angels seem to like me the way I am, I thought, I'll just have to leave that bit out and do my best. If I put rabbit-food in front of Derek when he was expecting a decent meal, there'd be hell to pay. We can have macaroni cheese once in a while, I reckoned, he'll eat that. And he's happy with egg and chips, with a bit of tomato; that's vegetarian too, come to think on it.

I got the Feng Shui book, and rearranged the lounge to help with my Chi. Fortunately, I'd unconsciously chosen a highly spir-itual suite, it's silver-grey velour printed with black bamboo. I was after harmonious, growth-oriented energy cycles, but I wasn't keen to redecorate, so I thought I'd better stick with moving things around. One thing they set store by is you aren't supposed to sit in a room with your back to the door, because it stops you getting all the positive energy circulating in the space, but I was at my wit's end what to do with the settee. We've a built-in entertain-ment area by the fireplace, so the telly's got to stay there, you want the settee handy, and I could hardly move the door, could I? Anyroad, I could do something about reflecting energy back into the room, so I took the picture over the fireplace down, and swopped it with the mirror from the spare room, which I reck-oned would help a bit. The trouble was, I wasn't fond of the thing, it was one which'd belonged to my mam, so it was a bit of a nega-tive symbol for me. From what the book was saying, I wasn't sure if that meant it was making things better or worse. So I bought three pot-plants with big round leaves, hung up some wind-chimes, and hoped for the best.

All that was by the by, really. The most important thing was I made sure I spent some time every day meditating. I'd read some-where that if you've got it in you, you can quicken your vibra-tions so you attract the higher beings to you – it's not ordinary will-power, you need, it's a sort of spiritual will-power. I thought I could see what they meant – it was some people called the Golden Dawn which sounded all right. So I knew I'd have to try and give my spiritual will-power a boost, but I was pretty sure I could do it.

When I looked into it all, I realised that first time, when I'd made a fool of myself, I'd tried to do too much, too quickly. I'd been right to go for the candles and the scent, it all helps, but I'd been straining, and you shouldn't do that. There was some good advice about breathing from one lady I spoke to: she said you need to breathe in deeply through your nose, count to five, then breathe out slowly through the mouth, and just let yourself go. I added a special touch of my own; instead of counting, I said, 'Ariel, Itheriel, Ariel, Itheriel' in my head all the time I was holding my breath. I knew the energy was out there, and they were trying to get in touch. I could trust it, so after a while, when I felt I was ready, I started working on my reception. I told myself, you are living and breathing light. I had this vision of little sparks, like living snow, the Chi energy, sifting down from the higher realms, attracted to me because I was there to receive it. I could just see Ariel and Itheriel with their lovely wings beating, pushing it all towards me; I pulled it in through my nose, and while I held it, I could feel it rushing through my body, all the way down to my feet. I wasn't moving, but I felt every particle of me was vibrating, totally still and at peace, and yet I was moving at incredible speed. It was wonderful, just beautiful, the first time it happened, soft airy energy, and me floating in it, and I realised I'd found my own path. Some people can do it without a guide, you know, and of course, I'd had the angels to help.

I'd been doing this for a while, and I gradually found I was getting better and better at it. I was finding I could hold the Chi trance for half an hour or more, when I suddenly found I'd progressed to the next stage. I kept my eyes shut when I was medi-tating, but I knew the light was all around me, I could feel it. But that time, I sensed something sort of *in* the light, and I saw a tiny little face, it seemed to be miles and miles away but it was coming towards me and getting bigger, and when it was the size of a postage stamp, I saw it was Ariel, looking at me and smiling softly, just the face and no body that time, although I didn't feel it made any difference. He was coming towards me, and I said in my head, 'Come down o soul divine!' – I don't know where that came from. There seemed to be light coming out from under his skin, I could hardly look at him, but I had to. I sort of wanted him to kiss me, and I couldn't think what it'd feel like. But when his face was ordinary sized, his eyes were bright as diamonds; I mean, it was just like looking at a car coming towards you at night. I knew he was communicating – I felt him saying, I am in heaven, beloved, and when you are ready, you will join me here, and then I knew he couldn't touch me the way I'd been thinking, my earthly body would've just shaken apart. I opened my eyes, and I could feel the tears leaking out of the corners. I must've been crying for a while, because I could feel the wet in my hair, just above my ears – I'd been lying down, you see.

That special moment with Ariel stayed with me all day. It's not everyone gets proof positive there's such a thing as heaven. I was very moved. I remember thinking suddenly that night, I'll never be shamed and helpless with two angels watching over me.

Anyway, that was a Wednesday, so the day after, I had my job to go to. I do Thursday, Friday, Saturday at the local chemist's, their busy end of the week. Now, I've always been friendly with the lady who's there full time – Jean Wilson, her name is. She needs the work, poor soul. Her husband just up and left, getting on for ten years ago now, and she's got two boys, so she's not had an easy time of it.

The first job of the day's restocking the shelves. I got the toiletries sorted out, and went to give Jean a hand with the baby goods.

'How's the Feng Shui?' she asked, while we put bottles of shampoo and stuff on the shelves. I'd told her a bit about it.

'I've done what I can,' I said. 'They must have very odd houses in China, that's all I can say. Nothing's supposed to be in a straight line, not even the path to the front door, if you please.'

'How's it supposed to work?' she asked, ripping open a carton of Pampers and handing up the packets so I could shelve them.

'It's about sorting out the energies around you,' I explained, stuffing them into place. 'You need to work out where your nine "life situations" zones are in the house, and then you sort of try and get the Chi energy to go where you want it.'

'Life situations?'

'Oh, Love, Finance, Spirituality, and all that.'

'Where d'you find your finance zone then? I need all the help I can get.'

'It's not as simple as that, Jean.'

'Nothing ever is,' she said. I looked at her properly. She was looking very tired and pulled down. She's subject to headaches, and I know she's having a lot of trouble with her younger lad. There were people starting to come in by then, so we had to leave it all there.

We had a bit of a lull mid morning, and I saw her getting paracetamol out of her bag. 'Have you got one of your heads again?' I asked.

'I was up half the night waiting for Michael,' she said. 'He's skiving off from school again. He can't wait to leave, and what His Majesty thinks he's going to do after that, I just do not know. I don't trust the lads he's going around with. They're not a nice lot. At least with t'other, it was computers, computers, computers, I always knew where he was.'

I thought of the stuff I'd found on Derek's machine, and I wanted to say something, but I thought better of it. I felt proper sorry for her. 'He's making good money now, isn't he?'

'He's not doing badly, but it's a chancy business, the computers. There's no security in it.' If you gave Jean a golden crown, she'd be saying it didn't fit right, that's the way she is. But she had that funny, squinty look she gets, so I guessed she was feeling poorly. No wonder she wasn't very cheerful.

A bit later, towards lunchtime, I saw her leaning against the wall with her eyes shut, massaging her temples.

'You should get Mr Bhatia to give you something.'

She swallowed and shook her head. 'There's nothing as helps, Wenda. I'm getting the flashing lights again.'

I knew I'd have to keep an eye on her. Any minute now, and she'd be off in the toilet chucking up. Migraine goes to her stomach. You could tell she was only just holding herself together, picking up everything as if it hurt her to touch it. It seemed so unfair, to my way of thinking. I mean, on top of having a lovely home, and Derek, who's been all you could really expect from a man, I had Ariel and Itheriel, whilst Jean's Norman turned out an absolute B. who ran off and left her dragging along with a pair of ungrateful great lummoxes to feed and clothe, and to put the tin lid on it, she was seeing flashing lights. I could only think there must be some great scheme behind it all, something you can't get a grasp on, but it made me feel very humble.

I was serving a customer when I saw just a sort of flicker of one of the angels out of the corner of my eye. I looked round and Jean had disappeared. Five minutes later she still hadn't come back. There was nobody in the shop, so I nipped back to the stockroom and there she was, sitting on the chair, looking the colour of porridge. I felt so sorry for her, then suddenly I felt the Chi energy starting to move in me.

'Jean,' I said, 'I'm going to try and help.'

I went up to her and just put my fingertips ever so lightly on either side of her face. It felt funny, I'd never touched a woman that way that I could think of. All soft, and a little bit clammy. Not like touching Derek at all.

'Ariel, Itheriel,' I prayed, inside my head. 'Help me to help her.' I sensed a sort of whooshing rush of energies, the Chi sparks gathering themselves together, like in that Lotto advert, coming down into me and out through my fingertips.

Jean opened her eyes. She looked as much surprised as anything. 'I think it's gone, pet. What the heck did you do to me?'

'Hoi! Shop!' Some cheeky so-and-so was shouting at the counter, and then I heard Mr Bhatia's voice, sounding pretty sharp.

'Ladies! Where have you got to?'

I hurried back through, Mr B. was serving, with a face like thunder.

'Sorry,' I said to him, once the customer'd gone and he'd shut the till. 'Jean was taken poorly.'

He wasn't best pleased. 'You must be available to do your work, Mrs Bootham. There are security issues.'

For heaven's sake, I thought, it was only a minute! I was going to snap at him, but then I looked at him, pompous little fellow like a bantam cock with pouches under his eyes. Have compassion, I thought, or maybe the angels were prompting me. He's a poor devil stuck on the material plane.

'Well, no use raking it over, Mr Bhatia. There's been no harm done.'

Just then, Jean came back into the shop. She'd washed her face, you could see the damp around her hairline. She still looked pretty washed-out, but her eyes were back to normal.

'Are you fit to work, Mrs Wilson?' he asked her.

'Yes, Mr Bhatia. I'm fine now. I just felt a bit faint.' She'd've said it anyway, she's mortally afraid he'll give her the sack, but looking at her, you could see it was true.

That night, she rang me up. I was surprised to hear her; she tries not to use the phone if she can help it.

'I've been thinking on what happened today,' she said. 'How did you know what to do?'

'It wasn't me,' I explained, 'I was just channelling the spirit. I was sort of moved to do it.'

'It didn't come back, you know, after you touched me. Are you doing a lot of that sort of thing?' she asked.

'No. It was the first time. I feel as if I'm learning. It's maybe meant to be my next step.'

'It's a precious gift, Wenda.' Then there was this terrible noise on the phone, one of those rappers, or rapsters, or whatever they're called, it was absolutely booming out. Michael must've come in. 'Turn that down!' she shouted; I could hear him giving her some cheek, though I couldn't make out what he said. Poor soul, no wonder she has migraines, it was giving me a headache and I wasn't even in the same house. 'Could we go for a coffee after work tomorrow? I'd like to talk.'

'Yes, that's fine. Derek's not usually home for a good hour or more after I get in.'

There's a little café just along from the chemist's, The Nook, it's called, it's quite nice and handy for the bus stop, so we went in there.

We sat down, and the girl brought us two coffees.

Jean surprised me. 'Wenda,' she began, as soon as the lass had gone away. 'I want you to tell me a bit more about t'other day. I know you. There's things you're keeping to yourself.'

I didn't know quite what to say to her. I mean, how can you

talk about this stuff without sounding as if you've got a screw loose? That's what I thought then. I put some sugar in my coffee, and stirred it round.

'What happened when you put your hands on my face?' she went on.

I was quite relieved. 'Oh, that was just channelling,' I explained. 'You just open yourself to the Chi energy and let it come out through your hands. There's nothing to it.'

'Oh, aye? So you think anyone could do it?'

'Well, I wouldn't quite say that,' I admitted.

'Nor'd I. So what's special about you? Look, Wenda. You've always kept both your feet on the ground. I mean, you've had your fancies like the rest of us, but nothing out of the way. And all of a sudden, you're talking about Feng Shui and there's this channelling, which is a heck of a gift, and you know it. So what's going on?'

'I don't know if you'll believe me,' I said. 'I haven't told this to a living soul.'

'Try me.'

'All right. I started seeing angels.'

'What do you mean, seeing?'

'*Seeing* seeing. I mean, they're as real as you or I. There's two of them, and they're called Ariel and Itheriel.'

'What do they look like, then?'

'Well, they're sort of twins. Both boys, at least, I think they're boys. You can't really tell with spirits. They've got long robes on, and their hair's sort of shoulder length, and they've got wonderful faces. They seem to shine from inside somehow, all golden.'

It was quite a relief spitting it all out. Jean looked a bit puzzled, but she was taking it all in. 'I've heard of people seeing ghosts, but it's not like that, by the sounds of it,' she said.

'Oh, no. They're much realler. And, I mean, ghosts, you'd get this negative energy feeling, wouldn't you? The angels are just incredibly positive. And anyroad, ghosts happen just in one place, don't they? The thing with your angels is, they go everywhere with you, and watch over you.'

'They're your own angels, then?'

'Oh, yes. Everyone's got them.'

'Can you see other peoples'?'

'No,' I admitted. 'Or maybe I ought to say, not yet. I've been working hard, but it's a slow business. They'll teach you, but you need to work out what you want to know for yourself. It's not like at school.'

'Does Derek know about any of this?' she asked.

'No, of course not. He'd think I'd gone off my rocker. If there's anyone breathing less spiritual than my Derek, you'd go a long way to find them. Mind you, I don't think a lot of men can tune into the higher energy levels. They've a lot more holding them back than we have. I've noticed it's mostly women, on the Net.'

'It's funny, that, when it's always been men who were priests.'

I remembered that Jean was brought up Catholic. 'Oh, no. You're all wrong there. Back in the olden days, it's women were the spiritual ones. Then the men put a stop to it because their noses were out of joint. They reckoned women had too much power, you see, and then cause they couldn't connect with the Chi energy themselves, they made up all this stuff about hellfire to keep us in our place. It's all there in history. I've read about it.'

'Hah. That makes sense. They don't let us have much, do they?'

That made me think of Derek, and I looked at my watch. 'I'd better be going, Jean. I'll need to be home to make the tea. But I'm glad we've had this talk. I've felt shy of saying anything.'

III

I don't like Sundays. Saturdays I'm in the shop, and we're very busy, so I'm always bone-weary come the evening. We were never really ones for going out on Saturday night, even before I started at Mr Bhatia's – sometimes we'll go down the road to the pub if we're in the mood, specially in summer, or sometimes Derek goes by himself, but if we do, we don't stay long. All I really want's a bit of a rest, so the evening just goes by, you hardly notice it. But the trouble with Sunday is, after we've had a bit of a lie-in, I've got him under-foot all day, watching the telly in his stockinged feet, or maybe faffing about in the kitchen if there's anything needs mending.

I used to be pleased he liked just stopping at home, but it really gets on my nerves now. I can't do my meditation with him about. I like to use the settee and of course there he is, sat there watching the motor racing or some rubbishy film. He messes up the ambiance, and I can feel all the energy in the room's got confused; it goes to where it's expecting to find me, and then sort of bounces back, as if it's saying 'What's this?' I mean, he's just a lump, like a rock or something, because he's an earthbound soul. I usually end up taking my little computer through to the kitchen and putting it on the table so I can see what's going on with my friends on the Net, but I can't get on with my own stuff.

It was specially annoying that week, because of the business with Jean. I wondered if I'd be able to do it again, how I could develop my talent. It'd make sense if all this ended up being *for* something. Because if it wasn't, why were the angels bothering themselves? I found some interesting bits and bobs when I was surfing. One thing I came across really stuck with me:

'As you attune to the angelic realms, you may find that some of your friends and acquaintances do not appeal to you quite so much. If someone is making you feel drained or depressed, try spending less time with him or her for a while. What is happening is that your aura is absorbing their negative energies so you are feeling bad. They, on the other hand, are absorbing your positive energies.'

That might account for a lot, I thought. I was definitely not wanting to spend time with Derek. Maybe it was instinct at work; unconsciously, I was trying to protect my gift. But I had a lot of spiritual energy. If Derek was absorbing it, there ought to be some-thing to show for it.

Talk of the devil. Just as I was thinking about all that, he came through to put the kettle on.

'Derek, how are you feeling in yourself?' I asked.

'Why d'you want to know?'

'I've been reading this stuff about energy.'

'Can't say as I think about it,' he said, 'and I suppose that means I'm not too bad, considering. I'd not've said that on Friday, mind, but after a couple of days to myself, I'll do. Don't you go messing about with what we eat again, Wenda, whatever they're telling you. Doctors don't know everything.'

'No, I wouldn't do that, Derek. People've been having roast beef and Yorkshire pudding for hundreds of years. There's nothing wrong with it.'

'That's right. You make a good Yorkshire, pet. I enjoyed our dinner. D'you fancy a cup of tea?'

'I wouldn't mind,' I said.

He made us a cup each and sat down with me, and we drank our tea together. 'I was going to nip down to Sainsbury's Homebase', he said after a bit. 'I thought I'd get some new handles for the bathroom cupboard, see if there's anything else we could do with. D'you want to come?'

'I won't, Derek. I was on my feet all day yesterday. I don't really fancy going out.'

'That's fine. Don't worry if I'm not back for a bit. It's a nice afternoon. I might have a bit of a drive around, go out to Beauchief, maybe.' He put his cup on the draining board, and kissed me on the forehead. 'See you later.'

Hum, I thought, when he'd gone. It's adding up. He looks totally depleted and exhausted when he gets in of an evening. Then after a couple of days in positively charged space, he's a different man. All the Chi energy's rushing into the vacuum, and that's why I'm cross and out of sorts.

Thank heavens he decided to go out. As soon as he was gone, I was straight into the lounge, picking up his little bits of mess, reclaiming my space. I lit my essential-oil diffuser, a drop of hyssop to exorcise bad influences, a drop of rose-oil to calm. Angels are attracted to the smell of roses.

Funny he was thinking of going to Beauchief. I half-wished I'd said yes when he asked me to come. I hadn't been out that way for goodness knows how long. It was late spring, so maybe the bluebells were out in Abbeydale woods. I hadn't seen them for donkey's years, but I remembered them like it was yesterday, that intense filmy haze of blue over the brown of the leaf-mould, shimmering under the trees as far as you could see. It was such a strong memory, it felt like a definite prompting, so I went and lay on the settee, let my mind clear the way I do when I'm channelling. Drifting back. Now, we got married in '83, so it must've been the year before. I was still at home, Mam needed an eye kept on her by then. The others'd waltzed off, of course. Catch them lifting a finger.

'I thought you might like to see the Abbeydale Works? They're very historic.'

'I suppose so.'

'I'll pick you up after dinner, then. We'll have our tea out, maybe?'

'That's fine. See you tomorrow.' I put the phone down.

'Is that your fella?' Mum said.

'Mmm.'

'Well, tell 'im 'e's not to keep you out too late. You've got your work to go to in the morning.'

'Yes, Mam.' I was thinking about clothes. He'd landed me in it properly, in a typical male way. If I'd understood him right, we'd be traipsing round some kind of open air museum, so I'd need comfy shoes, and then I'd want to be dressier later on and I didn't know where he was thinking of taking me. I could carry brighter lipstick and eyeshadow and put it on in a ladies' somewhere, but the rest of it was a facer.

'Give me a hand up, Wenda. I want to go and do the spuds.' She'd arthritis in her knees and hips and she could hardly move. They talked about hip replacements, but she'd been on a waiting list for two years by then.

In the end I started with the shoes. I'd a pair of wedgies with round toes and ankle-straps I could walk a fair way in, so I built up from there. A shortish skirt, sort of heather mixture tweed, and a clingy black roll-neck jumper which was smart enough for evenings. It'd have to do.

He picked me up a bit after two on the Sunday. He'd just bought an old VW Polo and he was dead proud of it, it was always immaculate. He helped me in, and off we went. I was looking at him, knowing he had to watch the road. He was wearing brown wool trousers and a tank top. His mum used to knit all the time, and he was never much of a fancy Dan, so he'd wear stuff to please her. He wasn't really handsome, more all right looking. He'd a pointy nose, but he was quite full in the cheeks. When my sister Michelle saw him, she'd christened him Hammy the Hamster because of the chubby chops, and that put me right off him for a while, but I'd got used to him over time. He was serious, and he liked things to be nice, just the way I did. He was quite ambitious, prepared to work for what he wanted, and I respected that.

The Abbeydale Works were sort of interesting. It's an old scythe-making workshop they've put back together; there's these huge waterwheels driving a pair of tilt-hammers. You could see the force of it, the way the bits joined together. Imagine if anything got under that hammer by mistake, nothing could stop it. It was shivery to think about. I wondered if there'd been accidents back in the olden days – even then, I knew I was sensitive to atmospheres. There'd been a charcoal burner burned to death in the wood once, they told you about that. Derek was in seventh heaven, he's a civil engineer, so of course he could see how it all worked; he was trying to explain it to me but I wasn't following. After a while he could see I was getting bored.

'Do you know, those hammers struck 126 times a minute? It must've sounded like a road-drill, only deeper. Lovely stuff.'

'Mmm?'

'Tell you what,' he said. 'It's a lovely afternoon. We could have a little walk in the beechwoods.'

We left the works, and got back into the car. Abbeydale woods are just a tiny bit further along the same road.

'Just look at those bluebells,' I said, when we'd got into the wood. They'd made nice wide paths with that bark stuff so you could take a pushchair along: with my wedgies on, I was perfectly comfortable.

'Fantastic.' He took my hand.

It wasn't all that crowded, considering it was a really nice day. We went along the path for a bit, and then he steered me off into this glade full of bluebells. It was like wading through a pond, blue up to our knees. We were going along carefully, trying not to stand on any, with the dappled sunlight coming down through the leaves; there were spots of light like gold coins on the tree-trunks. We were well into the wood by then, and nobody else seemed to be about. There was this enormous fallen beech, covered in moss, the trunk must've been a good four-foot thick. We climbed round the root end, Derek giving me a hand because of my shoes, and found this nice little spot on the other side, bare warm ground, and you could lean your back against the trunk as if it was a settee.

He pulled me towards him, and kissed me. I'd been expecting it, I could see him getting ideas when we saw there wasn't anyone about, and I found I was really enjoying myself. Some of my boyfriends had sort of rummaged round my mouth as if they were looking for something and put me right off, but Derek was sweet. He had his hand up my jumper, and I liked that too; he couldn't get my bra undone, though he'd had a go, but it was one of those lacy half-cup ones, so he was managing nicely. It was so peaceful, you could hear bumblebees droning away, Derek's breathing, even the little scritching sounds of cloth as we shifted about.

'I love you, Wenda,' he said, the first time he'd said it.

'Oh, Derek.' I kissed him back, and he put his hand up my skirt; I had tights on, of course, and I pulled away. 'Derek, you can't. We're in the open!'

'There'd not be much to see,' he argued. 'Anyway, who cares?'

'We'd get arrested.' I wasn't all that experienced then, but I knew what it was all about, and I was terribly tempted. He took my hand, and put it on his fly, and I couldn't resist undoing it. He felt nice, all warm and hard. 'Hang on a minute.'

'God, Wenda!'

It took a little while to get my shoes off, because of the fiddly buckles, but I got them undone at last, and quickly slipped my tights and knickers off and stuck them in my handbag. 'Fair's fair,' I said, sitting down again, and reaching out to him. 'I'll do you if you'll do me.'

I was so happy that afternoon. It was so strange, remembering that feeling of being safe and loved in a little private paradise. I'd fallen in love with Derek then; I'd thought, this is the man for me, and I'd assumed we'd go on being happy forever. I wondered where my angels had been. With me, of course, but I hadn't known it. I remembered those quivering, golden motes of light, the way it dazzled when I tipped my head back, letting myself go. There'd been angel faces in that light, loving me for just being a healthy young girl, doing what comes naturally. Of course when you're young you think sex is the be-all and end-all, it's hard to see beyond it, they'd've known that, of course. That was my animal phase, but I'd been privileged to evolve onto a more spiritual plane in time, and now Ariel and Itheriel gave me all that, and more. I wanted them now; thinking about all that made me sad, and stirred me up a bit; I wanted comfort. I settled into my breathing routine. 'Ariel, Itheriel, Ariel, Itheriel. . .'

'Hullo, love,' said Derek. 'Been having a little sleep?'

I sat up with a jump, and nearly fell off the settee. 'I was thinking. What's the time?'

'Twenty past six.'

'Oh my godfathers.'

'Never mind, pet. What are Sundays for?'

'Did you get what you wanted?'

'They didn't have the right size. I'll have to try in town. But I had a nice drive.'

'I'm surprised you're not sick of driving. You drive enough during the week.'

'It makes a difference when you're not needing to get anywhere in a hurry. We might take a run out to the Peak District next week, if the weather's like this. Or Chatsworth.'

'Maybe. If I'm not too busy.'

He came and sat down beside me, and put the telly on. After a bit of clicking about, he found something which took his fancy. I got up, and went back to the kitchen.

Monday, Tuesday, Wednesday I really worked on the chanelling. I wasn't sure about healing, but I knew I could channel. What I was working on mostly was getting my receptivity going when I wasn't lying down – I was thinking, if I was working with someone else, they'd be laid down as like as not, and we couldn't lie side by side like a couple of kippers.

I can't sit cross-legged or do a lotus position, my knees won't stand it, so I was just sitting on one of the hard chairs from the kitchen: it didn't feel right, and it looked funny. But I had a stroke of luck on the Tuesday, or guidance, maybe. There's a little place, a junk shop really but it has office surplus stuff, on London Road just by the railway bridge. They put it all out on the pavement, and when I was going past on the bus I noticed they had one of those balancing chairs, the ones you sort of kneel on so you can keep your back straight. Funny looking things, but I'd tried one once at a friend's and they're quite comfortable. I got off at the next stop, and walked back. It was just what I needed, and only fifteen pounds. When I tried it out, it worked really well. Getting onto it reminded me of getting on a bike when I was a kid, and that was right enough, a really helpful thought, actually. I was climbing into the saddle to start a journey: I imagined the breath of the Spirit blowing in my face, facing into the light, as if I was biking up, up, off the ground and into the air, past the stars and up to heaven. It was even better than lying down.

I'd picked up some hints and tips from some of the websites, and browsing around in the shops: there's a nice place in town where you can buy essential oils and those Red Indian smudge sticks and crystals, and there's a couple of stalls in the market that have stuff as well. Mr Bhatia shuts at midday on Wednesdays, so Jean came round in the afternoon. I'd never entertained her at home, Derek doesn't really like us having people in, and anyway, I knew she'd be embarrassed about having me back. She thought the house was lovely, she was full of praise, and that pleased me a lot.

'How've you been?' I asked, once we were sat down with a cup of tea. The room smelled nice, I'd been round with a smudge stick cleansing it of negative Chi just before she came in.

'Could be worse. But I'm having terrible trouble sleeping. It takes me ages to get off because I'm listening for Michael coming in, and then, bang: five o'clock, I'm wide awake, and I can't ever get off again. I get up usually, there's no point just lying there. It's pulling me down.'

'You think he'd show you a bit of consideration. You're the breadwinner. Can't you tell him to be in at a sensible time?'

She looked at me as if I was mad. 'You can't do that, Wenda. He's a lad. They need to assert themselves, poor little sods. I can't shame him in front of his friends. You've got to try and see it from his point of view. He's not got much.'

It wasn't understanding Master Michael needed, it was a bloody good hiding, I thought to myself. But that was half the trouble, he'd not had a father to sort him out.

'Well, I can't do much about Michael, can I?' I said. 'But I'll see if I can help with the other bit.'

I got Jean to take her shoes off and lie on the settee, and I put a CD on; I'd two or three special spiritual ones I'd picked up in the market which I kept for meditating, there were two Hildegards and an Enya, high, sweet voices all in harmony. I turned it down so it was just warbling really quietly in the background. I'd quite a collection of essential oils by then, so I chose the ones I thought'd do the trick and dropped them into the water-bowl.

'A drop of angelica,' I explained. 'That's the one which puts you in touch with your higher self. Clary sage for peace and harmony, rosewood to open the doors of the spirit, sandalwood to make a bridge to the spiritual realm, and dispel negative energies.'

'You know a lot about it,' she said.

'I've done my research.' I lit the tealight under the bowl of the perfume diffuser, and before it started getting hot, I stirred it round with my finger. Then I went over to Jean on the settee, and touched her forehead between the eyes, and both cheekbones.

'That smells wonderful.'

'It's not just for the pleasure, Jean. It all helps. Fragrance is a very powerful tool for drawing spiritual beings, and opening us up to our inner selves. So's the music. It boils down to harmonious vibrations, you see, and that's basically what angels are.'

She lay still for a bit, then she spoke again. 'It's peaceful here. You're lucky to be living in a cul-de-sac.'

I didn't reply, I was busy moving my balance stool. Once I was settled, I reached out and took hold of her stockinged feet. 'Just breathe in through your nose, count to five, let it out through your mouth,' I said. 'I'm going to start now.'

I began calling the angels, summoning up the Chi energy in the usual way. I'd not seen much of them for a while, though I sensed them around me a lot of the time. When I felt connected, I said, 'We're in the light. Feel it in your feet, where I'm holding them. You're breathing golden light. Every breath, feel it coming higher up your body. You're filling up with golden light.' I looked at her, chest rising and falling with long, slow breaths, she looked very peaceful. And there was Ariel suddenly, standing behind her head, looking down at her with such a sweet expression. I took that as my cue to move; I let go of her feet gently and shifted to the other end of the settee.

She needed to do her hair again, you could see where the grey was growing out. I wondered if I should mention it. Later maybe. I put my hands gently on her temples, the way I did before. For a while, we just breathed in harmony.

'How are you feeling?' I said softly.

'Getting a bit cold.'

I should've thought of that. Lying still like that, her feet'd be freezing, even with her tights on. 'Hang on a minute.' I slipped off my stool, and went upstairs to get a cellular blanket out of the drawer.

'Thanks.'

'I'll take a minute to get back into it,' I warned, but it was all right, the link came back in no time. 'Ariel and Itheriel, help me to heal the spirit of Jean Wilson,' I said aloud. 'Let her grow in the light.' The Archangel Raphael's the one for healing. I thought of a chain of hands, me holding Jean, Ariel holding me and Itheriel, Raphael holding Itheriel. Wings beating. You could feel the energy moving, as if I was an electric cable. 'Invite the angels into your heart,' I said. 'Can you feel them around you?' She nodded. 'Imagine you're putting your hands in their hands. Ask them for help. They want to help, if you let them.' I could feel her tensing up again, she was wishing and wishing. 'Relax. You don't have to shout, they can hear you. Listen for a still, small voice.'

After a while, I turned my wrist so I could look at my watch. It'd been half an hour or so since I started, which seemed about right. I got up again, and went round to her feet, just standing this time, and leaned forward to take hold of them. 'Return us to the physical plane,' I said. 'I thank you for your love and care for us. Now, Jean. Feel your hands letting go. Feel your feet, ready to touch the earth. I'll count slowly from ten to one.' I counted down, as slowly as I could, though I could feel the strain in my back, leaning forward like that. At one, I let go, and straightened up. Oh, the relief. 'Open your eyes when you're ready.'

It took a moment, but at last Jean opened her eyes, and boosted herself up, swinging her feet down onto the carpet. 'Oh, Wenda,' she said, and burst into tears. I'd a box of tissues sitting on the telly, fortunately, so I gave her a handful. I had tears in my eyes myself, I remembered how I'd felt that time I saw Ariel. She cried for ever such a long time, but I didn't try and stop her. There was nothing hysterical about it, she was just sobbing and sobbing and blowing her nose. I reckoned it was bad stuff coming out, and nothing to worry about. I put a couple more oils on the burner, hyssop and juniper, for purging and cleansing, in case it helped her get shot of it all, and a drop more of the clary sage. I had a smudge stick handy from earlier, so I lit it, and put some of the oils on it, and went round her with it, shaking the stick to release the scent.

When she stopped crying of her own accord, I said, 'D'you want to pop upstairs and wash your face? I'll get the kettle on.'

'Thanks, Wenda. I don't know what I must look like!'

Actually, she looked about ten years younger. Her hair was sticking up at the back, and her nose and eyes were red and a bit swollen, but basically her face was more relaxed than I'd ever seen it. When she came back down, she looked absolutely fine.

'I feel fabulous,' she said. 'Sometimes a cry really does you good. Thank you ever so much.'

'It's not me you want to thank,' I pointed out. 'I'm not doing it.'

'It's all coming through you, though. I feel a lot stronger. I'd like to come back, if you don't mind. You could really help people, doing this. You ought to think about it.'

'I don't know as I'd want people all over the house. I've got a lot to do as it is. And Derek wouldn't like it at all. What if they weren't honest?'

'I think you'd only get a very nice type of person wanting you to channel angels,' she argued. 'I'm sure it'd be mostly women.'

'There is that. But it's a big commitment. I like having my time to myself. And they'd be ringing up all hours, wouldn't they? Anyway, it's not free, you know. The oils cost a fortune.'

'I was going to ask you to let me contribute,' said Jean, quite stiffly, and I was furious with myself.

'I don't mean you, Jean. It was just a drop or two and it's between friends. I just meant, if it was every Tom, Dick and Harry, it'd add up, wouldn't it?'

'I don't see why you shouldn't charge,' she said. 'It's totally harmless, and you could do a lot of good.'

'Oh, I couldn't do that. How'd I set about it, anyway?'

'Ad in the local paper, and Homebase let you put up ads. And in the library. I could get Chris to design you a website.'

I was tempted by the idea of a website. You could tell there were people making good money on the Web: there were all sorts offering consultations, and they didn't even have to have people coming to the house. It seemed clean, somehow. I didn't mind touching Jean, I'd found it quite moving, but I didn't like the idea of having to touch just anyone. I've always been fastidious.

IV

'Over my dead body,' said Derek.

'Why shouldn't I? I've got a talent, Derek. I need to use it.'

'It's all a lot of nonsense. I'm not saying I mind you taking up new hobbies. I'll put up with all the chimes and the crystals and the pong, but this has gone far enough. I'm not having you filling my house with all sorts.'

'You won't be here. You'll be at work. I need to try my wings.

If it works out, I'll maybe see about renting somewhere else, but that's a big commitment.'

He stopped shouting then, and just looked at me for a bit. 'Look, pet,' he said suddenly. 'What's this all about? Have you got someone else?'

Funnily enough, I almost said yes, because it was sort of true in a way. I was furious with him. It was like talking to a post. Of course, he's a Metal person, born in the autumn, they don't change their minds easily. I'm Wood, so I'm creative. 'Oh, for crying out loud, Derek. I'm not that sort of person.'

'I don't think I know what sort of person you are, Wenda. I never thought I'd hear you saying you wanted all and sundry traipsing through your lounge. You don't even like having your sisters.'

'It wouldn't exactly be traipsing,' I argued. 'They'd just come in, and get their treatment, and that'd be the end of it.'

'It's never that simple. They'll be asking to use the lavvy, and filching stuff while your back's turned. What if there's a psycho? You'll be all alone with him, remember. I could come back and find you lying around in bits.'

'Don't be stupid! The angels wouldn't let him!'

'What the hell'd they do about it? Hit 'im with their haloes?'

'Now you're just being rude.' I knew I'd be guided right, but there weren't the words to tell him that so's he'd understand. There was something in my head I wanted to say to him, a quote about angels will bear thee up lest thee strike thy foot against a stone, but I couldn't get it straight, and the moment passed. I tried to make him understand. 'Look, Derek. Haven't you ever felt there ought to be a bit more to life? Isn't there anything deep inside you that's secretly looking for something?'

He looked at me as if I'd gone mad. 'Of course not. I thought I'd got all I ever wanted. A decent job, a nice house and a proper wife. I've worked to make you happy, Wenda. I thought we'd made a good life together.'

I was touched, even though I was still angry. 'You've been very good, Derek, I'm not denying it.'

'This isn't because we never had kids of our own? We're too old for adopting, but we could still foster, if you really wanted to.'

'No. It's not about kids. It's about spiritual growth. If you can't
see that, I can't explain. What I've realised in these last few months
is that the really important thing in this world is believing in yourself. If you believe in yourself, you can do anything.'

'But what if you're wrong?'

'I'm not.'

'Wenda, you need your head seen to! You haven't got the change
of life coming on, have you?'

'That's typical male thinking! None of that's got anything to do
with it.'

'Gah! I'm going out. Don't wait up. I'm not listening to another
word of this cack.'

He slammed himself out of the house, and I plopped down on
the settee, absolutely shattered. He was taking it all very badly.
There was negative Chi everywhere; you could feel this long, ragged
muddy streak in the air where he'd been raging, like the trail of a
speedboat. I smudged the room, which helped a bit, but it'd take
a lot more than that to set things right. I'd a Chocolate Orange on
the go, so I got it out of the fridge. I needed something to calm
myself down a bit. Chocolate's good for your nerves, that's scien-
tifically proven. A lot better than swilling beer. Ten to one he'd
have a head in the morning. He can't hold it the way he used to.
At least he'd have a chance to sleep it off, seeing as it was a Saturday.

I was properly angry with him: he was being totally unreason-
able. Jean had been back more than once, and she'd brought me
a couple of other ladies she knew. I really seemed to have a bit of
a talent for this spiritual healing; they'd all been very contented.
Jean was nagging me to get her Chris to design me a website, and
I was keen to do it, but it'd cost a bit of money, and I couldn't
keep it from Derek: we've got a joint account, and he's a careful
chap: he goes through the statement properly every month, just
in case. So I thought, if I didn't talk it through with him before-
hand, there'd be the mother and father of a row. And a lot of good
it'd done me, we'd ended up having the row anyway. I was very
upset about it. I know there are people who row all the time, but
we'd never been like that. He had his own interests, and I had
mine, but we'd always been polite. I couldn't think when I'd last

heard him raise his voice. But it wasn't as if I was beholden to him for every last penny. I earned enough at the chemist's to cover my own bits and bobs, and to contribute a bit. I didn't see why I shouldn't spend my own money how I liked.

I got my angel book, the one I write in. I'd given it a title by then, 'The Book of Life'. I didn't want to think about Derek any more, and I had an idea I was working on. I'd seen something of the sort in a shop, but I wanted to do my own version. Angel cards, sort of like the Tarot, something I could use with people. I could make them out of ordinary card: I'm not artistic, but they didn't need to be anything fancy. I could just write on them with coloured felt-tips, they didn't need to have pictures.

I'd found out a lot about angels by then: there's the four great archangels, Michael, Raphael, Gabriel and Uriel. They'd be the four suits, Hosts, I'd call them. They've each got their own special jobs, you see: Michael's the warrior, so he cuts you free from old stuff, Raphael's a healer, Gabriel's a messenger, Uriel brings love, so that's four key things. Blue, Green, Yellow, Red. Then there were all the ordinary angels, Israphel, Sandolphon, Leriel, Tabris and so on, they've all got their qualities as well: Israphel's the angel of music, and Sandolphon looks after children in the womb, for instance. I'd just have to intuit which one belonged in which Host, but with a bit of help, I thought I could do that. I'd put nine in each Host, the ones which felt right, and a quality alongside the name; Israphel's would be Harmony, I could see that right off. Sandalphon, Nurturing, maybe. Then I'd do three cards for each Host which were just qualities associated with that archangel, the equivalent of Queen, Jack, Ace: for Michael, maybe they'd be Courage, Strength, Power. . . I needed to do a lot of thinking, with Ariel and Itheriel helping me all the way, so I'd get every single one right. It made me so calm and happy, doing that angel work, I could feel the good energy just spiralling out from where I was sitting, even though I wasn't actually meditating, Ariel and Itheriel working with me, and fanning all the anger and the badness away from me and out of the house with their beautiful wings. 'Inspiration, Intuition, Joy', I wrote.

By the time I'd finished my Chocolate Orange and was ready for bed, I was clear in my own mind. It was a joint bank account.

Derek couldn't actually stop me writing Jean's Chris a cheque. He'd have to like it or lump it.

Things went quiet after that. We hardly spoke on the Sunday. I don't think he was feeling very well, and anyway, there was nothing to say. But at some point he must've gone whining to my sisters. Lynne, that's the middle one, lives in Manchester now, but Michelle's still in Sheffield, and she still reckons she can run everything and everyone. Nothing'll change her. She's hectored me about since the day I was born. When I got wed, I told her I wouldn't stand for her interfering any more, and we'd agreed to differ. Mostly we just saw each other at Christmas and special family occasions. Derek quite liked her, God alone knows why. He played golf with Brian sometimes.

When I picked up the phone and heard her voice a couple of days later, I knew what she'd be wanting to say. We weren't brought up religious, but she got quite keen after she married Brian – he's one of those born agains. I suppose there's a place for that sort of thing in your life if a person isn't naturally attuned to the astral realm. I don't hold with it myself. Frankly, I reckon the Almighty wouldn't waste his time on a long thin streak of misery like her, but it takes all sorts.

'Wenda, is that you? Have you got anybody there?'

'Oh, it's you.'

'Derek says you've taken up spiritualism,' she said, going straight to the point as usual.

I was very annoyed. 'Not spiritualism. I've been developing my spiritual side. He can't tell the difference.'

'You're going around telling people you're seeing things. It's the first sign of madness, you know.'

'I'm not seeing things. I'm just sensitive to angels. I don't expect you to understand.'

'And you understand, I suppose! Wenda, you're meddling with stuff you shouldn't be getting into. It's very dangerous, you know.'

'What's dangerous about it? I've developed a talent for channelling the basic energy of the universe. It's absolutely natural and beautiful, and now I'm a bit experienced, I've found I can strengthen people and make them happy. There's nowt wrong with any of that that I can see. You don't understand, cause you're not listening. You've never listened to me, and I'm not expecting you to start now.'

'Satan can disguise himself as an angel of light, Wenda. That's in the Good Book. When did you last open a Bible?'

'You know I can't be having with religion. All it does is lay down the law. The whole thing about spirituality is it tells you to listen to your own guidance and follow your heart. I've been blessed with the gift of opening my mind to angelic communication, and it's a blessing they want me to share. You're just jealous, because you know nowt about it, and never will.'

'Don't give me that. It's been self, self, self with you since the day you were born.'

'That's rich, from you. D'you remember the Christmas Mam made me give you my new Sindy? She always took your side.'

'That was cause you'd cut all the hair off my Tressy.'

'You were meant to cut the hair off! It said on the box it really grows!'

'Oh, for Pete's sake! And it wasn't yours to cut off, anyway. I'd cried about it all morning. You've forgotten that.'

'I'm not going to argue with you. I forgive you. Don't think I'm blaming you, Michelle. I don't expect you to understand. You're suffering from a lack of spiritual evolution.'

That shut her up. When she came back, it was on another tack. 'You can't be some kind of tuppenny-ha'penny priestess in Sheffield! Show some sense. It's just making a fool of yourself.'

'Why the heck not? Everyone's got to be somewhere. Bethlehem wasn't much of a place, by all accounts.'

'You blasphemous cow. I've had about enough of all this.'

I put the phone down. Good riddance. I wished I'd done it years ago. It started to ring again immediately, so I pulled the jack out of the wall. That was the angels, of course. I'd that new strength in me, to do what I thought was right. I'd knuckled under to her far too long, just because she was the oldest.

'Do you know what you want, Mrs Bootham?'

'Yes I do.' I got my notebook out. Jean's Chris worked in this funny little office, a couple of rooms over an accountant's. There were shelves all round and computers with their insides out, and bits of electronic doodahs piled all the way up to the ceiling. There were two or three lads working there, Jean said, but nobody else was about. I hadn't met Chris before; I'd seen his little brother Michael once or twice, and I thought he was a surly little B., but this one was quiet and shy. 'I want it sunshine yellow at the top, shading to sky blue at the bottom. And the bits where you'd click, I'd like them to be angels holding hearts, or candles or something. You'd click on the heart. Can you do that?'

'Oh, aye. That's straightforward, Mrs Bootham. But what d'you want it to do?'

'Be a website, of course.' I couldn't see what he was getting at.

He sighed in that 'older people are stupid' way young 'uns all do. 'What are you telling the punters about? What d'you want 'em to do about it?'

'Oh.' I hadn't quite looked at it that way.

'Okay. Let's come back to that. We'll have a think about design, since that's where you've got to.' He reached for a scruffy sketchpad, and drew on it. 'This is the basic layout. Everyone looks at the top left-hand corner first, so you put the name up in a bar at the top.'

'I'm calling it "Walking with Angels".'

'Fine.' He scribbled it in. He had dreadful handwriting, you could hardly read it. 'Now we gussy it up with a posh font. We could try Gothic lettering, it might have the right feel for what you want, or Celtic maybe, or a brush script if you want a more contemporary look. As fancy as you like, just as long as people can still read it.' He swivelled on his little stool, and woke up his computer.

'Let's try some mock-ups.' He typed in 'Walking with Angels', and started ringing the changes with different styles of writing. I was amazed at the difference it made. 'You can't get too complicated, cause not everyone's got all the same fonts.' He tapped the screen with his biro. 'If you go for this one, which is Lucida Handwriting, it comes as part of the basic MS Word package, so just about everyone'll have it. You can fancy it up a bit though, put shadows on, that type of thing.'

'I'll have Lucida, then.'

'Okay. D'you like these shadows under the letters? I reckon it gives you a nice 3-D effect, makes it stand out.'

'Yes. I'll go with that.'

'Fine.' He made a note. 'Well, next you want a visually distinct bar down the left-hand side, that's pretty standard now, so people know what to do with it. You can have a stripe of a different colour and put stuff on top of it, or if you like, you can make a column of data, just so long as it looks different from the text section. You stick your navigation buttons and links there; it's like a contents page for your site. Then text goes in the rest of the page, see?'

'It sounds straightforward.'

'It's not.' He took a drink from a mug which was standing by his keyboard, coffee, by the smell. He never thought to offer me one, not that I'd've taken it if he had. In a place like that I don't expect they wash the mugs from one week's end to another. 'The thing is, with a site like this, you're going to be dealing with pretty ignorant people.'

'What d'you mean, ignorant?' I was highly indignant. 'You don't leave your brain behind the door when you're dealing with angels, far from it. It gets very technical, and you need to do a lot of research. There's one lady, one of the top experts, who's got a PhD. Doctor Doreen Virtue.'

'Yeah, well. I meant, ignorant about computers. I mean, you're not trying to reach major-league geeks. They're more likely to be just people who use computers a bit.'

'Well, that's true enough,' I conceded.

'That means you can forget about things like pulldowns, they mightn't recognise them, and there'll be other constraints because we'll need to cater for non-standard browsers.'

'What's a browser when it's at home!' I was getting really annoyed with him; I felt he was just showing off, blinding me with science.

'You know. The bit that takes you where you want to go. It's usually Internet Explorer these days, but some people still use Netscape. But the thing is, punters on an angel site are just as likely to have crappy computers with bolt-on modems, because they still sort of work. So they could have anything, see? Mosaic, even. Basically, you're targeting users with an incredibly random subset of actual machines, so you can't get too complicated.'

I thought I saw what he was getting at. 'I've been on some really pretty sites,' I said. 'Angels who flap their wings, flowers growing and unfolding, and that sort of thing.'

'Don't go there. I don't think you can afford to get into anything more complicated than jpegs – jpegs are how I'm sticking on your angel pictures. You need to worry about slow connections, see? With an older computer, even a jpeg takes forever to download. You know what I mean – if you get onto a site and find there's a lot of blank bits and you have to wait around while it all downloads, you get pretty pi– fed up, don't you? So you'll lose people if you get too fancy, because they'll get bored of waiting and try something else. Your target audience won't necessarily have things like JavaScript and Quicktime, they're not tech-heads. So basically, there's no point making something which works perfectly here in the office, on a 120 gig state of the art Sony Vaio with broadband and all the trimmings, when the point is, the folk you want to reach are just as likely to have a ten-year-old pile of crap with 128k, a 14.4 modem, and a processor which came out of the Ark.'

I was beginning to feel quite discouraged. I'd had such a clear picture in my mind's eye, and it sounded as if it wasn't going to be like that at all. 'What about colours?'

'No problemo. All the pretty colours you like.'

That was something, anyway. We thought about colours for a bit. Blue and green have strong spiritual associations, so with the background being turquoise blue and gold, we settled on dark blue for the title, and the navigation buttons in bright green Lucida Sans. It was starting to look very nice already.

'Okay, Mrs B. What's it going to do?' he asked.

'I want a bit where I put down my experiences.'

'Great. Call that the first navigation button. Someone clicks that, they get a whole lot of text coming up, whatever you give me. Call it "Talking to Angels", or "Seeing Angels", or something.'

'"Guardian Angels",' I said. He typed that in. 'Then an ideas bit. Sort of, my philosophy. Call it "You and Your Angels". Then I need a bit explaining about angel cards.'

'And you need a contacts button, so people can get in touch by email. Mum said you thought you might make some money off of this?'

'I want to cover my expenses.'

'How?'

'What d'you mean, how?'

'Well, you want them paying for services, I suppose. But the key thing is, how do they do it? They can't shove a tenner in your hand. It's all got to be electronic, and there's security issues.'

'If I put my real address on, people could write cheques,' I said.

'Yeah, well, but that's not exactly immediate. If someone asks you for something, I dunno, maybe, do the angels reckon I ought to marry this bint or not? either you've got to give them their answer up front and risk them not paying, or you've got to wait for the cheque to turn up by snail-mail and then wait for it to clear. By then they'll've forgotten all about it. It all looks like too much trouble, see? And registering as a vendor with the credit card people costs a fortune, believe me.'

'But what am I supposed to do?'

'You need to get registered with PayPal,' he said promptly. 'All you need's a credit card. The beauty of that is, security's their problem, not yours.'

It was all so confusing, for two pins, I'd've told him to keep it. But I really wanted this to happen, and the angels wanted it too. I could feel them approving, and it kept me going, even though it wasn't at all my kind of place.

'That's pretty straightforward, then,' he said, scribbling. 'You've got the nav bar, or people can get the same info by clicking on angels. What about the angel pictures, though? Where are they coming from?'

It must've been a prompting: I'd never got around to throwing away that year's Christmas cards. There were some with addresses I'd been meaning to copy into our book, so I'd ended up just putting the lot in a cardboard box in the spare room till I had time to go through them. We'd had some lovely classical cards based on old masters, and there'd been any amount of angels. I'd selected out the best ones, and I had them in a folder.

'Can you copy these somehow?'

'Oh, yeah. They'll scan all right, and after that it's just a matter of selecting out the bit you want and making all the images the same size. Four of them are actually going to have html links, from what you're saying, then I suppose I sprinkle some more around for decoration.'

'That's right. With the ones you click on, can you put a little heart in their hands so people'll know where to go?'

'Piece of piss. I mean, not a problem. The hearts'd better be a uniform bright pink, so they're noticeable.'

'That's about it, then.'

''Cept for the text, Mrs Bootham. You've got a site that's all dressed up with nowhere to go.'

I was typing with two fingers, not one, by then, but it was still a bit of a prospect. Never mind. For Ariel and Itheriel, I'd go through fire and water, do anything. I'd just have to get on with it.

'I'll build your site,' said Chris, 'and send you my bill, but there's no point putting it on the Web till you've done the text, you'll just annoy people. Email the bits to me when you've got them the way you want them, and I'll do the rest. Best to do one file under each of your headings, then I won't make any mistakes.'

'What are you actually charging?' I asked. Jean hadn't been too clear on that, but she said he'd agreed to take something off since I was a friend of the family.

'Twenty quid an hour.'

'That's a heck of a price, from a lad of your age!'

'That's family rates, Mrs Bootham. I'm not charging my consultation fee.'

I was in the wrong business, and no mistake, I thought.

V

The next person to stick their oar in was my middle sister, Lynne. I was quite surprised to hear her on the phone. She doesn't often get in touch. Michelle's such a bossy little madam, there wouldn't be room for two like that in one family, so it's not surprising Lynne's one for the quiet life.

'Derek's told me a bit about what's going on,' she said. 'Channelling and angels and that. Wenda, I'm not sitting in judgement, but I think you ought to see the doctor.'

'If that's not judgemental, I don't know what is. You're saying I've gone doolally.'

'No, that's not what I meant. This has all come out of a clear blue sky.'

I wasn't actually quite sure about that: I'd been giving it some thought. 'I don't think it has, Lynne. I'm sure some things in the past were actually contacts. Do you remember, I used to have two invisible friends?'

'Half the kids in the world have invisible friends. That doesn't mean they up and start seeing angels forty years later.'

'Doesn't it? All the kids in the world have guardian angels. Maybe it's just that when you're young and innocent, you can see them.'

'I don't buy that, Wenda. It's just self-dramatising. Paul and Joshua used to do it all the time when they were little. Every time one of them broke something, they'd blame it on Pinky or Bodger, but I still don't think we had angels running round the house spoiling my lipsticks and kicking over plant-pots.'

'That's as may be. But what about when Nanna died?'

'What happened? I remember you had to sleep with Mam and Dad for about a week, cause you were screaming out at night.'

'That's right. I took it very hard. I'd always felt she was special for me.'

I remembered it very well. The dreams first of all, the reason Mam had to take me into her bed. They'd told me Nanna was in heaven, but when they came back from the funeral, Michelle said they'd put her under the ground. I hadn't gone, they thought Lynne and I were too little, so old Mrs Thorpe from down the road stopped in with us till everyone came back for the tea. I went into the yard, after Michelle said that, and put my hand into the earth in Dad's border. It was cold and dirty and sticky, and something moved, a big horrible worm squirming against my fingers. I wiped my hand down my front, trying to wipe off the feeling, and ran inside, and Mam gave me hell for spoiling my good frock. After that, I had dreams where I was lying down and people were putting cold earth on top of me, all dirty and wormy, and I couldn't do owt to stop it.

But then, one night, I was lying beside Mam; I remembered her big, warm, soft shape, and Dad snoring on the other side. She used to wear a brushed nylon nightie, it felt very nice to touch. They had the front bedroom, of course; and the curtains were thin, not lined or anything, so when the cars went by outside, you'd get a beam of light travelling across the ceiling. I used to lie and watch it. Then one time, the light seemed to stop, and get stronger, and I knew it was my Nanna.

'I miss you,' I said, just whispering.

'Don't fret, Wenda,' she said, or something like that. There was just a presence, this tremendous feeling of reassurance, and I knew she was all right. I went to sleep then, and that was the end of the nightmares. I didn't think anything of it, of course; when you're six you take things like that for granted. I don't know if I even told anyone. I'd've been worried Michelle would laugh at me.

'I got a definite message about Nanna,' I explained. 'That she was in heaven and everything was all right. That's why I stopped having the dreams.'

There was a sceptical sort of silence, but she didn't say anything, just sighed. That's where Lynne's different from Michelle, she lets you have your space. 'Okay. But granted you got a message, you didn't actually see her, did you? Cardie and stockings and all.'

'No,' I admitted, 'but I knew it was her.'

'Well, look. You're actually *seeing* these angels, apparently. That's something different. I really think you ought to have a check-up. You might have a growth or something. You haven't been getting headaches, have you?'

'Not unless I've got people nagging me to death.' I was worried, though. It's not a pleasant thought.

'Gareth's mum's sister started smelling things that weren't there. It was a bit of a joke in the family. She'd come in and say 'Who's been baking?' when there wasn't anything, in reality. It turned out she had a lump in her head, and it was pressing on that bit of her brain.'

I didn't like to ask the obvious question, but Lynne answered it anyway.

'She passed on a year or so after that, poor old soul. Mind you, she'd done pretty well. The thing is, Wenda, that kind of thing can happen at any age. It might be a warning.'

'I don't think so.'

'It's as well to check, though.'

'Maybe you've got the rights of it,' I admitted. 'I'll do that. How are Gareth and the lads?'

'Champion. Paul's started his course at Manchester Met, and Joshua's got a new girlfriend. We're crossing our fingers this one's a stayer, she's a nice lass, and he's besotted.'

I got her off the phone after a bit, but she'd given me a lot to think about.

'I reckon you ought to charge ten pounds a time,' said Jean. We were back in The Nook, after work one day in late spring. I'd no reason to hurry home, Derek had taken to coming in later and later, and we barely spoke. 'Not more, people won't pay more round here. It's got to be enough to be worth your while, but not enough to make people feel guilty they're spending it on just themselves. That's fair, anyway. You haven't a lot of overheads, apart from the oils and the candles, and since you're using your front room, and it's just money in your hand, who's ever going to know? One thing, though. If you start doing readings on the Net, you'll have to keep proper accounts, or the tax man'll come down on you like a ton of bricks sooner or later. You ought to buy an account book.'

'I wish I'd never heard of the flipping Net. It's been nothing but trouble.'

'Oh, I wouldn't say that. It's just the getting started. How's the writing coming on?'

'It's a nightmare. I never used to like English at school. It's funny. It looks fine in my notebook, but when I type it it looks all wrong, and I don't know how to make it better.'

'But you're really inspirational, the way you talk about it.'

'That's different. I can't think when I'm typing.'

'Tell you what. If you've got a tape recorder, do it that way. Dictate it. I learned how to type properly. I'd do it for four pound an hour.'

I thought about it. 'I know where there's an old cassette player upstairs. They record, don't they?"

'That'd do. D'you want to give it a go?'

I could see I might end up paying out a lot of money that way, but it was worth trying out, anyway, and Jean's as honest as the day.

'You might end up bringing in a lot more business that way,' she said. 'I mean, you've got the whole world out there, not just Sheffield.'

'I'll believe it when I see it,' I said. 'There's something else I've been thinking of as well. You know the Alternative Health Centre?'

'That place up by Meersbrook Park?'

'Yes. They do all sorts: Feng Shui and Reiki and reflexology. I went and had a word with them, and you can get the use of a room, with a share of the lady who's the receptionist and does the books. I was just asking if I could maybe have a day a week there, once I'd built up a bit of a customer base, and they were quite positive about it. I said it wouldn't be for a while, till I saw how I was doing, but it's something to build towards. I don't like having people at the house, to be honest.'

'Mmm.' I could see she was thinking. 'It'd still just be a pound here and a pound there, wouldn't it? I reckon you ought to develop the angel cards, Wenda. I think they're brilliant. Better than anything I've ever seen in a shop.'

'Develop them how?'

'You could make good money off them.'

'It's a thought. They'd need to be a lot prettier.'

'You could find a designer.'

'And then what, Jean?'

'See about getting someone to make them. The way I see it, there's two ways forward. You sell someone the idea, and that's that, it's them as profits. Or you market them yourself. It's harder, cause of the distribution problem, but if it works, it's all yours.'

'You've really thought about all this.'

'Yes. I have. Wenda, I think we ought to have a range of merchandise.'

'We?'

'You can't do it all on your own. You're the one with the vision, but you need someone to take care of the business end.'

'I've never thought of you as a business person.' I was surprised at her.

'You never knew me in the days of Norman. We used to make garden furniture, and I did a lot on the business plans and marketing. The thing is, since he walked out, I've never had a spare ha'penny, and with the boys round my neck, I hadn't the time. I hadn't any sort of special concept to sell, either. But you have, Wenda. We'd make a heck of a team.'

'What else were you thinking of?'

'There's the aromatherapy end. Those mixtures you make. You could market your mixture for calling angels into your presence, and maybe some others.'

'I could do one for purifying the environment, and a meditation mixture,' I said. I was beginning to catch on.

'And angel jewellery. Sort of talismans. I don't know, silver and enamel, maybe. Things people could wear, to remind them of their guardian angels. If you want prototype moulds made, I'm telling you we're in the right place to do it. There's little workshops all over Sheffield.'

'But I'm not artistic!'

'Ask your angels, Wenda. They'll tell you what they want to look like.'

'That's true.' I hadn't ever tried doing that, but I could see it might work.

I'd made myself a lovely altar in the lounge on a little table by the wall. Two gold candles, my essential-oil diffuser, a cut-crystal bud vase and ashtray – I don't let anyone smoke in the lounge, it was there so I could write messages to the angels and burn them, which is very efficacious. My angel cards were in pride of place, in a special gold box I'd got in the Oxfam shop, with a natural crystal sitting on top of it. I'd chosen Iceland spar, because the way it took the light reminded me how Ariel and Itheriel sometimes shimmer just in the corner of my eye.

When I got home, I got out The Book of Life, which I keep hidden away under a pile of clean sheets in the airing cupboard. I didn't want Derek anywhere near it – I didn't want it scoffed at, and I'd half a thought that if he saw it he might burn it or chuck it out. I'd developed a sanctifying routine by then. I used it on anything which had negative Chi, and just generally if I wanted to be extra careful. I laid the book reverently on the altar, with the crystal on top of it, lit the candles, and put some essential oils in the diffuser. I couldn't put the oil on the actual book; as I'd found out the hard way, it made nasty marks on the leatherette. Myrrh, frankincense, rosewood: if that didn't open up creative pathways, I didn't know what would.

I tried to keep a bunch of fresh flowers in the lounge, it's good Feng Shui apart from anything else. I'd some roses on the go that week, which are best of all from the angelic point of view; one in my bud vase, and the rest in a vase on the telly. I took the head off one, and sprinkled the petals over my book, thinking of Ariel and Itheriel, asking for their help and protection.

After I'd done all that, I pulled my balance stool up to the table as if it was a desk, blew the petals carefully off my book and opened it at a blank page. I'd a very good ballpoint which wrote nicely, so I put it there all ready. None of it's up to me, I thought. It's all up to you. Then I started my meditation.

There was nothing in my mind at all, consciously, I mean, but when I came out of the Chi trance, I picked up my pen and started to draw these little swirly figures. They just seemed to come out of the biro by themselves. I drew them again and again, they were somehow like little energy diagrams, and I really liked them. As I went on drawing, the concept got more and more refined. You could see the bodies and the wings, only abstract, but they came out sort of oval, a nice, neat shape, and they weren't quite like anything I'd ever seen, they were something new. A gift from my angels.

I did go to the doctor; Lynne had got me quite worried. I don't see a doctor very often. What with working in a chemist, I mostly just ask Mr Bhatia for advice if I'm under the weather. I had to wait for ages, in this room full of wheezing kids and old wrecks with varicose veins who smelt. I reckoned if you hadn't got anything when you went in, you would have by the time you came out. When I got into the doctor's, he was a young man I'd never seen before; he looked about seventeen come Sunday, which doesn't exactly inspire confidence.

'Well, Mrs Bootham. What can I do for you?'

'I think I'm perfectly all right, Doctor. The only thing is, I sort of see things other people can't see, but there's nothing wrong with my mind, I'm sure of that.'

He looked rather puzzled. 'You certainly don't sound as if there's anything wrong with your mind, Mrs Bootham. Have you had your vision checked? How old are those glasses?'

'This year's. I thought of that, of course, but I'm up to date with eye tests.'

'And your general health's fine? No headaches?'

'No, nothing like that.'

He did a few tests after that, felt my head all over, and got me to watch the end of his pen while he moved it to and fro.

He sat back after a bit. 'Well, Mrs Bootham, as far as I can see, you're absolutely okay. The thing is, I can't look inside your head, so even though I haven't found any evidence of anything, there's just an outside chance you might've had a tiny stroke and there's a blood clot roving about in your brain, or you might have some kind of a growth. I'm going to send you up to the Hallamshire for a CAT scan and a chat with a consultant, just to make sure. There probably isn't anything there, so try not to worry about it, but if there is, they'll find it.'

I told him it was a lot of fuss about nothing. I could do without wasting the best part of a day sitting about in the Hallamshire, but I wasn't sorry to be persuaded. Once someone's put the idea in your head, you want to make sure.

'All right. Thank you, Doctor,' I said. I felt absolutely fine, but I knew full well that doesn't always prove anything.

I tried to put it out of my mind after that. As the year went on, the angel therapy began to take off. The Alternative Health Centre let me leave some leaflets, and quite a few people got in touch from that, but mostly it was word of mouth. Some of them wanted the channelling, but quite often it was the cards that really interested them. I started to think Jean had a point and I ought to develop them. By July, I was in two minds about whether I ought to move to the Alternative Health Centre. If I did, I'd have to make quite a bit more, I'd need to start paying tax, and I'd be paying out for the room and the receptionist. On the other hand, it'd be a lot more professional. I was starting to get quite a lot busier, and I didn't want the neighbours complaining about me running a business in a residential area, it'd add fuel to the fire.

Derek and I were barely speaking; he'd taken to playing golf on Sundays, and I'd moved into the back spare room. But he couldn't say I'd stopped being a proper wife to him. I'm careful about things like that. By the time he came in of an evening, the house was immaculate, with nothing to show I'd been seeing my clients. I washed and ironed all his clothes, and I still made him his breakfast and his tea every day, but I didn't eat with him. I'd stop in the kitchen with my plate, and leave him in front of the telly. I'd no idea what he was thinking. He was like a dead weight in my life, and I hoped to goodness he'd come round to my way of thinking. There were all kinds of things I wanted to ask him. He'd always worked for a company, so I didn't think he'd have been able to help directly with getting me started, but all the same, I knew there were all kinds of things he knew about the world of business. He'd told me things from time to time, and I'd never paid him much heed. VAT, now, who pays VAT? When would I start being liable? I probably needed an accountant, where could I find a good one? I used to look at him sometimes, and think, there's all sorts of useful knowledge locked up in that head, but whenever I tried to talk to him about my angel stuff, he shut me up, or lost his rag.

Meanwhile, Jean and I worked and worked on the text for the website. By the time we gave it to Chris to post on the Net, I was very satisfied with it. It was a wonderful feeling, calling it up that first time, and just admiring it. It looked so professional and beautiful, a person couldn't help but be attracted. I started leaving messages in the chat rooms, telling folk it was there, and I had quite a few visitors. I even started getting people asking for more about the cards, and asking for card readings. All in all, it was starting to look like a success, and when I'd earned enough off it to offset what I'd had to pay out to Chris Wilson, it felt like one, too.

VI

One Sunday that summer, Derek had gone off with his golf clubs, and I was looking forward to having the day to myself and catching up on some of my Web business when I heard the doorbell. I could see someone through the patterned glass panel, it looked like a woman. I don't see clients on a Sunday, so I thought it must be Jean, but when I opened the door, it turned out to be Michelle.

'What the heck are you doing here?'

'Aren't you going to ask me in?'

'You can come in if you like. It's a free country.' She followed me into the kitchen, and I put the kettle on. 'Have you come to tell me I'm going straight to hell?' I asked.

'Don't talk daft. I've come round because someone in the family has to try and hammer some sense into you before it's too late.

Derek and Brian've gone off to Lees Hall to play golf, so we won't be interrupted. They've seen quite a bit of each other this summer.'

'Oh, aye?'

'You're playing with fire, Wenda. He'll leave you, if you go on fannying about with these angels, and then we'll have you round our necks for the rest of your life.'

I wanted to throw my cup of tea in her face. She's cruel, Michelle, she's always known how to put the knife in. My stomach was knotting up. 'He's not that sort.'

'There's a limit to how much a man'll stand. Take a proper look at yourself, and listen to reason. You're unskilled, and you're forty-six years old, and you've let yourself go.' Michelle's a PA, she never lets you forget she's got qualifications. 'What do you weigh now? You'd be in a pretty pickle without Derek's salary. Just face it, Wenda. You couldn't make much of a life by yourself. For God's sake, kiss and make up, before it's too late.'

'He's not got someone, has he?' I hated myself for asking, but I couldn't stop myself.

'Not that we know of, but it's a matter of time, isn't it? You can't neglect a man indefinitely. What Derek's put up with's nobody's business. You stopped him smoking, you stopped his football, and now you won't even give him bacon for his break-fast. He's a good man, but he's not a saint. He bottles everything up, so someone's got to speak for him. Whatever happens, you can't say nobody's warned you.'

'You're just jealous, because Brian treats you like a slave bound hand and foot,' I said.

'Jealous? Of a man as couldn't even give you kids of your own? I'm sorry, Wenda. You're on the wrong track there.'

'You're just being negative. That's typical of you. You've never believed I was worth anything.'

'That's cause you're not. You were a mardy, whining kid, and now you're a mardy, whining woman. You useless fat mare. Never in a million years will you get me to believe an angel 'ud waste his breath on you.'

'Get out of my house.'

'All right, I'm going. It's no pleasure to me to be talking to you, believe me. Just remember what I said.'

She picked up her jacket and marched out. I heard the door shut behind her, and the car starting.

I sat on where I was, finishing my tea and feeling like death. Of course I didn't want Derek to leave me. All I wanted was for him to see my point of view. Michelle was just being spiteful, she's always had enough bile and vinegar for half a dozen. But it was true, I didn't know what he was thinking. I put my cup in the sink and went up to the front bedroom.

I was in there every day, of course, making the bed and picking up after him, but I wasn't in the habit of stopping there to get an impression. The room looked funny without my stuff on the dressing-table, and it smelled of Derek. He's very clean, but he doesn't like to use a deodorant because he's got a sensitive skin; I have to do his shirts and underwear separately in Woolite or Stergene. He can't say I don't look after him. There was a jacket of his hanging up, and I went through the pockets. There were just petrol receipts, old Polo mints, a couple of restaurant bills. He'd spent a lot on lunch, if it was for one, but I knew he entertained sometimes. It wasn't necessarily a bad sign.

I sat down on the bed, on his side, trying to gauge the feeling in the room. Sadness, I thought. Anger. That's what I'm getting. We've a padded satin headboard, it's nice to lean against if you're sitting up. I noticed it was developing a greasy mark from his hair, it needed a drop of Dabitoff. He must've been reading in bed. But that could wait. I leaned back against it, literally trying to look at things from his point of view, and I started trying to think how long it had been since we'd had sex. It came as a bit of shock to realise that it must've been half a year. Certainly not since I'd found that stuff on his computer back in January. It gave me a funny feeling inside. It wasn't really that I wanted it myself, I'd sort of grown out of all that, but I didn't want to lose him. Only for the life of me, I couldn't think how to introduce the subject.

The computer. That was a thought. I went through to the little spare bedroom and turned it on, but he'd changed the password, and this time, I couldn't guess what it was.

I was looking out for him coming back that evening. You could see the golf had done him good, there was a spring in his step, and he'd caught the sun a bit. But I could see his expression sort of harden as he came up the path to the door. For a minute, I wondered if Michelle'd told Brian she was coming round for a word, and it put me off, but I realised that was foolish. I'd better stick with it.

'I've done a chicken,' I said. 'I thought you'd be hungry, you won't've had proper Sunday dinner.'

He looked at me oddly. 'Thanks, Wenda. I could peck a bit.'

I set the kitchen table for once, and when he came down from his bath, I opened a beer for him. I'd roasted a chicken and some potatoes, and we had peas and carrots, and I'd made gravy.

'Wenda, what's this about?' he said after a bit.

'It's not about anything. I just thought, we're not speaking. I wanted to get it out in the open.'

'Does that mean you've come off it?'

'Derek, it's not like something you can come off. It's a sort of mission. But one thing I haven't mentioned. I've got an appointment at the hospital this week.'

'Do they know what's wrong with you?'

'It's just tests. But don't think you can get out of it like that. I haven't got a screw loose, and I don't think I'm ill. Only, just in case . . . well, I sort of wanted you to know.'

'Oh, Wenda. I can't stand a lot of this, pet.'

He hadn't called me pet in a long time.

'We've got across each other,' I said. 'I don't like that any more than you do. It's not dignified. Listen, Derek. I'm going to start seeing people at the Alternative Health Centre. It's practically a business now, I've developed my client base, so I can start doing it properly. Then it'll be out of the house. I know you don't want me having people here. I haven't enjoyed it much myself, actually. It'll be nice to have the place to ourselves.'

'I still think this angel healing's a load of cobblers.'

'Yes, well, people're different. There's loads as think I help them. We're not all the same.'

'That's true enough. As long as it's out of the house. You're making a bit, are you?'

'Yes. Not a fortune, but just a little extra.'

'Well, that's something, anyway.'

'I put back what I had out of the joint account.'

'I noticed. It was very fair of you.' He put his knife and fork neatly on his plate. 'Is there a sweet?'

'Apple crumble. It's Sunday.'

We had a quiet evening after that, just watching the telly together. When he switched it off for the night, I said, 'I thought I might come back,' trying to sound casual.

'I wouldn't mind.'

I moved my bits and bobs back through, and put on a new nightie I'd bought in Cole's sale.

He was sitting up reading, one of those Ken Folletts, but when I got into bed, he put it down and turned off the light.

I felt quite shy of him. I just lay there on my back in the dark, knowing he was there, and then I moved my hand a bit, and found it was touching his. I didn't move mine away, and he started stroking the back of it, just with one finger. That's all it took. No explanations or anything, sometimes it's better not. He rolled towards me, and I felt his breath on the side of my face, so I turned my head.

I quite enjoyed it, I have to say. I didn't get there myself, but I hadn't expected to, not with all we'd got in the background. All the same, there's something nice about giving pleasure. I don't just lie there like a dying duck in a thunderstorm. It was good to know I still suited him. Even if Michelle thought I was a fat cow, he clearly had no objections. I went and had a wash afterwards – that's the bit I don't like, all that messy stuff. It seems to get every-where. By the time I'd tidied myself up to my own satisfaction and got myself back to bed, he was already asleep, I could hear him snoring.

It must have been quite a bit later, because it seemed to be light. I was lying there quiet and warm. Too warm, really; I could feel

my legs beginning to prickle with it. I pushed the covers off,
because my legs were itching like nobody's business. Then I saw
this thing tickling on my calf, like a grain of rice from a rice
pudding, only with a black head, and then I saw it was moving. It
was some kind of a maggot, ugh, I thought, flicking it away. But
my legs were still itching, and I started to realise that I could see
the black heads coming up under the skin, and I knew they were
coming out of me. I wanted to scream, but I knew I must be dead.

I woke up then properly, all hot and sweaty, it was about six in
the morning, and the sun was coming up; we hadn't shut the
curtains properly. Derek was still snoring. I had to get up and go
into the bathroom and take a good look at myself to be quite sure
I was all right. But then I thought: it's just this mortal body. And
then I wondered if Itheriel and Ariel really cared about me or loved
me at all, and I thought, they'd better, because if they don't there's
no point in existing.

We jogged on all right for a week or so after that. We ate together,
and we were a lot friendlier generally. Derek seemed happier; he'd
give me a kiss when he left for work, touch my shoulder, that sort
of thing, and we made love once or twice, but I knew in my heart
I could never go back to being just ordinary. It'd be spiritual death:
I'd had my warning, and I wouldn't forget it. But I was very worried
about moving to the Alternative Health Centre. I'd have to cover
overheads, and on top of that, I'd have to start paying tax. I'd need
to put my price up to fifteen at the very least, and I wasn't at all
sure my ladies'd pay fifteen. All in all, I was beginning to think it
might all be a terrible mistake, but I'd promised Derek, so I'd have
to do it.

At the same time, I dreaded the thought of the family all crowing
over me if it went wrong, and I really began to wonder if Jean
had the rights of it. I'd hardly make anything just seeing people
one by one. Where I'd really get somewhere'd be with a proper
angel business. I really liked the notion, anyway. It'd be one in the
eye for Michelle if I made something of it; I mean, she's lorded it
over me all our adult lives because she went to college, but basically, she's just a glorified typist. She hasn't had an idea of her own

in all her born days. There was Derek to think of as well. He was so sure it was all a load of rubbish, but he'd be laughing on the other side of his face if I started making real money. He'd have to admit I knew what I was about.

Anyway, it was a Tuesday, just after lunch. The doorbell rang, and when I went to see who it was, I found about six-foot-five of bugger-all in a dog-collar. Well, I know who's sent you, Sunny Jim, I thought.

'Mrs Bootham?' he said, peering down at me. 'Is this a good moment?' He was one of those tall men who tips his head back and seems to be looking at you with his teeth. Big yellow teeth like tombstones.

I looked at my watch. 'I've got a client coming in at three. You'll have to be out of here by quarter to.'

'Right. Fine. Can I come in?'

'Please yourself,' I said.

We went through to the lounge and sat down. I didn't offer him anything.

'Mrs Bootham. My name's Bob Young. I'm a friend of your sister Michelle.' No surprises there. 'She's very worried about you.'

'She's no call to be.'

'Mrs Bootham, we've all got a call to look after one another. Don't reject her concern.'

'Oh, it's not concern, Reverend. She just wants me to do everything the way she's laid down for me. She's always been like that.'

'Families can be difficult, Mrs Bootham. All the same, she's maybe got cause to worry. What's all this about angels?'

'I communicate with angels, Reverend. I'm not ashamed of it, and I'm not the first one, either. There's plenty of angels in the Bible, so that's proof if you like. Angels can come down and talk to us if they've a mind to. They talked to Joseph and the shepherds and the Wise Men.'

He flapped his hand, sort of brushing me away. 'But you're not setting yourself up to be Joseph, Mrs Bootham. Joseph was obedient to God's commandments. You aren't a churchgoer, is that right?'

'No. I don't hold with it.'

133

'I don't understand how you can believe in angels when you don't believe in God.'

'Of course I believe in God. I just don't see what He's got to do with anything.'

'But you're worshipping created beings, Mrs Bootham. You're breaking the First Commandment.'

'I'm not worshipping them. I'm communicating with them.'

He looked across at my angel altar. 'Praying to them.'

'Well, sort of. But that's not the way I look at it.'

'It's the way God looks at it.'

'And how do you know? Has He spoken to you lately? You're just going on what you've been told.'

'What we've all been told. We need to look to the Bible for our salvation. Come on, Mrs Bootham, you were properly brought up. I know that from your sister.'

'Well, I think heaven is within you. That's in the Bible too. Seek and ye shall find. I've been a seeker, and I've found everything I was looking for. Of course you don't like it. It'd put your sort out of business if people went around doing things for themselves.'

'Mrs Bootham, you can do yourself a lot of harm messing with this stuff. Don't forget Galatians 1:8 – "But even if we, or an angel from heaven, preach any other gospel to you than what we have preached to you, let him be accursed." And Colossians – "If an angel appears and demands that you worship him then it is not from God." '

'Oh, aye? And who are you to go finding fault? In the olden days, people like you burned people like me for witches. That's what religion does for you. People like me have never hurt a living soul.'

'That's just what you will hurt, if you don't watch out.' He was getting quite steamed up, I could see him starting to go red; he knew he hadn't a leg to stand on. 'Trust in the love of God, and open your heart to Him before it's too late.' It was hard to keep a straight face. I was thinking of him reporting back to Michelle, telling her I'd beaten him hollow.

'There's no call to be rude,' I said. 'Listen to me, Reverend. Religion's all about sitting in judgement, and you can get enough of that round here without going to church. The whole point about angels is that they've got to love you whatever you do. I mean, love's sort of what they are. They're pure energy and light, so of course they're pure love, it all goes together.'

'But I don't think these angels of yours are encouraging you to grow in humility and love, Mrs Bootham. From what I can see, they're stirring up your pride and desire for success. You need to be asking yourself about that. Don't forget, there's two sorts of angels. Some of them fell.'

'I'm not listening to this rubbish. I know they're good, for heaven's sake. You can tell by the energy. There's not a scrap of anything negative anywhere about them. And I'll tell you this for free: anyone who preaches hellfire and damnation is energising the darkness so whatever they think, it's the darkness they're working for.'

'Mrs Bootham, I don't think there's a lot of point prolonging this. But think over what I've said to you.'

'I'm sure you mean well,' I conceded, 'but you're stuck in your little groove. Life isn't all isn'ts and oughts. We aren't all the same. I reckon each of us is naturally attracted to a belief system that'll help us get the most out of our lives. It's our job to listen out for the messages.'

'I'll say goodbye now,' he said. 'But if you're ever prompted to open a Bible, do it. It's never too late.'

He went away after that, and good riddance. He could tell that skinny cow he hadn't got much change out of me. What call had he got to tell me what to think? What does a toffee-nosed so-and-so like him know about what it's like to be me? The angels don't judge. They don't upset you. They surround you with strengthening love. No wonder hardly anyone goes to church now.

The other thing that happened at the end of the summer was my visit to the Hallamshire. It always seems to take forever to fix these things up, but at last I got the letter telling me to come in for a CAT scan. After I'd had it, I had to go and have an appointment with the consultant. She turned out to be a little Indian lady called Dr Gupta, very smart. She'd a white coat on, of course, the way they all do in hospitals, but her face and hair were done up to the nines as if she was going to a wedding, and she was wearing the most gorgeous diamond earrings. Her office was very homey, with pot-plants and framed photographs, and I was thinking, if those were her own kids in the photos she must be a good bit older than she looked – I'd spotted one of those graduating photos with a lass in a mortar board.

She looked up when I came in and smiled at me, very polite. She had dark red lipstick on. 'Hello, Mrs Bootham. D'you mind if I call you Wenda?'

'Please yourself, Doctor. It's all one to me.'

She asked me a whole lot of questions: if I was worried about anything, if I slept all right, if I had trouble with my bowels, how I was getting on with the change of life; all the usual stuff doctors ask a person. She took a lot longer over it than Doctor Bathgate, but I kept telling her no, I had nothing to complain of. She made notes with a gold pen.

'How about your vision generally?' she asked. 'Have you had an eye test recently?'

I was ready for that one. 'I had new glasses this spring. I was getting a bit of eye strain, so they've given me special ones for reading.'

'But you don't get spots, or floating patterns, or episodes where your vision blanks out? Have you ever had a migraine?'

'No, I know what you mean, Doctor. My friend gets migraines, and she's told me what it's like. I'm sure I've never had it myself. Of course I get a headache once in a while, but they're nothing like Jean's – I mean, she's sometimes actually sick with them, and she can't bear the light. I've hardly ever had a headache I couldn't get over with a couple of aspirins, and I've never had the eye trouble.'

She drew a little flower on her jotter. 'So, Wenda, what is it you actually see?'

'Well, sort of people.' I felt a bit shy about telling her.

'Can you remember if they're pretty much the same each time? Or similar, anyway?'

'Yes, I'd say they were.' It felt funny talking about Ariel and

Itheriel like that, but I knew she wouldn't understand, I could see she'd an idea of her own and there'd be no shifting it. I don't know if you get angels in India.

'Do they look quite solid?'

'Yes. They look real, and I'm definitely sure they aren't a figment of my imagination. They're from outside, somehow.'

She looked me in the eye. 'Wenda, I think you may have Charles Bonnet Syndrome, which is very good news, because it's absolutely nothing to worry about. You're certainly not going mad, and we know from the CAT scan you haven't a growth on the brain or anything like that.'

'What's Charles Bonnet when it's at home?' I asked.

'It's a type of hallucination which affects people who've got all their wits about them. It's simply caused by a little disturbance in the activity of the brain, and it really isn't anything to fret about – up to twelve per cent of people have some kind of CBS experience before they're through. It sometimes comes on when people are getting a little older, especially if they've had a bit of trouble with their sight – you've had these visions for about a year now, haven't you, and there hasn't been anything like that in the past?'

'That's right,' I told her.

'That's fairly typical. So's the fact that it's people you're seeing. The commonest types of CBS hallucinations are people or faces, which we think is probably to do with the way the brain's wired up. The thing is, facial recognition is deeply imprinted in the neural pathways – I mean, their mother's face is the first thing anyone learns to recognise, isn't it? Then the next thing after that's other faces, and then people more generally. It makes sense if you think about what babies need out of life.'

'So that's why toddlers always do faces when they start drawing?'

'That's right. Basically, what your experience suggests is that you're getting a tiny bit of disturbance in the ventral temporal lobe. That's the bit of your brain which controls visual recognition. But it doesn't mean there's anything seriously wrong with you. We'd only be able to see anything at all if you were wired up to an EEG while you were actually having an episode, and there's no reason why we should waste your time. You needn't be afraid you're going to have a stroke, or anything like that. It's totally harmless. Are they nice people, by the way, or do you find them threatening?'

'I don't mind them,' I said. 'Actually, they're quite nice.' Sorry, I whispered inside my head. I love you.

'Well, that's fine, then. Enjoy it if you can, and if you can't, don't let it worry you.'

As she was speaking, Itheriel turned up, just behind her chair. He was smiling. I could see he forgave me, and he thought it was a great joke. That's all very well and good, madam, I thought to myself. But Itheriel and Ariel are as real as you or I. 'I'm glad to know there's nothing wrong,' I said.

'You're fine, Wenda. Your long-term fitness'd benefit if you lost a pound or two, as I'm sure your own doctor's told you, but basically, you're a perfectly healthy woman. Nice to've met you.'

'Well then, what did he say?' Derek demanded when he got home. I didn't care for his tone.

'For goodness' sake, Derek. She said I was perfectly normal. I've just got a brain that's very sensitive to impressions, that's all.'

'Soft in the bloody head, you mean.' We were going through another bad patch.

'I'm not talking to you if you're going to be like that.'

VII

All the while this was going on, I was still working in the chemist's half time. It didn't pay much, but although the energy work really interested me, there was no security in it at all, and the Alternative Health wasn't doing that well. I was seeing problems wherever I turned; I wanted more time for my own stuff, but the job with Mr Bhatia was the only money I had coming in I could actually depend on. I could see that if we got serious about Walking With Angels, someone'd have to work on it full time to get it all off the ground. It couldn't be Jean, until there was enough profit to give her the equivalent of a salary, so it'd have to be me. I wished I'd learned how to drive, I could see it'd be useful, but it was a bit late for that. Every time I went to work, I thought about it all over again, sitting on the bus, but I never got any further forwards.

Anyway, this particular day, there was a kerfuffle by the door, and I saw old Mrs Renshaw creeping in with her walking frame. Poor little soul, she's one of our regulars, and it's more a question of what isn't wrong with her than what is. She's got feet and legs like an elephant, she's so bowed over she's bent practically in half, and her poor hands are all twisted. She went to Mr Bhatia first and got her prescriptions; Lord knows what she's taking, but there was any amount of it, it took him ages. She can't carry anything with those hands, so she has to hang everything off the handles of her Zimmer. She wanted to get it all crammed into her handbag, so she got him to take it out of the paper bag he'd put it in so there'd be room. She ought to have one of those motorised buggies really, but she says she's afraid she couldn't steer it. I'll say this for Mr Bhatia, he can be a bit crisp, but he's very patient with her. Once she'd got everything stowed to her liking, she came toiling over to us.

'Hello, pet,' said Jean. 'Are you all right?'

'I'm not very good today, and that's a fact. Fit for the knacker's.'

'Never say die, Mrs Renshaw,' said Jean, jollying her along.

'If someone knocked me on the head, I wouldn't be sorry. I'd just as soon go. I'm sick of it all. My insides are bad again. I was up all night.'

'So is it the Milk of Magnesia you're after, or some Bisodol?'

'I want something for the belching. I can't sleep for it.'

'I'd try the Milk of Magnesia then, pet.' Jean fetched it down for her, and then she said, 'There's something else I want.'

'What is it, love?'

It's hard to see her little face, she's so bent she's practically got her nose on the counter, but you could tell she was bothered.

'I can't bring it to mind. And I don't want to have to come out again, my legs are giving me gyp.'

We suggested a few things, embrocation, aspirin, the usual, but nothing rang a bell, and she was starting to get upset. As we knew from past experience, it doesn't take much to make her cry.

'Might you have written it down, Mrs Renshaw?' Jean asked.

'I might've,' she said doubtfully. 'I'm getting so forgetful, it worries me a lot.' She fumbled her handbag off the bar of the Zimmer and put it on the counter on top of all the cold-cures and throat-sweets and stuff; she was sort of pawing at it, trying to get the clasp open – she's got no grip at all. The bag was a terrible old thing, flaking red plastic, with the gilt coming off all the trimmings. She's as poor as Job, of course. God help women on their own.

'Shall I take a look for you, pet?' said Jean.

'I wouldn't mind,' she admitted. So Jean opened her bag for her, and we had a look inside. There was her purse and all the prescription stuff of course, which had to come out because it was on top of everything else, and a paper bag of mint imperials and some bits and bobs – and a shopping list on the back of an envelope. You can hardly read her writing, but we just about made out, 'pills, burp mix, foot powder, corn plasters.'

'That's it, love,' she said. 'It's my feet.'

Jean went to get her stuff from the podiatric display, while I was getting some Nurofen and Vaseline for a lady in a hurry with three kids and a buggy, and of course the poor old besom and her Zimmer were in everybody's road, with all of us reaching over her little head.

Jean got her sorted out in the end, and got the money out of her purse for her, and rang it all up while Mrs Renshaw got everything stuffed back into her bag higgledy-piggledy. I was serving other customers all that time, so we were all sort of going round each other, and she was embarrassed.

Suddenly, just as she'd got herself away at last, I saw Ariel just out of the corner of my eye. He was standing by the counter and I couldn't think what he was doing there. He was looking very grave, as if there was something important he wanted me to notice.

Mrs Renshaw was struggling out of the door. Jean was showing someone where we keep the contact lenses stuff, Mr Bhatia was looking at the computer, and just at that minute, there was no one standing waiting to be served. And I saw that she'd left a white pack of prescription pills on top of the Strepsils. It was just instinctive. I slipped it into my overall pocket. It seemed like I was meant to have it. Mrs Renshaw'd never know where she'd lost it, or even if she'd lost it at all. A bit later, I took an opportunity to slip it into my handbag, and after that, I forgot all about it. It was a busy afternoon.

I was very thoughtful on the bus home. It was seeing Mrs Renshaw brought it on. I'd never seen inside her home, but I could guess. One and a half rooms somewhere, smelling of mildew and old clothes, with everything grey and peeling and a one-bar electric heater. You could tell that just by looking at her. God knows what she lived on. Stale bread, probably. Most of her pension must've gone on chemist's stuff. If Derek and I split up, what'd happen to me? I'd always worked, but not full time, I hadn't built up a lot of contributions. I'd get a share of the assets, but I doubted very much I'd get maintenance, with no kids involved. So assuming I got half the value of the house, I'd be able to buy – what? Some horrible flat, at best. The sort of place Jean lives in, with kids everywhere, and noise on all sides and all sorts and colours for your neighbours, with lifts that don't work and dirty, stinking stairs covered in graffiti. But even if I got somewhere to live sorted out, I'd be sort of all right as long as I was working, but what about when I stopped and I didn't have anything coming in? It was a thought to make you feel sick.

I got off the bus, and walked up Cartmell Road to Periwood Close. The sound of the main road faded out behind me as I walked. The street's very quiet, and the close is a cul-de-sac; apart from the odd learner driver practising three-point turns, it's so peaceful most of the time you'd honestly think you were in the country. It's a very good area. The house was illuminated in the last of the sun; we're west-facing. We've lived there nigh on ten years, since Derek was promoted to area superintendent, and we've got it exactly the way we want it. The house glowed at me; the nice red brick, the fresh paintwork, the clean picture-window, the good curtains just showing through my nets. I put my key in the lock and went inside. I liked everything about it. I'd washed, and vacuumed, and kept it spanking clean for all those years; it was part of me. The carpet's a deep-pile textured Wilton in a lovely shade of pale green, we'd liked it so much we got them to lay it throughout. It'd cost a fortune in Cole Brothers, but Derek said, you don't often buy a carpet, you may as well have the one you really fancy. He'd been quite right, it'd worn very well, and it still looked immaculate, even on the stairs.

I went into my lounge; it was a really beautiful room, with the crystals in the window catching the setting sun and throwing rainbows up onto the ceiling, and all the flowers, and my good suite, and the little mahogany tables. I used to do needlepoint before I got the angels, and I'd put two of my best creations up, a floral, and a lovely scene with a lighthouse, all properly framed and everything. We'd never been extravagant, but everything was good of its kind, and if it got worn or damaged, we threw it out and bought something better. We changed the wallpaper every two or three years, and the curtains as well. It was the lifestyle I was used to; I had a Zanussi fridge-freezer, and we ate real butter. I'd assumed it'd always be like that, but if I was going it alone, realistically, I'd be struggling to do as well as Jean.

I felt so sad and indignant it all got into my throat and choked me up. It wasn't fair. The angels had brought me so many blessings, I couldn't imagine they meant to see me reduced to poverty. I took my coat off and hung it up, and went over to my altar. I lit the candles, and wrote on a slip of paper, 'Please open Derek's eyes and make him understand.' I put a drop of oil on it to help the communication, melissa, which is a wonderful 'bridging' fragrance, and set it alight. Because of the oil, it caught very quickly, and the piece of paper fluttered up out of the ashtray as it consumed away. It was just a wisp of grey stuff really, but funnily enough, I could still see the writing. I caught it before it got onto anything, and it turned into a smear of ash in my hand. The way it had been drawn up seemed like a good omen.

I was beginning to calm down, and remember some of the things I'd read. Fear's not always a bad thing. When you feel afraid of anything, it's a good time to stop and look around, and listen to your higher self. The angels will bring you what you want, if you let them. I wondered if I was just being too impatient. It's part of their role to guide you in the things of this world, and after all, I was doing their work. It had all been going on for less than a year. It was only natural to want to do everything all at once, but perhaps it was wrong. 'Don't let me be poor,' I wrote on another bit of paper, and sent it after the first. They're spiritual beings, they don't know what it's like being a mortal. I wondered if perhaps they were overlooking that aspect of things. It wouldn't hurt to remind them.

By the time Derek came in, I'd sorted my ideas out a bit, and made the tea.

'There's a fish pie,' I said, but he only grunted. Honestly, I thought to myself, here's me trying to meet him halfway and what do I get? He was a bit more civil later on, when we were eating.

'That bloody car's started making a knocking noise every time I turn right,' he told me. 'I'm not going to have time to get it seen to this week.'

'It's not anything serious, is it?'

'It's just the bearings. I can live with it, but it's distracting. I'm beginning to think I ought to get something newer. We've had it three years, and the amount of driving I do, I need a car I can rely on.'

'What d'you want this time?'

'Nothing fancy. I'd just as soon have another Astra. It's not been a bad motor. Or a Mégane, maybe. It's a question of what comes up at the right price, I'm not thinking of buying new.'

It seemed reasonable enough to me. We'd had the outside painting done in the spring, but we hadn't had a big expense since then. There was no reason he shouldn't, that I knew of.

But all that set me thinking. We had quite a bit of savings, but how much, I didn't know. We've never been the sort of folk who spend every penny that comes in; at the end of the month, what's left in the current account goes into savings. Obviously, I knew what went into the current account, but it's Derek who balances the books. And he gets bonuses and things, and they just get put away. If I want something big, new curtains or anything like that, I ask him. That's the way it's always been, and I've never objected, because he's never refused me. I know there's a building society account with a couple of thousand in for real emergencies, and a seven-day account for big purchases, and more in some kind of funds where you can't get it out, that's all set to mature when he retires, I think.

All that money. If I could only get him to see the point of Walking With Angels, I'd be able to get it off the ground in a year. It was utterly galling, like being on the wrong side of a pane of glass. I hadn't much of my own. I'd always thought of my little job as pin money, and put it straight into the current account. I bought things for the house, my clothes, and had my hair done, and it paid for all that. It was only recently I'd opened a savings account of my own – I'd a bit coming in from Internet clients, which I needed to offset the shortfall with Alternative Health. But all in all, I was messing about with a few hundreds, and I knew we had thousands.

'I could help with the car, maybe,' I said.

'Eh?'

'You've been deceived in the past. Remember that blue Vauxhall we had. It was never out of the garage.'

He poured out the rest of his beer, and said nothing.

'When you get to the point where there's one particular car you fancy, I could ask the angels about it.'

'For crying out loud, Wenda, I'm sick to death of bloody angels!'

'There's no need to shout! I'm trying to help!'

'Well, you're not. Look, Wenda. Just stay out of what doesn't concern you. I'm not having you meddling.'

I could have cried. He pushed his plate away and went through to the lounge to put the telly on. I did the dishes, and got my computer and the angel cards out. There were a couple of people wanting readings; that'd take me through to bedtime.

I just couldn't understand his attitude. It wasn't as if Walking With Angels was just a pipe-dream. I'd asked around friends of friends and found a designer, just a young lass, but she was very clever. She'd charged thirty pounds for doing a sample card, back and front. I'd asked her to do Michael, because I was coming to feel a special affinity; I thought if I had a connection with one particular archangel, it'd be Raphael because of my healing work, but it had turned out not to be, and I was pretty sure by then that Ariel and Itheriel belonged to Michael's Host. The back was a wonderful Celtic knot pattern, you wouldn't think anyone could have the patience, all in red and gold. Michael was in blue. I'd told Carron that blue was his colour, and she'd got him absolutely bang-on; he was perfect, with his beautiful sword and his lovely stern face. It was truly inspired work, and I was ever so pleased with her. It meant we had something to show in the meantime, and as and when we could afford it, I'd just give her the word and she'd do the rest. The angel oils I could make up myself; Carron quoted me a price for doing fancy labels, and I knew where I could get little bottles wholesale; we have them as a line in the chemist's, people buy them to put a bit of shampoo in if they're going away for a weekend. I could do all that out of the back spare bedroom, to start with.

The big expense would be the angel jewellery. Carron had a friend who was a jeweller, and she made some proper working drawings from my sketches, two versions, a brooch and a pendant, and helped us cost them, I wanted to do them in white metal, silver, and gold plate. We thought they shouldn't get too expensive, but even at that, there'd be a lot of outlay; I'd copyrighted the designs, and I knew where I could get the moulds made, and the jeweller had pointed us towards someone who'd manufacture the things. I'd got quotes for an initial order of a thousand of each, and it all added up to a heck of a lot of money up front.

Jean was putting a lot into Walking With Angels as well. She came round one Wednesday with a business plan she'd worked out. I was dead impressed. There were spreadsheets and all; she showed me how they worked. She'd thought of everything, as far as I could see; what we knew about the market and the competition, the start-up costs, which I'd been worrying about, and the marketing and advertising, which I hadn't got around to at all. I could see it might all work, but I'd have to borrow, and I was ninety per cent certain they'd want the house as collateral. I could just hear Derek saying, 'Over my dead body.'

We sat side by side at the kitchen table, and looked at cashflow forecasts for the first two years, budgeted sales, overheads and profits, with different projections depending on what we were charging.

'It's like magic. Honestly, Jean, I never knew you knew about any of this stuff.'

She looked pleased. 'It's not difficult once you get your head round it.'

'We're going to need a lot of money to get started. There's going to have to be a lot of knocking on doors, persuading people to give us a try.'

Jean said nothing, but I knew her; she was thinking, you're sitting pretty. The money's here. The thing was, she was right.

'I can't do anything without Derek,' I said, once I was sure she wasn't going to speak.

'It's all in his name? That's what Norman did to me.'

'Well, he's not like Norman.' It sounded a bit weak, even to me. 'He's not an imaginative person. He doesn't like taking risks.'

'Who does? But honestly, Wenda. You've really got something going here. I absolutely believe in it. It's better than anything Norman and me ever came up with, and we made good money, you know.' She fished around in her bag. 'I wanted to show you this,' she said, quite shyly. 'I wrote it last night. I wondered if you might put it on the website.'

I took her bit of paper; it turned out to be a poem.

> They stand there at the door
> Of happiness and light,
> And watch the stars flicker,
> As souls descend to night.

> A light descended earthward,
> Come down from heaven's hall.
> It was an angel coming,
> To answer to a call.

Spread over all the earth
Are souls who'll understand;
Who'll welcome them into their hearts,
And want to lend a hand.

While angels walk beside you
In love, it's always true:
You'll always find it's easy
To care in everything you do.

'Jean, that's beautiful,' I said. 'I never knew you were a poet.'

She tried to pretend it wasn't much, but I could see she was happy. 'You never know till you try. It just came to me. Maybe it's the angels at work.'

I was sure she was right. The whole thing was opening up her creative side, and she was blossoming. I'd never seen her looking better, or more cheerful, and now all of a sudden, she was writing poetry. It made me sure I was doing the right thing. There was so much good Chi and harmony and creativity around us, it just had to be right.

VIII

'I'm afraid there's not a lot you can do without involving your husband, Mrs Bootham. With a loan this size, we'd need security, and that means the house. You'd need to be joint signatories.'

He was quite a young chap, a spotty Herbert in a brown corduroy suit, not my idea of a bank manager at all. I suppose it wasn't a very big branch.

'Couldn't you ask someone else?' I said. 'I wanted it to be a surprise.'

'I'm afraid that's company policy, Mrs Bootham. You might be able to find an unsecured loan, but it'd be very expensive. I really wouldn't advise it.'

'Is there anything else you can think of?'

He looked at me. 'No. Not really. It's quite a good proposal, and with a bit of work, you might make something of it, but it's not sure-fire. The bottom line is, one in ten new businesses fails, so we've got to be careful. And with someone like yourself, it's difficult.'

'Why with someone like me?'

He looked a bit shifty. 'Well . . . I mean, you don't really need the money, so you might change your mind when you find out how much work this is all going to take. Or hubby might put his foot down when he finds you're away all the time.'

'I'm never, ever going to change my mind.'

'Listen, Mrs Bootham. Try and talk him round. It's the best way, believe me. You might get him interested.'

I might as well've been talking to a potted plant, I realised. A proper waste of a morning. He'd taken one look at me, and thought, it's just some silly old mare with a hobby. I wished I'd had Jean there, she's got a tongue on her. I was brought up too polite, that's my trouble.

'If that's your last word . . .'

'I'm afraid so, Mrs Bootham. Go on. Chat up the old man. It might all work out.'

I wasn't surprised, I was just downcast. I went home, and I decided I'd better try and see what the angels thought about it all. I reckoned I'd get the clearest answer from the cards, so I lit the candles, put on some oil, and got myself into the right frame of mind.

I shuffled the cards, and chose three: I was making a 'focus' layout, which is how I ask Ariel and Itheriel where I've got to and what I ought to do about it. I turned them over, and somehow I wasn't surprised to find that they were all blue: Barchiel – Purification, Azrael – Release, Aniel – Spiritual Growth. Well, that seemed plain enough. And they all came under Michael: when I was asking the cards something about myself, it usually was Michael, and I started to think what that was telling me. Michael's the Angel with the Sword who you invoke when you need to cut etheric cords which are binding you and draining your energy. So the whole thing was obvious: the angels were saying, purify your life. Release yourself from dead relationships, and it'll lead to a surge in spiritual growth. Well, that was clear. I knew exactly who was holding me back.

All very well, but I couldn't think where to go from there; there wasn't any guidance. But I was supposed to start with purifying, so I decided to have a bit of a tidy. It's very good for your Chi; the Feng Shui people are always on at you to throw stuff away, they reckon clutter breeds 'poison arrows'. I always try and keep the place nice, but odds and ends mount up all the same. I got a black bin-bag, and started going round with it throwing things away. There were some clothes which didn't fit me any more and books we'd finished with, those could go to Oxfam, and there was all kinds of actual rubbish, ends of bottles of shampoo and hand-cream and stuff, a silk flower arrangement Michelle gave me that just gathered dust. I'd take it all out with me when I went to Alternative Health, and put the rubbish in the wheelie-bin.

Last thing before I went out, I emptied my handbag onto the kitchen table. It always gets cluttered up with till-receipts and sweetie papers, all that might as well go too. But when I turned it out, I found Mrs Renshaw's pills. Now, that made me feel really peculiar. On the one hand, there was me saying I wasn't getting any guidance, but maybe I'd already had it? I remembered very clearly I'd seen Ariel and I'd definitely been prompted.

Ooops. I was going to be late. The Oxfam stuff'd have to wait. But as I ran down to the bus stop, I did find myself sort of thinking. If I didn't have Derek, I'd have the house and the money. And he carried quite a lot of insurance, I knew that: he once told me I was well provided for if anything happened. But the angels couldn't mean that, surely.

I turned it all round and round in my head. The thing with angels is, they can't possibly think just the way we do. They're on a different energy level: I mean, to them, this mortal body's just a veil. They don't really understand about mortal stuff unless you tell them; I'm not sure they think bodies really matter. If you know for a fact there's another life, everything looks a bit different.

Once I got to the Alternative Health, I was into the thick of it

all, I had no time to myself till five, which was maybe a good
thing. Sometimes you think better when you're not thinking, I've
often noticed that. The notion which came to me on the bus home
was, maybe Derek wasn't meant to understand in this life. He's a
Scorpio, so he's as stubborn as anything, and in Feng Shui terms,
he's Metal: that means he's organised and methodical and logical,
but on the down side, he's inflexible and he can't imagine alternatives – metal people aren't really creative. So Derek was in that
groove from the outset. I shouldn't expect him to be different all
of a sudden, he wasn't made that way.

If I understood rightly, and it did all seem to fit together, we
each progress in our own way till we turn into Ascended Masters.
It all happens for a reason, but the way it works is, there are lifetimes when you progress and develop really quickly – obviously,
I was having one of those – and lifetimes where you don't, and
that was Derek. My spirit was like a beautiful winged horse, struggling to fly with a ball and chain on its hoof. Maybe another time,
Derek'd make more progress. Perhaps that's how the angels saw
it. Just a matter of shifting from one state to another so that I
could spread my wings and fly.

When I got back home, I locked myself in the toilet and looked
at the leaflet which was in with Mrs Renshaw's pills. They were
something to do with her arthritis, and they were obviously strong.
The instructions were very definite that you weren't to exceed the
permitted dose; there were various things you had to watch out
for, headache, double vision, dizzy spells. If you got anything of
the kind you were to stop taking them and consult your doctor.
They weren't to be taken with alcohol, and you weren't to drive
or operate machinery within 24 hours. All that was no problem
for the poor old soul, of course, she couldn't afford to drink, and
she never did anything, but they obviously weren't meant for
anyone who was out and about in the normal way.

So the question was, what was I going to do? I put the pills in
the drawer of the back spare room bedside table – I knew I'd have
to get on with making Derek's tea in a minute. But as I was about
to go downstairs, I stopped; for some reason, the Reverend's words
had just came back into my mind. 'If you're prompted to open a

Bible, just do it. It's never too late.' My Bible's on the shelf in the spare room. It's the one I've had since I was a kiddie, black, with gold on the edges, my Nanna gave me it. I sat down on the bed with it in my hands, shut my eyes, and cleared my mind, just let it all go. Then I opened the book about halfway, and looked to see what my eye fell on.

I was in the middle of Psalms, and this is what I found: 'For He shall give his angels charge over thee, to keep thee in all thy ways. They shall bear thee up in their hands, lest thou dash thy foot against a stone.' It was the exact same verse I'd tried to call to mind when I'd been arguing with Derek in the summer. There was all sorts on that page I couldn't help noticing. 'He shall cover thee with his feathers, and under his wings shalt thou trust' and 'O Lord, how great are thy works! and thy thoughts are very deep. A brutish man knoweth not; neither does a fool understand this . . . the righteous shall flourish like the palm tree.' It all seemed to fit. What I reckoned was, I'd have to put the whole thing in the hands of Ariel and Itheriel. I seemed to be being told that if I'd got it all wrong, they'd look after him. 'He shall call upon me, and I will answer him.' But on the face of it, it seemed pretty clear that in this life, he was one of the foolish men who can't see what's straight in front of them, like the psalms said. It wasn't his fault, but perhaps he'd done his bit. He'd looked after his old mother, nobody could've asked for a better son, and he'd put me in a position where I could do the angels' work on earth. He'd done well, and perhaps, in another life he'd have a chance to grow and develop. I took the pills out again, and put them in my pocket.

I thought we'd have a chicken curry. We don't eat a lot of spicy food, but it's all right once in a while. He's not fond of rice, but you can have it with oven chips. Curry's handy, because it does quite slowly, and it'll stand a bit of waiting about; I could make it, and then just hot it up again while the chips were cooking, after he'd come in.

'I don't think much of this,' said Derek, after a mouthful or two. 'Are you trying something new?'

'There's a new spicy range at the Co-op, it comes in sachets. This one's supposed to be Goanese.'

'Where's Goa, then, when it's at home?'

'How the heck should I know?'

'It's not very nice. I reckon you should stick with kormas and tandoori,' he said. 'You don't seem to think much of it either. You're not eating.'

'I'm not hungry. I had a sandwich when I came in, because I was absolutely dropping, and it's ruined my appetite. If you don't fancy the curry, don't have it. I'll do you an egg or something.'

'It's not that bad. I just don't think I want it again. There's a funny aftertaste. Are you sure it was inside its sell-by date?'

'Oh, for heaven's sake, Derek! I'll get the sachet out of the bin if you like, and you can have a look at it.'

I was beginning to feel really peculiar, watching him forking it all down. Derek eating's never an attractive sight. He's still got hamster cheeks, after all these years, and he tends to put too much in his mouth at once and then work away at it, nibble, nibble. It's always annoyed me the way he chews at his food. But I'll say this for him, he's never been fussy. His mother taught him to eat up what was put in front of him; he complains a bit if he doesn't like it, but he gets it down him.

He got his plate cleared at last, and belched.

'Pardon me. It's the spices.'

'Do you want anything else?'

He considered. 'If you've got a yogurt or something in the fridge, I wouldn't mind. It was a bit heating. And I wouldn't mind another beer.'

I got up and took the trays through to the kitchen. 'There's a strawberry and an apricot,' I called.

'I'll have the apricot, thanks.'

I brought it through, on a little plate with a spoon beside it, and gave him a can of lager.

'Ta, Wenda.'

He settled down to watch the telly. I didn't know what to do with myself. I was looking at the screen, but it could've been *The Magic Roundabout* for all I knew. I was wishing I hadn't done anything, but what could I do? He'd eaten it. I'd just have to trust it'd all work out for the best.

I couldn't bear it; I went upstairs and started sorting out the laundry. There was a pile of nice clean shirts waiting to be done; I took them through to the back spare room which is where I do my ironing, it keeps it out of the way. I'll get on with them tomorrow, I thought to myself, when I come in from work.

Then it just hit me all of a sudden, it was like an actual knock in the chest. By tomorrow evening, there mightn't be anyone to wear them. I nearly fainted, I had to sit down suddenly on the bed. Derek. My husband. I'd washed and wiped-up and cooked for him for twenty-one years. I just couldn't imagine what it'd be like being a widow. I slipped down onto my actual knees beside the bed, and prayed: 'Ariel. Itheriel. Don't let anything happen to him. Please don't. There must be another way.'

I went back downstairs after a bit, once I was calmer.

'Have we got any paracetamol, pet?' he asked. 'I'm not feeling quite right.'

'Maybe it was the curry,' I said. 'You're not feeling sick, are you? Maybe you should get it all off your stomach.'

'No, it's staying down. But I don't want it again.'

I got him a couple of paracetamols, and a glass of water.

'I think I'll have an early night,' he said. 'I'll feel better in the morning.'

I heard him moving about upstairs, the toilet flushing and so on. I did all the washing-up, and put everything away, and did the top of the stove really thoroughly, and washed out the grill pan, and emptied the crumbs out of the toaster, and wiped down all the cupboard doors, and set the table for breakfast. I couldn't bear the thought of talking to him. I wanted to be sure he was asleep by the time I came upstairs.

He was, or at any rate, he'd put his light out. I wasn't sure he was actually asleep because he wasn't snoring. I didn't think I'd get a wink myself. I was listening to his breathing, feeling so awful you can't imagine, but in the end, I did get off.

He was looking quite poorly in the morning; his eyes were a bit funny.

'Take the day off, Derek,' I urged, when he came downstairs. 'You're not looking well.'

'I can't do that, pet. I've got a lot on. I'll try and get home early. Have we any more paracetamol?'

I gave him two, and he asked for the packet, and put it in his pocket.

'Don't you want your breakfast?' I asked.

He shook his head. 'I'll get something later, once my head's settled.'

'Derek, I really think you ought to stop at home!'

'Wenda, don't fuss.' He walked past me, and got his coat down, and went out to the car, leaving me standing.

I rang the Alternative Health, and told them I had flu. I was like a cat on hot bricks; all I wanted was to see him safe home. When I went into the lounge, I saw Itheriel; he was smiling, and I thought, all right for you, you're a spirit. The way he looked so beautiful and serene absolutely turned my stomach, I had to go and be sick.

Once I was out of the toilet, I went and lay down. I was praying, let him be all right, but I didn't know who I was praying to. I had nothing to hold on to any more. I was following the Astra in my mind's eye. Out of the close, up to the Chesterfield Road, then he'd be going along London Road and Bramall Lane, the traffic thickening at every junction, everyone pouring into the city to go to their work. He was on a job at Owlerton, so I knew he'd be going right through the middle of town, which is diabolical first thing. That horrible roundabout at St Mary's Gate, four lanes, hundreds of cars coming at you from all sides. Then there was Hanover Way, God help him. Just one little misjudgement, and anything could happen, just in a second. I was crying as I lay there. Maybe the angels thought it was all worth it, but I didn't. I stared at the ceiling, feeling the thud and the crunch in my bones, the car spinning across the road and all the glass crumbling and scattering like hailstones, and I was so lonely I wanted to die.

I'd been lying there for ages when the doorbell rang. I knew it'd be the police. Coming down the stairs, I saw two people through the glass, a man and a woman. I could see those hats they wear, with the black and white checks. They always send a lass if it's bad news.

Garden Guerrillas

I

Lythrum salicaria requires temperatures above 20°C and moist open soils for successful germination, but once established, seedlings grow rapidly (more than half an inch a day) and plants can flower in their first growing season. Established plants can tolerate very diverse growing conditions, including permanent flooding, low water and nutrient levels, and low pH. Plants can grow in almost any soil, and develop a large, branching root-stock weighing up to three pounds which stores starch to safeguard the plant. Mature *Lythrum* can produce more than thirty annual shoots reaching more than six feet. The plants are long lived, and mature specimens can produce more than two and a half million seeds annually, which remain viable in the soil for many years.

I was in the garden when I was tempted, so naturally, the only thing to do was to give way almost immediately. Since events were conspiring to throw me out of paradise anyway, there seemed no very pressing reason not to.

It would've been nice if there had been an apple tree handy, but it wasn't that sort of a garden. In fact, I was standing under, or properly speaking, in, my 'Persian Musk' rose at the time, that is, in an overarching wave of crumpled, grey-green leaves and thorny stems, tying her in to her old and mellow brick wall. Not a rose for everyone, but I'd put her in a very carefully chosen spot, and she grew very nicely for me; by June, she would be a mass of soft, just-pink blossom with an extraordinary tangy, spicy perfume.

What it's hard for people to realise now, even David who was brought up there and ought to know better, is that you didn't exactly need to be a millionaire to buy a house on Kew Green in 1962. Geoff, my late husband, bought it from a very old lady because I'd absolutely fallen in love with it, and it was in the most terrible condition. It was one of my blasted romantic notions, as he reminded me for a goodly number of years. Most of the woodwork was riddled with dry rot, and there was no source of heat or hot water except for an old-fashioned, coal-fired range in the kitchen. I spent half of that first winter grovelling on my knees in front of the damned thing, trying to get it to stay alight, with David crying miserably in his Moses basket; I was terrified he'd get TB, with the cold and the damp, and of course, if anything happened to him, it would be all my fault. Geoff had wanted somewhere newer, smaller and easier to maintain, but I talked him into Kew Green. Always a mistake, really, however much you want something; it leaves you in a position of apology till the last syllable of recorded time.

It was a year or two before we could afford to do much. Sometimes it was all so awful I'd stick David and a book in the pram and go into Kew Gardens and sit in one of the hothouses all afternoon, just for the warmth. It was thruppence in those days, and when we decimalised, it was one new penny, the only thing I ever heard of which went down when we decimalised. One's not supposed to ramble on about the past, I know. When I do it in front of David and Karen, I can see their faces going blank; they switch off, waiting for me to stop. There's a very annoying thing David says sometimes, 'That was then, this is now.' But we spent a lot of time in Kew together when David was a baby. He could recognise and name a dozen different orchids before he went to primary school. The orchid house was lovely and warm.

I will admit that it's now that's the problem. Well, to be strictly accurate, it's me that's the problem, or so it seems. Forty years on, the erstwhile wreck is a beautiful Georgian house on three floors, a bit tatty-Habitatty, I admit, but David and his huge galumphing friends were not kind to it in their teenage years. I can see Karen thinking of skips whenever she visits, marking things off on an invisible checklist. Her beady little eyes tick round the room, missing nothing. Is there real parquet under the fitted carpet? There is, actually, but when he was five or so, David managed to knock over a five-litre tin of dark blue gloss – it was fashionable then, I'm sorry to say – and we decided to cut our losses. He'll have forgotten all about it, doubtless, so it'll be a lovely surprise for them in due course. And the kitchen lino's on her hit-list; you can see it's got to go. It's dark brown, and was considered rather chic in its day, actually.

Whenever we make a cup of tea, I can see wheels turning in her head: I'll rip that awful breakfast bar out, she's thinking, and put in – oh, I don't know. Do people still have central islands from Smallbone of Devizes in their kitchens? They're probably so, so, five years ago by now, but I neither know nor care. Unlike Karen, I do not read *The World of Interiors*. I prefer plant catalogues. Anyway, the point is, the house may be a little shabby, but it is wind- and water-tight, it has been properly maintained, and it is now worth an absolutely obscene amount of money.

I wouldn't like you to think that I didn't love Geoff, or that I'm blaming him in any way. We were married for forty-three years, after all. He was a large, kind man, and rather practical, and we had a good life together. He played cricket on the green in the summer. But the thing is, he thought money was virtually sacred. I don't mean he wouldn't spend it if there was good reason to. As and when we could afford it, we got round the house, updating the kitchen, putting in the heating, renewing the roof; we went on holidays. For our silver wedding anniversary, he bought me a diamond eternity ring, which I never wear, because my hands are dirty so much of the time, and they're so battered-looking even when I'm scrubbed up I don't care to draw attention to them. But by 1990, it was clear that houses on the Green were going for £200,000, or even a quarter of a million, and the new people who were moving in weren't couples with young children, they were investment bankers. The value of the house seemed to me unreal, or even mad; it was totally incommensurate with the life we actually lived there. But the thought of all that money going on death duties simply appalled him.

'You see,' he explained, again and again – Geoff never argued, but he repeated his point of view with great patience until opposition somehow evaporated, which it did, because otherwise you could look forward to having the same conversation for ever – 'Looking to the future, if we both make our wills in favour of a family trust, we get two lots of tax-free allowances. It's a significant advantage. We can't get round the whole problem but that's half a million that won't be paying death duties. It doesn't make any difference, really. The property'll be owned by the trustees, that's you and me and David and perhaps Karen, for our common benefit. It's completely straightforward, because Davie's a sensible chap. It's just that in the end, it's his patrimony.'

'Nobody did it for us,' I said.

'But Alice, darling. It's a different world. How's he going to get a start in life, the way things are?'

So in the end, that is what we did. He came down from university, and lived with us for a while, saving money, though I was glad to have him at home, of course. In 1990, he married his girlfriend of two years, Karen Shattock, and we set up a trust with the four of us as beneficiaries, understood by all of us as a purely formal gesture. Karen worked, naturally, and still does; she's some kind of manager in a cosmetics company called Urban Suicide which sells bruise-coloured gloop to self-pitying teenagers. It's all a lot more sophisticated and packaged than it used to be. Do you remember the way mascara used to come in a cake, with a sort of miniature toothbrush? You weren't supposed to spit on it because it was unhygienic, but we all did, I'm afraid.

The boys, they're twins, came along in '93, and she found them a childminder. I really don't think mothers ought to work, at least not when the children are little, but that was another subject on which I was not encouraged to have an opinion.

'I don't know what you think we can do, Mum,' said David, when I ventured to say something. To him, not to Karen, of course. 'It takes both of us to keep this mortgage going.' They had just moved to somewhere a bit bigger, because of the twins, a rather dreary little terraced house off the South Ealing Road. What I was brought up to think of as a tradesman's house, but it had cost them £135,000.

'Well, you shouldn't have had children,' I said. 'I mean, you could've waited a bit, till you were more on top of things. You're only thirty-one, and she's twenty-eight.'

He looked completely affronted, an expression I remembered from those moments in his babyhood when I had tried to persuade him to eat strained spinach. 'But they're your grandchildren,' he said. One of us was clearly missing the point, and like his father at such moments, he took it as self-evident that it was me.

Geoff said, 'At least the girl wanted children, Alice. We should think ourselves lucky. A lot of them can't be bothered.' He had a soft spot for Karen, generally. 'That young woman's got her head screwed on the right way,' he would say, which is true enough. If she ever asked me to get the children's fishfingers out of the freezer, I couldn't help noticing that everything in there was neatly labelled and dated, using that special marker pen you're supposed to have. My own freezer contains rather more unidentifiable snowballs than it perhaps should, and I have not the faintest idea of how long they have been there. I could see that when they were littlies, she rather disliked the children eating anything I'd prepared, but I will enter in my defence that never in my life has anyone actually been poisoned in my house, and that I did, in fact, successfully rear a child. The young are rather more tolerant of such things than some people believe.

Will and Jamie were the joy of Geoff's life, a cliché, but in this case, true. They gave him a purely masculine kind of pleasure, which I found touching; there was always a certain simplicity in him. As soon as they were born, he became in his own mind a man with a son and two grandsons; and thus one who could see the line of Wrights extending itself confidently towards the future. People have said a great deal about 'patriarchy' in my hearing, but they have seldom mentioned that it is, for certain men, an abiding source of personal satisfaction. Our drawing-room gradually filled up with photographs, the two little round faces endlessly repeating on every available surface.

Everyone took it for granted that I adored them; it is part of the natural order of things that grandmothers dote. I do love them, of course. They were dear little boys, sweet-smelling like healthy puppies, and when I saw them squatting together over their toy cars, the way their soft, feathery, light brown hair just wisped down onto those pathetic, stalk-like necks that young children have completely melted my heart. They have given me considerable pleasure over the years, and sometimes they have even surprised me with a moment of fantasy or a quaint turn of phrase, which of course I then repeat to all my acquaintances in quite the approved manner.

I was even moved to buy a pad of cartridge paper and some Conté crayons when they started toddling about, though I'd hardly touched a stick of charcoal for decades. I made one or two sketches I was really quite pleased with, but of course, Geoff had gone straight out and bought the Pentax as soon as we knew for sure they were on the way, and he was keeping a proper record. He really did adore them, and of course, women are more sentimental, so it followed that I adored them too.

In fact, they did not occupy my every waking thought. David had, when he was a baby; like any young mum, I had tiptoed into his room in the small hours just to see if he was still breathing, but that, as he says these days, was then. It seemed to me that Will and Jamie were Karen's job, and within her own terms, she was doing it very well. The boys began their lives surrounded by bric-à-brac from the Early Learning Centre, they were happy, and she kept them immaculately turned out. There hardly seemed much point in anyone else worrying about them unduly, in the circumstances. In fact, I came to realise that I rather disliked seeing them in the garden once they were toddling; the sight of a determined little fist closing round the stem of a *Paeonium veitchii* just as it was coming into flower and ripping the head off did not immediately cause me, unlike the rest of the adults present, to go into raptures at how their co-ordination was coming along.

'That's not poisonous, is it?' Karen asked, as Will bumped down onto his bottom and began industriously picking the flower apart.

'I've never grown poisonous things,' I said. 'I thought about that when David was at the toddling stage, and I've kept on keeping them out out of sheer force of habit.' Not growing euphorbias and hellebores had been a source of regret once, but I had learned to manage without them. There was a distant yell from behind the treillage. 'There are plants with thorns, of course,' I added to her retreating back, as she dashed to Jamie's rescue, 'but I believe you call that sort of thing a valuable learning experience.'

Geoff was an insurance broker, and when David was a baby, he was working all the hours God sent, building up his business. That meant I spent a lot of time on my own with David, and there wasn't any spare money to go and do anything with. So, in a way, it was sitting in Kew Gardens which gave me the initial impetus to start on our own patch, but it was also sheer lack of alternatives. There was a dear old duck a couple of doors down from us called Mrs Tolland who was a great gardener: we got talking because of the baby, and when I started getting interested in what she was doing, she took cuttings for me and lent me some tools till I could afford to buy my own. That's one of the lovely things about gardening. People are very generous, and you can do an awful lot with not very much. And anyway, living where we did, one sort of had to do the front garden, because everybody on their way from the bus to the Main Gate automatically looked at it, so the whole thing started as tidying up and generally fulfilling expectations, but it gradually turned into something else. A lifeline.

And, virtually, a life. It struck me, as I finished with the 'Persian Musk' rose and started taking my bits and bobs back to the house, that for forty years, I had spent at least some of almost every single day in that garden. Whereas the house was to a great extent the way Geoff had wanted it, with a strong flavouring of having brought up a boy there, the garden was entirely mine, and though I say so myself, it had turned into something pretty wonderful. I had used trellis, climbing plants, and a couple of small trees to make the longish space into three compartments, with stepping-stones winding from one to the next, which made it all feel much bigger than it was.

I paused, as I could never resist doing, to admire the absolute star of the show in that bit of the garden at that time of year, my special moutan, 'Dou Lou', which was covered in light green, crinkled satin flowers a good four inches across. I had supported it with oriental poppies in white and a sort of muted, ashy purple, and some greenish-white *Iris sibirica* – suffragette colours, I remembered, looking at it approvingly, though that had not been in my mind when I did the planting. In a couple of weeks, that show would be over; although I would still have the benefit of the moutan's intensely sculptural leaves, that corner would stop drawing the eye. I would cut the poppies to the ground, let alchemilla and *Allium schubertii* take over their space, and meanwhile the viewer's attention would shift elsewhere, to the early roses, which by then would have started.

It was the endless dance through time which drew me out into the garden every day; the constant recomposition of the picture as one element receded and another came forward. It was beautiful every single week, even in winter, but it was never beautiful in exactly the same way. I couldn't paint worth a damn, as I discovered in my far-distant youth, but in that garden I had become an artist. Kew had taken me and taught me.

But it was time to go in. I needed to sort out the papers; in our bit of London, they come and collect paper for recycling periodically, but it all has to be organised and put in a special bin. There'd been so much to do, I'd just given them the *Guardians* for a while, but it was high time I tidied out the magazine rack, cut out the articles I wanted to keep, and heaved the rest out. So I made myself a cup of tea and settled down with my garden-notebook, my file, and the scissors. I suppose I'd been working for about an hour when I picked up a *Gardens Illustrated*, and out slipped one of Geoff's repeat prescription forms. It was such a jolt to see that infinitely familiar piece of paper, with the words Mr Geoffrey Wright written at the top; he'd been taking seven or eight different pills towards the end, so I'd been back and forth to the chemist's. His not-thereness overwhelmed me, and I started to cry. There was nobody to tell me to pull myself together, so I didn't, I just shook and sobbed and knocked over the remains of my tea. When the storm finally began to blow itself out, I realised that I was very, very angry. And what I was thinking, as I blew my nose and started mopping up, was, 'It's only been six months!'

I never drink during the day. Once I had washed my face, I poured myself a glass of white wine, warning myself not to make a habit of it. My lovely Burmese boys appeared from nowhere the way cats do, and jumped purring into my lap as I sat down again, with intent to comfort. 'O kitlings,' I said aloud, cuddling them, 'what the hell are we going to do?'

How much did I dislike Karen? It was a serious question, and with wine and the cats to help me, I started trying to think about it. She is a practical girl, and the practical facts were undisputed. She and David and two lively boys were living in a nasty little house off the South Ealing Road, getting on top of one another. She and David were two out of three of the beneficiaries of a trust which represented a Georgian house on Kew Green with four bedrooms and a proper attic. I had some rights, at least in theory, but it was two to one, so they had a great deal of practical power. It was natural enough for her to start thinking that they ought to be living in the house. She hadn't dared to suggest it when Geoff was alive; there had been a few delicate manoeuvres in the way of suggesting that with his heart, the stairs were perhaps getting to be a bit much, but there it had ended. Now, though, it was just me.

I have noticed again and again in mothers that the possession of young children seems to cancel out all other moral considerations whatsoever. She and David 'owned' a much better home for Will and Jamie than the one which they now occupied, it followed, therefore, as Karen saw it, that they had an absolute right to it. I suppose I ought to think myself lucky that she hadn't broached the subject just after the funeral, but I suspect that David had put his foot down. He is not an imaginative man, but he is kind.

Had I been like that myself as a young mum? If I am honest with myself, I have to say that yes, I probably was. David was more important than anything. I would have gone through fire for him, and if I had had a chance of giving him a better life, I wouldn't have thought twice about heaving out my mother-in-law, or anyone else for that matter. The question hadn't arisen, of course; Geoff had been the first generation in his family to buy his own house. He had worked his way up; something David and Karen were very much inclined to discount: it was the Kew Green effect. David thought of himself as upper-middle-class; he thought Carlyle Road was a comedown from an established, secure position. Geoff, of course, had not challenged this notion; in fact, he was immensely pleased that he had contrived to give David as his birthright a version of the unexamined self-confidence which powered posh boys up the ladder of success. In our time, we had seen plenty of complete twerps who believed in themselves, effortlessly overleaping the merely able; Geoff had wanted that for his son, and thanks to Mrs Thatcher and the rise in house prices, he had got it.

When had I started to feel the pressure of Karen's expectations? It was certainly some weeks previously, the last of the tulips were still out, I remember. She'd done something rather helpful, changing a light-bulb, I think (I don't care for ladders), and when she came down and I thanked her, she replied, 'It's getting to be a lot for you to manage.' I pretended I hadn't heard her. Later that afternoon, slipping quietly up to the loo, I'd heard the boys' voices from David's old bedroom. 'You can have this one. I'd rather have the attic.'

'I think we'll both be in the attic. They're going to make two bedrooms, and Mum says we can have our own shower. It'll be dead-mega-cool.' All of which gave me furiously to think, as we used to say.

When they had gone, I walked round the house, trying to see it through David's and Karen's eyes. Everything needed redecorating. We had seriously considered making a proper job of it when David left home, but we'd helped out with the deposit on his first house, of course, which had made rather a hole, and then a couple of years after that Geoff had his first heart attack, so we pulled in our horns a bit. It seemed only sensible to avoid unnecessary expenditure. Consequently, nothing had been done upstairs since the late Seventies. It still looked all right to me, though of course, when we were younger, one didn't redecorate every five minutes. I suppose the drawing-room looked a bit old-fashioned.

We had a lovely suite in black leather which had been wildly expensive when we bought it in Heals in 1974, and despite the cats, it was still in good condition, and very comfortable. The curtains were a really super, heavy, hand-woven linen I'd bought in Bourne and Hollingsworth's closing-down sale; they had been thought terribly arty at the time; proper people had velvet or damask, and I'd had a terrific row with Geoff before I got my way. Even after all this time, I am still fond of them. The plain taupe carpet had suffered a bit from cats and boys, but there were rugs over the worst bits, and it was plain and dignified; I don't care for clutter. I have to confess that once Geoff was gone, the photographs of Will and Jamie had been pruned with some severity. For the life of me, I couldn't see what Karen might find to object to, but I knew that she did.

I didn't have the family every weekend, far from it. Their Saturdays were consecrated to the Waitrose run and the boys' mini-rugby, or tennis in the summer, and on Sundays they generally went and did something purposeful, rollerskating or visiting a stately home, or God knows what. Leisure seems to be so much like hard work these days. So I was a little surprised, but in the circumstances, not very, when they proposed themselves for Sunday lunch a mere fortnight later.

I gave the meal some careful consideration, since I could guess what was coming. Geoff and David were both very partial to mutton, and one can still get excellent meat in Kew, so I got a nice leg of lamb, and did it with sauce soubise, roast potatoes, frozen peas for the boys because they don't really like anything else, and courgettes for the grown-ups. There was an apricot frangipane tart for afterwards, with cream or ice-cream. As the meal progressed, I could see that David had something on his mind.

'Eat up, Karen, darling,' I said. 'You've hardly touched your lamb.'

'I try not to eat too much red meat. David shouldn't either, specially with heart trouble in the family. We're trying to get our cholesterol intake down.' Which on the face of it, was tantamount to suggesting that I had directly contributed to Geoff's death: David, after one glance at my face, intervened hastily.

'It's very good, Mum. I shouldn't really, but I'll have a bit more, since it's carved. We can have salads for a couple of days, Kay. It'll even out in the long run.'

My daughter-in-law entirely failed to argue the point, which put me on the alert immediately.

Once we were at the coffee stage, the boys were allowed to get down and make themselves scarce. At their age, David had littered the garden with bamboo-cane teepees and cardboard-box space rockets, but Will and Jamie hardly ever went out at all. They seemed to have lost all their interest in running-about games when they discovered computers. At ten, the pair of them were waifish little souls stumbling about in huge, flapping trousers and base-ball caps, clicking obsessively at hand-held electronic devices, Pokémons and what-have-you. It sometimes occurred to me that the Japs had avenged themselves very effectively for what the Americans did to their country. At least it meant that I need have no fears for my 'Nora Barlow' aquilegias, then at their absolute peak. The stems are brittle.

I saw David swallow, and at last, the conversation which I had been bracing myself for began. 'Mum, we've been thinking that this is all an awful lot for you to manage.'

'It's no more than when your father was alive,' I pointed out. 'Considerably less, actually, seeing as I don't have to pick up after him.' If anyone but me had so much as lifted a tea towel, other than on Mother's Day, they'd've had to bring me round with brandy.

'But you're not getting any younger. I don't know if you've seen those new flats they've built down by the river? They're really very nice, and they'd be so easy for you to look after. It's not very rational, really, you rattling round here all on your own, and frankly, we could do with the space. I always thought that was what Dad wanted.'

Had it, in fact, been what Geoff wanted? I had a dismaying feeling that David was quite possibly right. Geoff had had enor-mous difficulty in seeing me in any other way than in relation to himself, and I am certain that if he had outlived me, he would have missed me so badly that it would not have been long before he followed me underground. It seemed to me highly likely that when he thought about 'after I'm gone', David and the boys had been far more visible to his imagination than was I. He might not, I think, have perceived my disloyally surviving him with any clarity. And anyway, as he so often said, we were all reasonable people.

Meanwhile, David was still being reasonable at me, in very much his father's manner. 'I picked up a brochure for Riverside Walk, it's in the car. I'll leave it with you if you like, so you can have a look.'

'Just how is this supposed to be achieved?' I demanded. 'Geoff left me a little money, as you know of course, but I'm not exactly rolling in the stuff. Most of it's in a trust fund for the boys' education.'

'That's part of it as well,' said Karen. 'If we were on this side of the river, I could get them into St Paul's. I wouldn't like you to think we were just being selfish.'

'I'm not talking about putting you out on the street, Mum,' David protested. 'We'd sell Carlyle Road, of course. The house next door went for two hundred and sixty, and if we got that for ours, we'd make £125k over and above paying off the mortgage. We'd need to keep a little bit of that to pay off the credit cards, but we could certainly afford to help out very substantially. After all, it's all in the family; I mean, it's an investment.'

As if I needed reassuring that he was not going to lose by the deal. I considered biffing him over the head with the bottle of Beaumes de Venise, but decided against it. After all, I had spent his entire lifetime acting as if I thought his needs were more important than mine, which on the whole, I did. No wonder he had such faith in me.

'It's for the boys, really,' said Karen, playing her trump card.

I played mine. 'But what about the garden?'

'But we *love* the garden! Don't forget, Kay's a great gardener.'

It was true: B&Q did not lack for her custom, all part of keeping the Carlyle Road house done up to the nines to enhance its value. Whatever this year's look was, she faithfully attempted to achieve it. That's not entirely fair; she did care in her way. Following an unsubtle hint from David, I had bought her a huge amphora from Pots & Pithoi for their tenth wedding anniversary, and she had been very pleased.

'I'll look after it, I promise,' she said. 'You've got it so nice now, it pretty well runs itself.'

I looked at her, appalled. It seemed more than likely that she believed what she had just said.

'Anyway, if you were living in Riverside Walk, you could pop over whenever you felt like it, and tiddle around,' said David.

I was in such a state of fury that I was bereft of speech, which is perhaps just as well. I could feel veins throbbing in my head, and I began to wonder if I might have some kind of a stroke. You'd better not, I told myself grimly, it'll just play into their hands, and with that, I began to cry. I never used to be a crier, but that's the one good thing about losing your husband, you find yourself getting weepy at odd moments. It's sometimes very useful to be embarrassing, I find; David hastily poured me another glass of wine, and came round to give me a hug.

'Poor old Mum. I'm sorry if we've upset you. We won't talk about it any more just now. Kay, let's just clear away and get the dishes done, eh?'

Even after forty years, I have never lost the habit of nipping into Kew Gardens when I need to think. When they had all gone away and left me in peace, I slipped a cardigan round my shoulders, and went down the road. I have a Friends ticket, of course.

'Afternoon, Mrs Wright,' said the gatekeeper. 'Lovely day for it.' After all these years, they all know me on the gate.

The trouble is, I have been going there so often that I hear and see the ghosts of former selves on every path. I steered clear of my usual haunts, and went off to the grass garden. I had been wondering for a while if I used grasses enough. I had Bowles's golden grass, of course, and the *Miscanthus* that Miss Jekyll liked, but that was about it. Perhaps I should be more adventurous. Grasses are quite wonderful in their own way, and I liked the thought of Bacon and Shakespeare peering through the stems like miniature panthers. I might try *Calamagostris brachytricha*, perhaps, I thought, surveying the clumps; the leaves were a very good colour, and there would be the added bonus of flowerheads later in the year. Then another one caught my eye, what was it? I stooped to look at the label, it was *Chasmanthium latifolium*. Automatically,

I reached into my pocket for my notebook, which I was not carrying.

Then suddenly the thought came over me: what the hell was the point any more? 'How dare she!' I said aloud. Fortunately, there was no one to give me a funny look; Kew in lilac time is pretty busy, but grasses aren't everyone's cup of tea, and I was alone. She seemed to think that it all just happened like that! Didn't she know I spent hours and hours thinking and planning, quite apart from the hours I spent weeding and pruning and trimming and dead-heading? A garden can't be made to stand still; plants go from too small to too big, you have to keep thinking and moving stuff around, or it starts going wrong.

And she'd take the credit for it! I could just see what was coming. The house would be totally remodelled. Whatever David might be thinking at the moment, I wondered just how much of the hypothetical £125k I was likely to end up with. There would be a great many bills from Fired Earth, Farrow & Ball, Colefax and Fowler, VV Rouleaux and the General Trading Company – or whoever next year's purveyors of must-haves turned out to be – and they would need to be paid. They could always remortgage, I suppose. But the garden was perfect. It wasn't just that I thought it was perfect myself; as Karen was very well aware, everybody on the Green thought it was perfect too, so she wouldn't go messing about with it. She had a good instinct for the socially acceptable, and a very considerable stake in impressing upon the Green, highly exclusive social enclave that it had become, that they were a nice young couple and 'persons like ourselves'.

But once the old house was to her liking, she'd fill it with people, and they'd all be yipping in chorus, 'Darling, you have done absolute wonders.' She is not the sort of girl to reply with, 'Actually, it's all my mother-in-law's work'; the whole thing would be ever so casually annexed as part of her general act. In a way, it was that which upset me more than anything. I had had plenty of practice in being taken for granted, but I drew the line at being eradicated. None of them seemed to have the faintest realisation that the garden was *mine*. Not just something that had happened, but my creation, a work of art, and not the automatic result of existing on Kew Green. And as for David's luckless suggestion that I might keep myself busy working as her unpaid gardener ... ! Words absolutely and definitively fail me! And what were poor Bacon and Shakespeare meant to do with themselves, stuck in a tiny flat with a sad little litter tray? Or were David and Karen to have my cats as well? – One mustn't be selfish, must one, they were used to an outdoor life, they would have to stay on the Green.

'Sod that for a lark,' I said explosively.

'Sorry?'

I smiled at a worried-looking black girl with a baby buggy. Without my noticing it, my feet had taken me out of the grass garden and back to more populous regions. 'I do apologise, my dear. I was just working something out in my head.'

She smiled back, a real smile, revealing gappy, strong white teeth. Relieved I wasn't a loony, I suppose. 'That's right. Don't let the bastards grind you down.'

'Do you know,' I told her, 'unless the world changes a very great deal, you are liable to find that when you get to a certain age, people will simply start to believe they're *entitled* to push you around.'

'You don' have to be older,' she said dryly. 'The trick is to push back.'

'Thank you, my dear. I think that's very good advice.'

'You take care now,' she said, and strolled on with her baby. He looked rather a sweetie, and I hoped he was enjoying the gardens.

When I went back to the house, I noticed the brochure for the Riverside Walk development on the tray in the hall. I knew about it, because I'd looked at the billboard as it started going up; it was a warren of tiny studio flats purpose-built as retirement homes, with the added inducement of a warden, for that extra peace of mind. I ripped it in half, and dropped it in the bin.

It was getting towards six, but there was still quite a lot of light. I looked out into the garden, as I had done so often, and noticed that the 'Persian Musk' rose was falling forward from the wall and needed tying in. A nice one-off job, which would neatly use up the last of the day. I got my raffia and secateurs, and a hammer and some vine-eyes, and stuck them in various pockets, and went out to deal with it.

'She'll find out how easy it is,' I thought sardonically, from the depths of the bush, wherein I had wormed myself by gradual degrees. The 'Persian Musk' is thorny and temperamental, and if you don't get her well secured early in the season, she sprouts huge, waving, sappy branches, wastes half the energy she ought to use on flowering, and savages passers-by. There was, however, a regrettable core of truth in what Karen had said. It was an established, mature garden; all the architecture, the box pyramids and so forth, was in situ and in excellent condition, and the shrubs and trees were full-size. It wouldn't be as nice as if I was hovering over it on a daily basis, but even with a pretty conservative programme of weeding and sorting out, it would coast on for quite a while looking fine, by most standards. It was then that temptation came to me, in the form of a little voice which whispered, 'And what if it wasn't quite that easy?'

Some ideas are like weeds. They blow into your mind from somewhere or other, looking terribly innocent, and then suddenly you find that they have laid down a large and complex root system and generally they're acting as if they've come to stay. While I was boiling an egg for my supper and buttering some bread, I found a number of strangely appealing notions floating up from the depths. I used to have a very appealing bamboo called *Sasa cernua* 'Nebulosa', but after two or three years, I ripped it out, not without effort, because it had a terrible habit of coming up where it damned well pleased. I started to think about reinstating it. And what else, on the same lines? Over the years, I had gradually banished forget-me-nots, nasturtiums and cosmos because they self-seed with such tiresome abundance that they make a nuisance of themselves. There might be a case for bringing them back; they're all quite attractive, but after a year or so of uninformed gardening from Karen, I rather thought that the word among the Greenites might be, 'You should have seen it in Alice's day'. Just a little, very small-scale changing of the balance, you understand; nothing poisonous or awful, and certainly nothing which might put the boys at risk. Just very subtly making the point that it takes more than wafting about with a pair of secateurs to make a really good garden.

I had supper, watched the news, which was dreadful as usual, read a book for a while, and went to bed. I had the most terrible dreams, mostly about Geoff, the ones I'd got used to where he was drowning or something and I couldn't rescue him, and some new ones I hadn't had before: one in which I went to meet him at Kings Cross and he walked straight past me, even when I screamed and cried and everyone looked, and another one, where I was in a burning building, shouting from the bedroom window, and I distinctly heard him saying to the fireman, 'It's all right, there isn't anyone there.' I woke up covered in cold sweat at ten to four, so disturbed that I had to go and make a cup of tea. I sat up in the cold, pre-dawn light, wrapped in a shawl, with Bacon and Shakespeare snoozing comfortably on either side of me, drinking my tea, and coming to terms with the idea that deep down, I was absolutely livid.

I finished my tea and hauled Bacon into my lap for comfort. He went 'mrrr', half-awake, and relaxed into a heap again, utterly limp and confiding. He was a bit like a silky bagpipe when he was as sleepy as that, a completely inert, apparently boneless structure, with a bundle of long limbs which seemed to have been attached at random. I sat stroking his resilient little body, thinking that cats share many of the most attractive features of babies, while being infinitely less trouble.

Other plants began coming to mind as I sat there thinking and cuddling my cat. Anchusa; 'Loddon Royalist' is a good form, a lovely clear strong blue, but try getting rid of it once you've got it: if you ever let it set seed, you're finished. I had some, and made sure that I cut it down the minute it stopped flowering. I wondered if Karen would be as careful. There's another rather super bamboo called *Yushania anceps* which clumps nicely and looks quite handsome and harmless, but it has a nasty habit of sending a stolon underground once in a while and throwing up another plant as much as twelve feet from the parent, in the middle of the lawn, for example. I'd never fallen victim to it myself, but I knew someone who had. And there was the rover bellflower, *Campanula rapunculoides*, which lives up to its name, and *Anemone tomentosa* 'Robustissima', which is lovely to look at, but belongs in light woodland and not in a garden at all.

I was beginning to feel sleepy at last, and a great deal calmer. I moved the slumbering Bacon carefully to one side of me, without waking him, and slipped down the bed between the pair of them. I have spent an entire lifetime unobtrusively making things easier for people and, over the years, I have developed a certain talent for it. So although I had no actual practice in making things unobtrusively more difficult, I suspected that I wouldn't find it came all that hard.

II

Phyllostachys aurea spreads by means of long, underground stems, or rhizomes. It does this so successfully that it rapidly invades areas where it is not wanted, including your neighbours' gardens. Before planting, you should be aware that if plants from your garden damage a neighbour's property, it may be regarded as a breach of your civil duty of care (a 'tort of negligence'), and you may find that you are legally liable for the damage caused by the plant, even if you were unaware that a problem was developing.

When I woke up properly the following morning, my night thoughts were still with me, and I went on brooding all through breakfast. It was, after all, my own garden, which I had made so beautiful: the idea of sabotaging it, after a lifetime of loving care, went deeply against the grain. But on the other hand, I argued with myself, it would be wrecked anyway. The anchusa would seed. The 'Persian Musk' would misbehave, the *Clematis recta* 'Purpurea' would get leggy and horrible, and the *Cornus kousa* which was threatening to get too big would get too big. Somehow people don't think enough about pruning trees, or at least, not at

the point where it will do any good. One way and another, there
was a lot to get out of hand.

If David and Karen had not made it so unfortunately clear that
they thought of me as a kind of machine for acting in the best
interests of my son, grandsons, garden, house, and cats, with no
will or desires of my own, then I could never have done it. But I
was not quite ready to be put in a hygienic cupboard overlooking
the river, to be brought out whenever Karen needed a babysitter,
and every time I thought of Riverside Walk, I got angry all over
again.

While I washed up my cup and plate, I started to wonder
precisely how one might set about anti-gardening, if I can call it
that, since none of my usual nurserymen were likely to be of any
help. But the *RHS Plantfinder* is an exceedingly comprehensive publi-
cation. I settled down with it in my favourite chair, and started
looking things up. If you don't happen to be a user, the key fact
here is that beside each plant, there is a little list of the nurseries
which supply it. All the things I wanted were perfectly good plants
in the right place, so they were all in there, and I was pleased to
see that there was one place which seemed to have them all: GarGo,
in RHS shorthand.

I turned to the back, and looked it up. GarGo was Garden
Gorillas, a nursery specialising in tough plants for difficult sites,
which made every kind of sense. The address was Alston, Cumbria,
with a Carlisle postcode, which also made sense; I rather suspected
that if you could grow a plant in Alston, you could grow it just
about anywhere, though you'd need rather a hair-shirt sort of
personality to try it in the first place. I wondered why I had thought
that, and realised that a faint memory was stirring, something to
do with an old motoring holiday; I got up to get Geoff's Shell
gazetteer, and looked it up. 'The highest market town in Great
Britain.' Ouch. That would mean long, hard winters, especially
that far north. I couldn't remember if we'd ever actually been
there, but I must have read the entry. We had done Barnard Castle,
Kendal and the Lakes once, so I had probably noticed it then, even
if we hadn't actually got there.

I was relieved to see that the Gorillas dealt by mail order. I do drive, but it had been years since I had driven at all far; I had taken over the car in latter years, once Geoff had stopped feeling able to trust himself behind the wheel, but like a good many men, he detested being a passenger. That meant that a little spin out into the country, the sort of thing we had done quite a lot of when we were younger, was no pleasure to either of us any more. Later that morning, I wrote away for a catalogue, and when I dropped the card in the box, along with my other letters, I felt a little glow of absolutely private satisfaction.

How much of my life could you say that of? I thought a bit later, when I was back home. It wasn't that I was naturally secretive, or at least, I didn't think I was, but I had gradually fallen into a mode of life which was solitary and contemplative. Geoff, or so he claimed, had been attracted to me initially because I was 'arty' and 'different', but once he was thoroughly used to me, other connotations of 'arty' also surfaced in his mind, such as 'not really practical', and even, 'not quite all there'. He and David, who was a chip off the old block, had gradually formed the habit of gently discounting my opinions. They were very masculine men, and I had come to find it easier to keep my thoughts to myself and transfer more and more of my interior life to the garden, where I could match my will against the gentle, persistent obstinacy of the vegetable kingdom with rather more chance of achieving something. I suppose if I had taken up a hobby which was a bit more intrinsically social, the Cats' Protection League, or bridge, perhaps, I would have developed a more communicative habit of mind.

I rang David a couple of days later and left a message on the answerphone; he called round on the way home from work.

'Lovely to see you, Mum,' he said, giving me a kiss. 'I thought I'd bring you some flowers. I know you don't like cutting stuff out of the garden.'

Actually, I don't like cut flowers at all, but neither he nor his father had ever perceived this. It was one of those rather awful mixed bunches you buy in garages, but there was a surprisingly attractive picotee carnation, I noticed; a charming, very pale sport of the yellow one you often get, and I pointed it out to him. 'You can often get carnations to root off a stem cutting, you know,' I told him. 'It's worth giving it a go. I could use this.'

'Good old Mum,' he said. 'Nothing goes to waste.'

I poured us both a drink; I felt I could do with one, and David could certainly drive on one glass of wine. It wasn't as if he had very far to go, at least in terms of geographical distance.

'Now listen, David,' I said. 'I won't keep you very long, I know you're tired, and you need to get home. I've been thinking long and hard about what you were saying. I can't say that I'm very happy about leaving this house. I've been here nearly all my married life.'

He automatically opened his mouth to start being reasonable again, and I held up my hand.

'Be quiet, David. I'm not saying I won't. But you mustn't rush me.' I could see the words 'Riverside Walk' forming on his lips, so I was rather firmer than he was accustomed to. 'I mean, we don't want to end up going to law with each other, or anything awful like that, though as a matter of interest, I think the concept of "the matrimonial home" gives me certain rights, you know.' He blinked a bit at that; it wasn't quite what he was expecting from dear dreamy old Mum. 'But we need to avoid all that if we possibly can; I see no reason why we can't achieve a good-humoured settlement, agreeable to both sides. But that means I'm going to have to give some careful thought to what I really want, I haven't moved house for an awfully long time.'

'Did you –'

'David, I am not going to go and live in Riverside bloody Walk and that's final!' He looked absolutely astounded; I doubt very much if I have had occasion to shriek at him since he was about sixteen, and perhaps not even then. As a teenager, he was, in retrospect, worryingly little trouble. 'Be sensible. The bottom line is that I need a place where the cats will be happy. It doesn't need to be huge, but I must have some kind of a garden.'

He looked rather dubious. 'That's not going to come cheap, in this area,' he objected.

'Does it have to?' I asked. 'You're putting in the money from Carlyle Road, after all, and it's an excellent investment. I should hardly need to remind you that we own this place outright, we paid off the mortgage years ago, and the last time anyone thought about it, it was worth more than a million. If you want to do a little work on it, as I suppose you will, it won't hurt you to remortgage for a while.'

He didn't like that at all. 'It's not at all advantageous to run a mortgage,' he grumbled.

'Well, for heaven's sake! Just live in it, and redecorate as and when you think you can afford to! What's *wrong* with you children?'

'For God's sake, Mum! We can't live in it, looking like this.'

'It's perfectly serviceable. You lived here for twenty-seven years.'

'You just don't understand.' Things were getting tense; I could see him assembling Karen's list of the things which made my home impossible for civilised people. In a minute, we'd be screaming at each other like fishwives. Anyway, I wasn't at all sure I wanted to know. Fortunately, he remembered that this was supposed to be a diplomatic mission, so rubbishing my taste in furnishings would be best left for another occasion. 'Let's just let it be, eh? I'm going to have to think about all this.'

I took a reviving swig of my wine. 'Of course, David. Nothing needs to be decided in any sort of a hurry. But I suggest we do things this way round. You decide what my budget is, and I, meanwhile, will start looking for somewhere. I'm the one who has to live in it, remember. Then we'll see if there's a possible fit beween what I want, and what we can afford.'

'You've got some money of your own,' he reminded me hopefully.

'I'm going to need it. Investment income's gone through the floor, and I'll need to maintain the place. I've only got the pension otherwise, so what am I supposed to do if the tiles start blowing off?'

'Fair enough,' said David. 'Actually, there's not a lot of point having money in the bank, is there? It makes much more sense to keep it in bricks and mortar.'

'As long as it's kept up,' I said pointedly. 'You redid your living-room last year, but when did you last clean out the gutters?'

He looked a little shifty, and I promptly followed up. 'If you do get this place, you can't afford to treat it like that, David. I may not've changed my cooker since you were wearing grey flannel shorts, but Mr Bryce comes every year to do the gutters, regular as clockwork.'

'It's true,' he conceded, 'you've been very good about all that. I should take a leaf out of Dad's book, really. The trouble is, anything someone's got to wait in for's so bloody difficult.'

'You could've asked me. I'd've come over to house-sit.'

'Thanks, Mum. But there's just so much to think about.' He sounded rather defeated.

'You work awfully hard. Geoff was very like you, when he was your age. You're looking tired, darling.'

'It's been a long day,' he admitted. 'I'd better get myself off home.'

I watched him out of the house and into his car; he tooted the horn and waved as he drove off. His tiredness was something more than just the end of a long day; he was starting to look middle-aged, poor boy. All that struggling and striving, and for what? I wondered if he ever thought for two minutes about where he was trying to get to; probably not. He couldn't afford it.

In the following weeks, I started looking in house agents' windows, and found it depressing but instructive. I'm not good at actually throwing things away and the house had filled up with junk over the years, but when I thought about it, there wasn't all that much of it I felt sentimental about; a couple of pictures, my gardening books, some bits and bobs, like my Jensen silver candlesticks. Most of it could go to Oxfam. All the same, I was used to a fair amount of space, and I was reluctant to move too far out of the area. If I wasn't going to be gardening on any great scale myself, I would hate to be too far from the solace of Kew Gardens. As I began looking for a place, and realised how truly awful it had all got, I became tense, and miserable, and depressed. I even began to see why David had been pushing Riverside Walk, though nothing would induce me to go and look at it. I could not possibly live in a place which had become for me the symbol of defeat.

Meanwhile, the Garden Gorillas catalogue turned up. When I riffled through it, they struck me as quite a sensible outfit. The catalogue was very thoughtfully laid out, and they had a surprisingly good range of plants, leading, of course, on ground cover for various types of site, trees for exposed, windy situations, wind-break hedging, and they made some very enterprising suggestions about things to do with tough, fast-growing greenery.

The catalogue sat about for a while, and after an exceedingly discouraging morning, on which I had spotted a rather nice but absolutely tiny cottage not too far from the Lion Gate – I mean, a hanky-sized garden, and basically two up, two down – which was on at £345,000, I was in such a mood for hating Karen, I sat down and started filling in the order form. Two bamboos – rather dear, but they were supplying good big plants – three campanula, three *Anemone tomentosa*. And there I paused, biro in hand, contemplating *Rosa filipes* 'Kiftsgate'. 'Kiftsgate' is an extraordinary rose; it popped up at Kiftsgate Court in Gloucestershire, as a sport of the ordinary *R. filipes*. It's a handsome brute with glossy, dark green leaves and huge trusses of single white flowers, very much the kind of rose I like, at first glance. Only it's a Godzilla of the vegetable world, and almost unbelievably vigorous. I saw it in its original habitat at Kiftsgate about ten years ago, by which time it was about three hundred feet long, had eaten one side of the avenue, and was beginning to look speculatively at a range of stables. Buying the garden a 'Kiftsgate', therefore, would represent a significant escalation of mischief. I had a 'Mme Alfred Carrière' showing symptoms of senility which I had thought about having out, so I had a space where it could go, in theory, but within four years, a 'Kiftsgate' would have undermined the wall and climbed the neighbours' pear tree, and where it would be four years after that is anybody's guess. To hell with it. I completed the order, totted up, wrote a cheque to Garden Gorillas, and sent it off.

After a series of rather difficult conversations, I extracted a pledge from David that he would let me have £300,000 to spend on an alternative home. I had quite a lot of leverage, of course, since he desperately wanted the house, and he was also concerned about his standing with the neighbours: going to law with one's Mama to put her out of her own house would very definitely *not* start him and Karen off looking like the kind of people the Greenites liked to make friends with. I am considered a touch eccentric locally, but highly respectable. David was not in the least pleased, but I pointed out that one of the reasons I had relatively little disposable income was, after all, that I was effectively poised to pick up the tab for the children's education as soon as they went into big school. And of course, as we did not say in so many words, it would all come back to him in the end. Or to Will and Jamie, perhaps: that occurred to me, and I waited for him to suggest it, which rather curiously, he didn't. Personally, I was past caring. But I insisted that we go to a lawyer together, and get the agreement down in black and white. He didn't like that either, but I didn't trust Karen an inch, and I did make him see the point that if I did find somewhere at all suitable, I'd need to be able to make a commitment very quickly, and since I couldn't, myself, get a mortgage, the vendors would have to be convinced that I was capable of raising the money.

So that was where things had got to, when one day, the phone rang, and I picked it up, with no very great expectations. There were a couple of estate agents who rang when something possible came up, or possible by their standards, at least. I was sick of saying that no, I did not want to live in Maidstone.

'Hello?' said a rather cultivated voice. 'Mrs Wright? Garden Gorillas here.'

'Oh, hello. Yes, what can I do for you? Did I forget to bung the cheque in?'

'Oh, no. Nothing like that. Erm. I've just sorted out your order, and so of course I noticed the address. I mean, Kew's pretty bijou, I don't suppose you've got all that much space? And this lot you've ordered, tough and rampant isn't in it. You do realise what they're going to do?'

'They're going to do exactly what I want them to,' I said firmly. There was a short bark of laughter from the phone. 'Christ almighty. I'm sorry, Mrs Wright, you must think I'm round the bend. It's just that something about the way you said that gave me the most incredible *déjà vu, déjà entendu* you'd have to say, I suppose. Just one of those moments of weirdness.'

'Who am I talking to?' I asked. I was beginning to get a most curious feeling that I really wanted to know.

'Oh, I'm sorry. The name's Martin Walker.'

'Oh, really. Well, you might care to know that I used to be Alice Caudwell, before I was Mrs Wright.'

'Bugger me sideways.' I burst out laughing. I hadn't heard anyone say that in years. Come to think of it, it was probably Martin who had last used the phrase in my hearing. 'Do you realise that's almost exactly what you said when you told me you were going to marry that twerp Steve?'

'Geoff.'

'Geoff, Schmeff. So tell me. What happened in the end?'

'We got married. We were pretty happy, really, only he died last year.'

'So you're on your own. You okay? Are there kids?'

'One boy, David. How about you?'

'I did go to America, and I got married a couple of times, but it didn't take. There are kids and grandchildren, but I don't see them. Their mums married again, and they all seemed to have enough parents to be going on with, so I sort of drifted away.'

I wanted to ask if it worried him, but it seemed such an intimate question. Geoff would have been absolutely horrified. 'When did you come back?' I asked.

'Early Eighties. I've been up in Alston ever since. My roving days are over. D'you know, Alice, I'm sitting here remembering exactly what you used to looked like? Black stockings, a pencil skirt, and a black sweater, *très* radical-chic. You did your hair in one of those French rolls, didn't you? The sort of hair any right-thinking man wants to take the pins out of. You were a proper little popsy in those days. I lusted after you wildly.'

It was as if he was talking about somebody else, and in a way, he was. I hadn't thought of myself in that sort of a way for so long I felt a little bit stunned.

'Did he do exactly what you wanted him to?' he asked, after a brief silence, making me jump.

'I'm sorry?'

'That was what you said, when you were handing me my cards. You were so absolutely sure of yourself, I just couldn't think of a comeback. Are you still like that?'

'No.' What a snippy little miss I must've been. The mind boggles. 'I've mellowed, I think.'

'Shame. Listen, Alice. It's been fantastic talking to you, but I've got some blokes due about now to come and talk to me about new plastic for the polytunnels, and I'd better get off the phone. Why not hop in the car when you've a day or so free, and come up and see me? You know where I am, and I'd be happy to give you lunch anytime.'

'Thanks. I might take you up on that, you know.'

'You do that. And I'll get your order off this afternoon – tell me what the hell you're up to sometime. God bless.'

I sat there for a long time just staring into space. Martin. He'd been in my painting class at Chelsea, and he was miles better than me. We all thought he'd be the one to really make it. We knocked around together for years after college, back in the days when I was scratching a bare living doing grisly illustrations and graphics for *Chat* and *Ladies' Home Journal*, and he was doing the same with *Popular Motorcycling* and its ilk. He was sort of my best friend, really, rather than my boyfriend; it was all a bit different then, if you were a nice girl, which I was, I'm afraid. I ate with my land-lady's family in the evenings, and she ran a respectable house, i.e., you weren't allowed visitors in your room. He'd been a rangy, strong-looking boy with rough, curly hair the colour of dead beech leaves, and lively greenish eyes, and I knew perfectly well he fancied me. I used to cherish a little fantasy in which Martin'd start putting a bit more effort into his painting and make a name for himself, and we'd go and live in Cromer or St Ives, surrounded by canvases, babies and espadrilles.

But then Jack Kerouac published *On the Road*, and he was completely sent. It left me cold. To me, Bohemia was one thing, hobo was another. He was determined to go to America and bum around living life as it came, and I couldn't see how girls fitted into all that. In the end, he told me I was just a square at heart, and we had the inevitable row.

Later in the day, I went up to my bedroom. Geoff used to tease me about the way I hated throwing anything out. I had to burrow right to the back of the wardrobe, but I found them at last. My old party shoes from before I married; they were from Anello's, and they'd been terribly expensive, twenty-two and six, if I remember rightly. They were black lace stilettos, with needle-sharp toes, size five, 'AA' fitting, and I'd loved them so much I'd never quite brought myself to discard them. Actually, they were a bit dusty, but still quite wearable; I'd looked after them. Proper Beatnik girls wore open-toed sandals or ballet shoes, but that was never my style. Gosh, they were narrow. I could see myself in the wardrobe mirror, where I sat on the floor cradling an old shoe in my hands: bobbed grey hair, a Breton tunic, jeans, Birkenstocks. With every passing decade, I have got more comfortable. In '57, I had a twenty-four-inch waist, and my bust measurement was only thirty-four 'A', but I wore a girdle all the same. One did. I wondered if I could still get the shoes on; I still took size five, but my feet seemed to be much wider these days.

I didn't try the shoes on, but I didn't put them away either. I left them on the rug in front of the gas fire, where I could see them. I'd bought them for the Chelsea Arts Ball, I remembered suddenly, just blown my winter coat fund on them when I saw them in Anello's window. They looked a bit disconsolate, standing there empty, but sexy.

The next time I was passing the discount bookstore, I noticed that they had a window full of road atlases. I had one, miles out of date, but these were this year's, and only £2.99, so I bought one.

What the map made me realise, very acutely, was what a long time it was since I'd been out of London. We'd hardly gone anywhere for the five years before Geoff died, and of course, I'd done nothing since. I spread the thing out on the kitchen table, and looked at the road up to Alston. God, it was daunting. Alston was practically on a level with Durham. It would mean the M1, the A1 and even a bit of A68, then an A road over the Pennines, or using the M40/M6, which was just as bad if not worse, coming off at Penrith. The journey planner seemed to suggest that it would take about six hours, but the journey planner was not seventy years old and unused to long-distance driving. I was very sad about it, but it was simply unthinkable. Anyway, the cats had never been left on their own for a night. I couldn't think of deserting them.

The stuff arrived from Garden Gorillas the following day. It's always been an absolute rule of mine to get plants in straight away, but I was grievously tempted not even to open the package, just to let them quietly dry out. There's such a difference between theory and practice, when it came to the point, I was completely in two minds. The package sat by the back door all morning. Once they were in, I had committed myself to leaving, and I had also declared war on Karen, even if nobody but me actually knew it, or ever would. Traditional notions of vengeance always involve an actual *moment* when the victim suddenly comprehends what has happened to them; some kind of 'for the love of God, Montresor!' climax, but I had spent my life among plants, and I had come to understand something of their methods, which are quiet, subtle, and infinitely tenacious. The victim perceives nothing at all, but begins, in a slow, bewildered fashion, to die. Not that I wanted Karen to die, of course, David and the boys loved her, even if I did not. I just wanted her to find herself battling a garden which was inexplicably difficult to manage, to have to ask David to help her eradicate lumps of surplus bamboo, only to have him say with that tact which only men can achieve, 'It never did that to Mum.' A little coolness with the neighbours over the variety of rogue and bandit seedlings which came boiling over the walls might be no bad thing either; I was reasonably fond of George and Harriet, Piotr and Christoph, and the Yamashitas, to name only the most immediately proximate, but they could all afford to give their gardeners a little more work, or even a lot more work.

I had ordered the damned things myself, no one had made me, but I found I was tiptoeing around the parcel as if I thought it might explode. In the end, after a day of worrying, I was forced to open it. The plants themselves exerted a sort of moral pressure, of a kind which was very familiar to me. They were beautifully packed in little plastic capsules, and as I set them out in a row, I found myself thinking about Martin, and wondering what he looked like. Gardening tends to keep you fit, even if it does play merry hell with your hands and your complexion. My invoice was in the box, sealed into a plastic bag with parcel-tape to protect it from the plants, and there was something else, also bagged. I ripped it open, and out fell one of those silly little brocade cases you get in Indian tat-shops, a bright red one. They're meant for a lipstick, I believe. I opened it, and out fell – what's the word? A reefer? or is it called a joint these days? I sniffed it to be sure, though I was pretty certain, and it was marijuana, all right. I hadn't smoked in years, and I'd certainly never smoked dope. There was a certain amount of the stuff around in my youth, especially in the jazz clubs, but I'd steered clear, which is just as well. The one time Geoff had caught David with a little bit of hash in a pillbox, the row had gone on for weeks. I don't know when I'd ever seen him so upset. I dropped the thing straight into the bin, but as I planted my plants, I found myself thinking of it from time to time, and it made me smile. Shakespeare came to peer into the hole I'd made taking out the 'Mme Alfred Carrière'. 'Buzz off, sweetling, you're in my way,' I said, flicking a drop of water at him from the can. He flounced off, affronted, and jumped on his brother; a pretty sight. They still played with each other like kittens, though they were nearly three, and the squabbles were strictly on the surface. Like my grandsons, they were companionable together.

I was doing quite a bit more driving than I had done in a while, because of looking for a house. I agreed to look at some places quite a lot further out. There was a little place in Esher, I remember, which I considered a bit more seriously than some others, since I'd at least have the Claremont Landscape Garden to walk in, and I also drove out to Guildford and Reigate to have lunch. This might strike you as frightfully un-thrilling, but for me, at that time, it was an adventure. I started to feel that I was getting to know South-West London like a taxi driver, and I also started to ask myself the essential question: how far could I trust myself? The answer seemed to be, a great deal further than I thought. I sometimes despaired of David because it seemed to me that never in his life had he tried to do anything which was too difficult for him, but I was, myself, very much out of the habit of risk-taking. And I began to realise as I battled through the London traffic that with my distance glasses on, my vision was perfectly good, and I was gaining confidence by the day.

I was in the front garden dead-heading the lavender and thinking about all this when I saw Ludmila coming back in with Sophie. The people immediately next door, George and Harriet, are far too busy and too grand to be about during daylight hours. They have two highly superior boys at boarding school, but much to everyone's surprise, especially Harriet's, they suddenly popped another infant when they were both in their forties. Ludmila was promptly introduced into the domestic equation, a nice, four-square, fair-haired girl from Croatia, who was, to all intents and purposes, my actual neighbour. There was also a relief nanny who covered evenings off and weekends, though I was fairly sure that Harriet would be able to identify her daughter by sight, should this ever prove necessary; at least if they gave her a bit of time to think.

I had become very fond of Ludmila. When I first saw her, she had an air of solid misery, like a poor little Jersey calf in a crate, and when I said hello and tried to cheer her up a bit, I realised what the problem was: no English. But it turned out that she had pretty good French, so I dusted off my old *Que Sais-Je?* and did my best to talk to her. I hadn't tried to speak French in decades, but we all used to think Paris was the centre of the universe, so I went to conversation classes for years and years. Only of course, when I finally got there with Geoff, it wasn't the way I'd imagined it at all. But you can't be a flâneur and sit about smoking in cafés when you're with a six-year-old. The awful truth is, if you have a young child in tow, everywhere is really very much like everywhere else.

I couldn't comprehend entrusting one's child to someone one couldn't talk to, but in this case, it had worked out very well, Ludmila is the salt of the earth. She had been with the Mathesons for four years at that point, and had got over the language problem, though I know Harriet still likes her to speak French with Sophie, to give her a head start. I suppose they'll try and iron out the Dubrovnik accent later on.

'I say, Ludmila,' I called. 'Can I have a word?'

'Look, Sophie,' she said, 'it is Auntie Alice.'

'Come and have some orange juice, sweetling,' I said to the

child. I got on rather well with Sophie; Ludmila being a sensible person, the child was quite an agreeable and well-disposed little soul. She seemed to think well of the invitation, so Ludmila wheeled the buggy into the garden, and in they came. We settled her down with some orange juice and an old bulb catalogue to look at, and I made us both a cup of tea.

'Ludmila, dear, I am in a bit of a quandary,' I said, *'devant un dilemme, comprends?* I have heard from a very old friend, and I'd very much like to go and see him. But he lives a long way north, and I need to take plenty of time to get there and back, I'm not used to driving for more than an hour or two at a stretch. So I think that if I go, I'd better plan to stay away for a week. Could I possibly ask you to feed Bacon and Shakespeare, and keep them company a bit?'

'But of course, Mrs Wright,' said Ludmila. 'It is a pleasure. Sophie and me will come and sit in your garden when we go out in the afternoon. And I will take dead flowers from your roses.' She is thoughtful in that way, bless her. 'We will visit with the little cats, *mignonne*, you will like that,' she added.

'Ludmila, you are an absolute star,' I said.

'Bacon an' Shakespurr,' contributed Sophie, gravely.

'Shakespeare, darling.'

'I can have a cat tea-party.'

'Of course you can, Sophie. I'll leave a tin of sardines and some kitty-treats on the table,' I said to Ludmila. 'And you know where I keep the b-i-s-c-u-i-t-s.' It was a charming thought. My boys like Sophie, who is a slow and rather gentle child, probably not a future Brain of Britain, but a very sweet little girl. In any case, they're both anyone's for a sardine. There would be much purring and weaving about and general harmony. 'If you really don't mind, that would be absolutely super. And if you could just pile up the papers and any letters on the hall table, I would be most grateful.' At least there weren't milkmen any more, so that was something one didn't have to worry about.

'It is no problem. Just tell me when you wish to be away, and Sophie and me will look after Bacon and Shakespeare.'

It's awfully nice when problems just evaporate; so many of them don't. But I trusted Ludmila. When they had gone, I rang David and left a message on the answerphone to say that I was expecting to be a bit tied up for the next couple of weekends. I wasn't expecting to see them, but it is as well to make certain. They would assume I was looking at houses, doubtless.

Then in the evening, I rang Martin.

'Alice! Great to hear from you. Are you coming up to see me?'

'I wouldn't mind. Would it suit you if I came on Friday? I'd quite like to spend a couple of nights, if I'm coming all that way. Is there somewhere nice and reasonably economical where I can stay?'

'You'd be perfectly welcome to stay here, but if you want to be independent, book yourself a room at the Blue Bell Inn. It's a nice little place, sixteenth-century I think, and I've heard the B&B side spoken well of.'

'That sounds just about exactly what I want. I take it I can get hold of them through Directory Enquiries?'

'I'd've thought so. If you have any problems, give me a shout, and I can always nip across and have a word with them. I'll book us a table at the pub in Nenthead for Saturday night, that being our local posh eatery, and I'll just have something for you here on the Friday.'

'I'm sure that's wisest. I don't know the road, you know, and I'd hate to feel I was driving against the clock.'

'Fine. There'll be something cold in the fridge, and then you won't have to worry.'

He blew me a kiss down the phone, and rang off. I sat feeling – affronted? Disconcerted? I couldn't put my finger on it for a moment, and then I realised what it was. Geoff or David would have asked which road I was thinking of coming on, recommended a route, and offered reams of good advice along the lines of 'try and be the other side of Birmingham before the rush hour', etcetera, etcetera. Martin, on the other hand, seemed to be under the impression that I could solve my own problems. Had I given the impression of being fearsomely independent in my twenties? It seemed quite possible, even though, in my own recollection of myself, I had been timid and conformist. Given the absolute pittance which girls were paid in the Fifties, I had never imagined a future other than marriage and motherhood, and if you're on the look-out for a proper man, there are things you don't do. Or at least, you didn't do them then.

But at last, after all these years, I was hitting the road, an easy rider in a ten-year-old Rover; Greater London glowed red before my eyes, as Kerouac almost said. There was no problem with the Blue Bell Inn; and as far as the actual journey went, which I proposed to take two days over, I had decided that I would simply find a B&B or a hotel as I went along, since I was not entirely sure how far I would get.

The thing which exercised me most was packing. It's all very well for a young man to stick a toothbrush in his pocket and head on out, but once you need three different pairs of glasses, two sorts of pills, and your moisturiser to get through a day, you might as well pack a suitcase. Boys, moreover, can be squalid with a certain grace, but a person with wattles and liver-spots who is planning to go on the road needs seven pairs of knickers and socks, pyjamas, tights, four blouses, two sweaters, a pair of smart trousers, a cashmere twinset and a raincoat, unless she wishes to be mistaken for a bag lady. After some hesitation, I decided I would wear my pearls. And then, of course, there was the dreadful question of shoes. Ecco lace-ups, of course; the Birkenstocks I find a bit heavy for driving. But I was meeting Martin and going out to dinner, so what the hell should I take? The lace stilettos were out of the question, I wasn't taking a cocktail dress, and while I had found that I could still just stuff my feet into them, I doubted if I could keep them on for five minutes; if I slipped them off in the restaurant I would have the considerable embarrassment of not being able to get them back on again. I had party shoes of more recent vintage, of course. There were, for instance, beaded, kitten-heeled mules which I wore to the Christmas dos on the Green. But I thought they were too dressy for wearing with trousers, so I settled on a pair of flat, bright-red pumps, cut like ballet shoes, with a fine line of white piping. Demure, comfortable, but a little bit gay, as one's not allowed to say any more.

On Thursday morning, I looked at the cats with great misgiving. My most faithful and constant companions, how could I do this to them? But they had learned to tolerate my long absences, house-hunting, I was sure they could cope. 'Oh darlings,' I said to them, 'be good. Try not to worry.' They stared solemnly back at me, round-eyed, aware, I think, that something was up. At least there were two of them, so they could keep each other company. It was nine o'clock in the morning; I had been awake for hours, but there was no point in trying to leave before the worst of the rush hour was over. I went out to the car rather quickly, before I changed my mind.

I had been over and over the route until I practically knew it by heart; I have a good visual memory. With nobody to navigate, I knew that I would need to know what I was doing in good time. I wrote down the junctions I intended to come off at, and taped the bit of paper to the dashboard. That was all I could do. So I stuck the key in the ignition, crossed my fingers, and went. The getting out of London bit was appalling, as I had fully expected. The incredible dreariness of the way factories, streets, a parade of shops, repeat seemingly endlessly was actively oppressive; as if the road from Kew to South Ealing had been duplicated by some insane three-dimensional Xerox machine and set out in rows across the countryside. By the time I was definitely free of London, I was just about halfway to my first stop.

I had a tremendous stroke of luck on the M40, a lovely lorry. It sat in the slow lane, puttering along at sixty mph, and when we got to the bit around High Wycombe where the road climbs, fifty. Nobody actually *makes* you drive like a maniac, I realised, with great relief. I sat just behind the dear thing, admiring its backside, which was decorated with a picture of cows and sunlit uplands and said 'Devon Churn', a species of margarine, I believe. With its help, I drove tranquilly to Oxford, letting everyone go round us. My plan was to go off the motorway there and look at the gardens at Waterperry, but I realised I would miss my lorry's protective cover when I resumed my journey.

It was all terribly interesting. I hadn't ever been on the M40, which hadn't been built when I last did any travelling in Britain, and there was plenty to see; it meanders through rolling, park-like country, for the most part. Waterperry gave me a much-needed break and an early lunch. Then it was back to the motorway. I had half a thought of going off again at Banbury and visiting Hidcote

Manor and Kiftsgate Court, if only to say hello to the *Rosa filipes* and see how big it was, but shelved the notion with some reluctance. It would take me forty miles out of my way, and I needed to be sure I was as fresh as possible when I negotiated the completely terrifying-looking maze of motorways around Birmingham. I consoled myself with the thought that Piotr and Christoph had been to Hidcote in the reasonably recent past, and said it was suffering from being over-visited, and generally not what it had been; the planting was getting rather coarse.

Of Birmingham, I would rather not speak. It was horrifying to think that people actually lived there. But I got from the M40 to the M6 without making a single mistake, though my nerves were in absolute shreds. I had to stop at the Cannock service-station for some coffee and a scone, simply unable to contemplate going any further for the time being; if it hadn't been for the knowledge that if I turned round, the whole hellish experience would necessarily be repeated, I would have fled for home there and then. As it was, there was nothing for it but to buy a bag of mint humbugs and tell myself to have a bit of backbone.

I finally stopped for the night in a perfectly pleasant B&B in Knutsford, rather prone to dollies, doilies, pot-pourri and itsy-bitsy patterns, but clean and comfortable. It was still fairly early, but I didn't think I could deal with Manchester until I'd had a good night's sleep. As I didn't fancy the idea of a proper dinner, I wondered what to do with myself. Some of the shops were still open, and there was a Marks and Spencer's; so I had the brainwave of going and buying myself a chicken sandwich and a quarter-bottle of wine with a screw top. What is more, after a little bit of pottering around the town to stretch my legs, at a suitable hour, I went and found somewhere reasonably nice to sit, ate my sandwich, and drank my wine from the bottle, for want of anything to put it in. I nearly made myself choke the first time I tipped it up, because I found a giggle forcing its way up as I was about to swallow. An old lady in sensible shoes, sitting in the public street swigging wine out of a bottle! It was really the thought of Geoff's face if he could have seen me at that moment which set me off. Dear Geoff. It was, I think, the first time since he had died that I remembered him simply with affection rather than with an atrocious upwelling of grief and loss. Don't be such a prune, darling, I admonished him silently. No one thinks anything of it. True; I attracted no more than a passing glance from anyone.

The next day saw me leaving the motorway at Penrith, and taking the road across the North Pennines. An enormous amount of England had passed before me; impressing upon me the sheer, dismaying density of the population between London and Preston. Soon, the way things were going, it would be one vast, amorphous city. London and Birmingham had already swallowed countless nice little market towns, like *Rosa filipes* on the rampage, but in the not too distant future, Metropolis Britain would swallow even London and Birmingham as perceived and separable entities. I found it a frightening thought. There were simply too many people.

But after Preston, the scurrying traffic thinned dramatically. The Lake District humped up on our left, turning its shoulder to the road like a sleeping man, and as we all toiled along, the cars started to space themselves out properly, as if the idea of sensible stopping-distances had been dropped back into circulation. When I came off at Penrith onto the Alston road, mine was the only car.

The A686 meandered across a reticent landscape of moorland, drystone walls, raggedy sheep, and bog-cotton, climbing ever higher. In the hour that followed, I met two other vehicles, both battered, muddy, four-wheel drives; a wry reminder that they are not an exclusively urban phenomenon. I noticed that in the more sheltered areas, there seemed to be a surprising range of plant life. At one point, there was a sort of intense, mauvish-pink flash in the corner of my eye, and I jammed on the brakes. When I walked back, there was a whole splendid drift of wild orchids in a hollow, rising straight and proud out of the grass; just ordinary *Orchis mascula*, but the most wonderful sight en masse. I got right down and sat among them cross-legged, so that I could look at them properly. They had a faint, very sweet scent, coaxed from them by the warmth of the afternoon, and I stayed there for a long time. One's pleasure in wildlings is very different from one's pleasure in a garden, I think. From my lowly vantage point the orchids, the grasses, the heartsease tangling through with its little cat-faced flowers, and the marguerites waving against the blue sky, were unimprovably lovely. I would not have dreamed of taking a single plant; and the scene could evoke no possible thoughts of how it might be tended or made better. It was, I think, the purest enjoyment of flowers that I had ever experienced.

When I got back to the car, I realised that I had forgotten to lock it, and the keys were still in the ignition. But that was all right, nobody had passed, let alone stopped. I drove slowly and soberly the rest of the way, in a terrible mixture of emotions, chiefly shyness, and also, now I was approaching my destination, concern, since it occurred to me then that Martin hadn't given me precise directions and I hadn't thought to ask. But I soon realised why not: there was a sign for Garden Gorillas on the road, and when I got into Alston, which in my state of mind at the time I barely noticed other than to register that the high street was ludicrously steep, there was another one further on, pointing the way down a little lane. A big sign marked the nursery itself, and the gate stood open. It was the usual sort of place, long benches laden with labelled plants, tall stuff standing in pots, a prospect of polytunnels. I stopped the car and looked around. There was a smallish house off to the left, a long, low, grey stone affair with a little porch, so I got out of the car with butterflies raging in my tummy, and went and rang the bell.

'My God,' I said, when he opened the door, 'what's happened to your hair?'

'Hello, Alice,' said Martin.

III

Polygonum cuspidatum establishes a system of rhizomes which can extend at least eighteen feet from the parent plant, and reach a depth of at least eight feet. The shoots which emerge in spring become six- to eight-foot canes.

Any fragment which is left in the soil can grow into a new plant. The crown (at the base of the stem) resists composting and easily produces new plants. Any small portions of cut, flailed or mown stem which reach soil, compost, or even water will also grow into new plants. Contact the Environment Agency prior to moving soil contaminated with *Polygonum* off site.

I followed him inside, and he poured me a glass of red wine. The living-room was exceedingly shabby, but clean, with a dreadful grey and pink uncut moquette suite which reminded me of my landlady's back in the days before I got married, and a very worn Turkey carpet over a slate-flagstone floor. There was a lovely view out into the blue distance from the low window. That was all I noticed at the time, because my attention was entirely taken up by Martin. He had put on quite a bit of weight; he wasn't ridiculously fat, but he was certainly chunky, not lean, and made more so by a fisherman's oiled-wool sweater with holes in the elbows and at the hem. His face was a deep reddish-brown with tan and windburn, which set off his white hair, a fleecy ruff from ear to ear, and his short white beard. He looked a bit like Captain Birdseye. Only the eyes were the same, though long crow's-feet radiated from their corners, and his brows were comically tufted.

'Why do men's eyebrows get longer as they get older?' I asked him, when we had sat down.

'I haven't a clue. Personally I think hair's migratory. I remember, when I was in my teens, I had shaggy legs and a smooth chest, and twenty years later, my legs were lots smoother, but I had plenty further up, and outcrops on my shoulders. Now I'm seventy and it's all gone south for the winter, as you can see for yourself. Alice, darling, why are we having this damfool conversation about hair? It's very nice to see you. Bottoms up.'

I drank some of my wine. 'Cheers. Martin, shouldn't I go and tell the Blue Bell people I'm here?'

'What for? They know you're having supper with me. They won't be bothered.'

I was starting to take stock of the room. There was a wood-burning stove in the hearth, a bookcase and a couple of tables, as well as the suite, but almost nothing that looked chosen. Just stuff you could put things on, with an air of having been bought at auctions. There were no pictures on the wall, and no photographs. If Martin had told me he'd only been there for a couple of weeks, I wouldn't have been at all surprised.

'Do you still paint, Martin?'

He shrugged. 'Not really. I went back to it when I moved up here, but it was no go. You'll remember, they taught us that very academic, precise approach? It was a kind of classicism, really.'

'You were very good.'

'Could be. But when I started again in '83, I realised you couldn't do well-mannered Fifties paintings any more, because meanwhile that kind of classicism had been flushed down the pan. There wasn't a point of connection between what I'd been taught to do and what was really going on by then, d'you see? We were modern kids, Alice. Post-modernity's something else again. Sometimes you just have to recognise you're an old fart with nothing to say, and leave them all to it.'

'But I can't think why you ever stopped.'

He poured himself some more wine. 'The truth is, darling, I didn't want a painter's life. It was a freedom thing. I wanted to be able to be out in the world, going to and fro and walking up and down in it, as the man said. I really wanted to write – I had that idea of cutting loose with a notebook in my hip pocket? Unfortunately, even I could see I was crap. After a year or two, I realised I hadn't had a single perception that the big guys hadn't had before me; it was all coming out pastiche Kerouac, practically pistachio Kerouac, if I'm going to be brutally honest.'

'I think that's terribly sad.'

'I don't, not really. There's enough paintings in the world. I don't think about it much.'

He put his glass down on the adjacent bookcase, and sat forward. 'Alice, would you like to stretch your legs? It's a very pleasant evening.'

'I'd enjoy that,' I said.

We went out into the sun. When we emerged from the porch,

a curious animal got up from under the shade of a cotoneaster, stretched front and back legs, and mooched over to join us. He was fairly large, with a wiry grey coat and white eyebrows, not unlike Martin's own.

'What is he?' I asked.

'I dunno. Some kind of dog, I assume. Basically, he's a mutt, so I called him Jeff.'

'Hello, Jeff,' I said. He sniffed my hand politely, and wagged his tail. 'There's Airedale in there somewhere, I think,' I said to Martin.

'I shouldn't be surprised,' he said. 'He's very strong.'

It was an oddly peaceful and beautiful spot. I wondered if it had been the site of a smallholding, in the past. As a lifetime user of nurseries, I sensed that it was a very no-frills operation; my guess was, it was economically viable but only just. 'Oh, is that your cat?' I asked, as a burly tabby swaggered across the space from one polytunnel to another. 'Puss-puss-puss.'

'Sort of. There's a gang of feral mogs that live around here. I put down a bowl of food for them every evening to keep them around. They keep the rodents down, so they're well worth their kibble.'

'Haven't you made friends with them?'

'They're wild animals, darling. They don't do "friendly". If you corner one in a polytunnel by mistake, it hisses and streaks for the exit.'

'Have you got onto the Cats' Protection League? You know, you can get them spayed, and wormed and so forth, without it costing you anything.'

'No need. Something must eat the kittens, I think. They litter like buggery, but at the end of the day, I've been feeding a stable population of six to eight cats for the last twenty years. They seem to've got themselves sorted.'

I was a long way from Kew, as I needed to keep reminding myself. In fact, I realised desolately, I had come up prepared to be charmed, but the thought which had just arrived in my mind was: I don't think I like this man any more. We've got absolutely nothing in common. It was hard to talk to a man of my own age who apparently wasn't worried that he hadn't achieved anything; frankly, I

found him disorienting. He guessed this, I think, because he didn't
try to talk to me. The two of us and Jeff wandered out of the
nursery, and back down the lane. There was a wonderful view down
the steep, cobbled high street in the early evening light towards a
stone market cross, with crookedy yellowish-grey stone houses on
either side. A Hovis advertisement sort of place. But quite well serviced; I noticed a baker, an off-licence, a little supermarket, a bookshop, a butcher, a couple of antique shops, places to eat . . .

'The Blue Bell Inn's round that corner,' said Martin, pointing.
'It'll take you two minutes in the car. We can walk down there
now if you like, and they'll give you your key.'

I hadn't got my handbag, I realised at that point; and we had
ambled out of Martin's nursery leaving everything unlocked
behind us. I terribly wanted to go back and get it, but I didn't want
to look as if I was fussing.

The landlady of the Blue Bell greeted Martin like a friend, and
seemed perfectly happy to take me on trust; she issued me with
my keys, and showed me which door to come in by. 'Just stick
your head round the door of the bar and give us a shout,' she
said, 'if it's before eleven. If it's later than that, bring Martin down
to carry your bag.'

'I won't be that late,' I promised. 'I'm rather tired.'

It was a bit of a hike back up the hill; I could feel my knees
creaking in protest. I was glad to get back to the cottage, and
discreetly check that nothing had been disturbed. Laid-back is all
very well, but I'd spent a lifetime in London. Martin picked up the
bottle of Beaujolais, and led the way through to the kitchen. The
scarred and pitted walls were a curious, spectral light blue I remembered seeing before in the far distant past; there was an elderly
Rayburn, and a collection of Utility cupboards; and a scrubbed
pine table, upon which Martin set out plates and glasses, brown
bread, cheese, salad, and fruit.

'I remember places like this from when I was a child,' I said.
'It's just caused me to reflect that the Farmhouse Kitchen Look is
a complete fantasy. You know, wicker and gingham and red
pelargoniums. D'you know why real farmhouses had these blue
walls?'

'Someone told me there was a theory it discouraged flies. It's just a bit of Reckitt's Blue in the limewash.'

'I'd forgotten about blue-bag.' In the olden days, you put one in with your white wash, to keep the sheets looking fresh, before there were modern powders. 'This is very nice cheese, Martin.'

He looked pleased. 'It's our local specialty, Cotherstone. We've got a sort of wholefood co-op and deli now. I help out once in a while.'

'You're very well supplied, I was thinking. Pretty well everything's to hand.'

'And there's something else I like about it. Had you noticed, apart from the supermarket, there's no generica? That was something which got me down when I came back to England, and travelled around for a bit. Wherever you went, there was a Dolcis and a Boots and a Smith's. Any town I went into, I hit the high street, and just about all of it was like the last place I'd stopped. It depressed the hell out of me. We thought life was pretty damned grey in the Fifties, but at least you could tell Boscastle from Newcastle.'

'Why did you come back?'

He sighed, thinking it through. 'I'd no very pressing reason to stay, really. My second marriage had gone pear-shaped, and I just found myself thinking one morning that it was maybe time I gave over here another go. I was growing almonds along with a couple of other guys, so I sold out my share and got on a plane. Bought myself a second-hand camper van, and took a look around the country for a while. My mother came from round here, Garrigill in fact, and I'd always meant to pay it a visit some time. When I got here, I found I liked it, and property was incredibly cheap. I could stretch to this house, five acres, and the plant and equipment, so I reckoned I'd just settle for that. I've never regretted it.'

'What about the winters?'

'They're cold. And there are things you don't try to do. We don't get completely cut off. I don't risk my old jalopy in the worst of the weather, but I can always get a lift from someone with a Range Rover if I really need anything.'

I thought of him hibernating, contentedly dormant, just

accepting staying at home while the wind and the rain lashed down, and for a moment, I saw the old Martin in him.

'It was a bit of a brainwave, specialising in ground cover,' I commented. 'It's turning disadvantages into advantages.'

'Actually, I like my thugs,' he confessed. 'The way they're feral and opportunistic. They sneak along underground and come up where they like. It started as defining a niche market, but it didn't take me long to realise that I'd got a sort of built-in sympathy for them.'

'So in a way, it's as if you're thinking of them as Beat plants?'

'Right! It's that concept of furtiveness and rebelliousness, and colonising the margins. It's interesting you saw that.'

I was enjoying the evening, though I was not entirely at my ease. I was asking far too many questions, but I couldn't think what else to do, since he didn't seem to want to volunteer anything. But he was asking none; and of course, one doesn't just start chattering on about oneself. I didn't want to bore him. In a way, I wished I was at home, watching the TV with Bacon and Shakespeare. I hoped Ludmila was being nice to them.

After supper, he put the kettle on, reached down a battered tin tea-caddy which turned out to be full of dried marijuana, and started rolling a joint. Then a second.

'Do you grow your own?' I enquired.

He shook his head. 'I'm a bit too visible. When you've got people wandering round the polytunnels all the time, it's not too clever. But I've got a mate who does. D'you want one?'

'No, I don't think I will.'

He put the spare back into the little tin where he kept his papers and so forth, and pocketed it. The kettle was just coming to the boil, so he dropped a couple of bags of Yorkshire Tea into mugs, and took me back to the sitting-room. I can't remember what we talked about; by ten o'clock, I was dropping. Martin drove my car down the hill for me, and took my suitcase upstairs. I flopped into bed, and dreamed about nothing at all.

I got up late the next morning, had my breakfast, and at about ten, strolled up the hill to Garden Gorillas. I found Martin in a polytunnel, pricking out anemones.

'Can I help?' I asked. In reply, he handed me a pile of black plastic pots and a tray full of seedlings, and moved over a little so I could reach the compost. We worked side by side for a while. 'I think I've forgotten how to talk,' I said. 'As opposed to making people tell me things.'

'Nobody says you have to.'

'But I want to.'

I watched his hands for a while, the absolutely practised movement which disentangles wee white roots without breaking them and sets out each plantlet in its own little pot with the compost firmed to precisely the right degree to sustain it and give it the best possible chance of getting away. I was doing exactly the same, with rather less mechanical skill and precision. I'm a wizard with cuttings, but I don't grow much from seed. A couple of dozen plants later, he began to talk to me.

'I've been thinking about what I used to be like, when we knew each other. When you gave me the heave, the one thing I knew for certain was that if you were going to be a real writer, you had to hop the freight trains. London was dead, it was the past, so we all went to look for America. But somewhere hidden in that notion was the assumption that the experience was in itself so necessary and so authentic it would somehow teach you how to write, do you see? Anyway, my visa was running out when I met this girl in The Griddle. Ellen was quite sent by the idea that I'd given up painting for the sake of all of that experience; it showed I was an artist, and pure, I suppose, so she married me so I could stay in the States. Well, I told you what happened. After a couple of years, I still couldn't write, and I couldn't paint either. Ellen stayed in New York while I was on the road, working in an office, and I came back to her there once in a while.'

'It all sounds a bit rough on her,' I said, 'if you were never there. Or was it just a relationship of convenience?'

'No. We did care about each other. But that's the way things worked then. The rule was, you didn't take your girl on the road, because if you did then things had to start getting organised, and the whole point was to enter the flux. I don't suppose Ellen was having a very wonderful time, but it was what she wanted. Anyway, once that phase was over, we took her savings, and went down to Taos together, and met some other people, and some of us ended up living together on a farm in upstate Florida, permanently stoned, growing oranges and dope. We had a couple of kids together; all the Beat girls were popping them out by then. The place was crawling with babies.'

I was listening in a sort of horror. Apart from the way it had all been such a waste of talent, if everyone was permanently stoned, who had poked Farex into the littlies and taught them to brush their teeth?

'What happened to them?' I asked. 'Your children, I mean.'

'They turned out fine, as far as I know. One of them works for the National Parks Department, and the other's in sales. If I fast-forward a bit, Ellen took up with someone she met in town, and left us, taking the boys. She'd gone off being a bride of art by then. Man number two was a square, a stable sort of bloke, and he seems to've made a pretty good job of them. I wasn't exactly good father material.'

What struck me more than anything was the way he didn't seem inclined either to condone or condemn his earlier self; it shook me. But he'd been like that in the Fifties, as I could remember very well; once something was done it was done, and all he worried about was whether you'd done it as hard and as well as you possibly could. 'There's nothing in the world except work, maintenance and crap,' he declared. 'You owe it to yourself not to let the crap take over.' Nothing got his goat except hypocrisy and worrying about what people might say. We wrangled about that all the time. 'Women can't ever be artists,' he once told me, with absolute, evangelical certainty, 'because you hedge your bets.' I had been quite sure he was right. Artists could wear blue suede shoes, in certain circumstances, but never black lace stilettos from Anello's.

'I never thought you were interested in plants,' I said.

'You weren't either, back then,' he reminded me. 'I'll tell you what happened to me, and I've never admitted this to a living soul. After three years stoned out of my brain in Florida, America taught me something else. It finally dawned on me I found oranges more interesting than beatniks. There was this little Mexican bloke, an illegal immigrant, who did most of the work around the place, and I got him to teach me about pruning and grafting.'

'I love pruning,' I said. 'It's something you can get exactly right.'

'Exactly. You've got it. You need to have a deep comprehension of growth, the shape the tree is, the shape you need it to be, and then you cut. By the time the whole thing broke up in 1970, I was a pretty competent orange farmer.'

'It sounds as if you were the only one doing any work.'

He shrugged. 'That was okay. It wasn't anyone else's thing, and the whole point about all of that way of life was it wasn't about ownership. But I had a skill by then I could make a living off.'

'It's not just that.' As we spoke, we were still mechanically pricking out seedlings, and setting the pots into plastic trays, twenty-four to a tray. Our hands never stopped moving. 'Around the time when my little boy went to school, I began to realise that nobody listened to me any more, but I was somehow in dialogue with the plants in my garden. I started to feel that was the only place where I was really communicating.'

'I know that feeling.'

'I can't help thinking, in retrospect, it was lazy of me. The world was changing, and I just disappeared out of my own family and cultivated my garden like Candide. The trouble is, all that women's lib stuff didn't seem to have anything to say to people like me, unless we actually left our husbands and went to live in lesbian communes, which somehow never appealed.'

'I met some of the lezzies here and there, the ones who'd talk to men, that is. On the whole, I liked the ones who lived with other women because they fancied them, and I thought the ones who were doing it out of political theory were a pain in the neck. You've never fallen in love with a woman, have you?'

'No. To be honest, I've never seen how anyone could.'

'Then it would've been wrong. So why not cultivate your garden?'

There was a pathetic squeak from somewhere to my right, and I looked up just in time to see one of the tabbies streaking past with its mouth full of something brown, a vole or a fledgeling, and I remembered that hunting was their job. I habitually went to great lengths to rescue little birds from Bacon and Shakespeare, and I had a sudden qualm that this was nothing more than sentimentality. Of course if one doesn't, then someone has to clean feathers, blood and giblets off a carpet somewhere, which is also a consideration, at least in Kew Green.

It was a really lovely day. The sky was an intense speedwell blue, and there was a little wind, but not much. Quite a few people came in to buy plants, and when the nursery shut for the evening, Martin changed into a more respectable jumper, I put on my twinset and pearls, and we went out in the Rover, first of all to Garrigill, down a road whose verges foamed with *Geranium pratense*, to visit a friend of Martin's who ran an outfit called Pennine Perennials.

Garrigill was a village round a green, like home, but more private and more introverted; the whole place was huddled into a dip, guarded against prevailing winds. People were playing bowls on the grass, and a gardenless little house with its front door at first-floor level displayed a plant-pot on every step, which, quite clearly, no local youth ever kicked off. Llamas grazed on the verge, wearing collars and chains, tall and lovely creatures with heavy-lidded, long-lashed eyes and tiny, discreet feline smiles. The friend I thought was super and very knowledgeable, and she had a pair of lovely, friendly cats – after Martin's dégagé establishment, I was quite relieved to find that plantswomanship and pampered pusskins were part of the local scene. She was able to grow what seemed to me an astonishing variety of things, despite the rigours of the climate, and I could have talked to her all evening, if Martin hadn't had a booked table waiting for us and dragged me away. I have always longed for *Meconopsis baileyi*, which she had in profusion, but it won't go in London.

After Garrigill, we went to Nenthead on a nearly vertical road for dinner in the pub. I was a bit taken aback by the décor when I walked in, it was so old-fashioned-looking, terribly dark with leatherette benches, horse-brasses and carpet tiles, but it was also cosy, and as I rapidly discovered, the young couple who ran it combined an unfeigned warmth with the production of remarkably good food. I have to confess also that I enjoyed being out

with a man. Martin gallantly offered to drive back, so that I could
have more than one glass, and I found after a while that I was
talking; which is to say, neither reminiscing nor imparting information.

'I've been thinking, over the last twenty-four hours,' I said, as
he poured me more wine, 'you can talk to someone who's from
your own background and your own generation in a way you can't
talk to anyone else, however much you love them. It's not even a
question of personal affinity, it's to do with the shape and size of
your unexamined assumptions. I don't think I've put that very
well.'

'No. I agree with you, Alice. I'm enjoying this, you know.'

'Martin, can I say something really foul?'

'Of course. The whole point is, we don't have to pretend.'

'You know when you ran off to discover America and be an
artist? Could you really be authentic even to yourself, if you'd
abandoned everything you actually knew anything about?'

'Oooch,' he said, grimacing. 'Well, Alice darling, there you put
your finger on it. Only the trouble was, you couldn't be Beat and
English, it was just impossible, and I was absolutely positive that
you couldn't be anything as important as Beat starting from where
we were. But you know what? The freedom was important, and
so was the sex. As you may remember, nice English girls used to
be welded at the knees, or so they led us to believe. It shook me
out of all kinds of respectfulness, and that's got to be a good thing.
But Jesus, Beats could be dull. I mean, just insufferable. There were
some very pure spirits, like Kerouac. But there were some pretty
desperate little fellow travellers, and I wasn't exactly an alpha Beat.
I was too late hitching a ride on the bandwagon, and I was English.
The people I went around with were sort of zeta Beats, to be
frank, hippies waiting to happen, really, and I woke up one day in
about 1963 to realise that they weren't at all interesting.'

'Poor old Martin. What a terrible waste.'

'Absolutely not. I had a life, and I lived it.'

'So did I, in my way. I had a baby, and I made a garden, and I
was a good wife. I don't feel sorry for myself either.'

He leaned his elbow on the table, and put his chin in his hand, looking at me steadily. 'Question for question, darling. Why did you want a "Kiftsgate" and some *Sasa*?'

So I told him. It took the rest of the main course, all the way through dessert, and a small malt whisky afterwards. He listened, and made no comment. Later on, he drove me back to the Blue Bell, and walked home up the hill. I had opened my window, and in the intense stillness of the summer night, I could hear his footsteps receding up the street.

I went back to the nursery on Sunday morning, to find Martin dealing with a customer who wanted a pretty sizeable order. I heard the voices from the office, and once I had worked out what was going on, I didn't disturb them; I just started making myself useful. Plants growing in pots always need tidying up; you dead-head, remove dead leaves, get moss and lichen out of the pots, generally improve matters. Some time later, he came out and saw what I was doing.

'This is great,' he said. 'I can't afford to hire anyone, and there isn't time to do everything myself.'

Some more people arrived, and then more. There was a lull at about quarter to two, and we retreated to the cottage for a quick bite of bread and cheese and some tea.

'You're being absolutely incredible,' he said. 'I'm very grateful. It's a pity you're not going to be here on Monday. It's my closed day, so I could've taken you around a bit.'

I goggled at him. 'Oh, no. How completely stupid of me.' I simply hadn't been thinking. Of course nurseries are open on a Sunday, that's when people have time to visit them. I'd thought in terms of staying a weekend because that's what one does, and I'd actually landed on his busy days. I wished he'd said.

'You'd be welcome to stay another day, darling. There's nothing you have to rush back for, is there?'

'Not as far as I know,' I admitted. 'I rang Ludmila yesterday, and she says the cats are fine.'

'Well, then.'

I threw in the towel. 'I'll just hop in the car and see if Mrs Thorpe can manage me on Monday night.'

'You do that.'

But this was where it all started, as Martin put it, to go pear-shaped.

'I'm terribly sorry, Mrs Wright.' She sounded genuinely regretful. 'We've got a block booking for all the rooms from some walkers doing the Pennine Way. I'm afraid we just can't manage it. I could ring round for you.'

'No, no. Please don't trouble yourself.'

I drove back to Martin's place, downcast, and told him the bad news.

'Don't be daft, Alice', he said. 'You can stay here. Or if you don't fancy it, there are other B&Bs, but why bother? It's not smart, but I have hot water and clean sheets.'

I gave in. 'All right then, I'll do it.' I thanked my stars that I had packed a dressing-gown. 'Sorry, that sounds terribly ungracious. Martin dear, I would be delighted to accept your invitation.'

He made a small, derisive noise, a sort of subdued hoot.

I moved my stuff over to the cottage on Monday, having said goodbye to Mrs Thorpe. We set off on a drive around the Pennines; we were going in the Rover, and Martin got in on the passenger side. He was a very good navigator. We went to Melmerby, and bought a picnic and various other bits and bobs at the lovely baker's there, which I had heard of even in Kew, and then we drove down to Appleby, across the moors from Brough, and climbed back up the valley of the Tees. We stopped at High Force in the early afternoon, and went to look at the waterfall, which I found almost frightening; it was such an awful, battering weight of water hammering against the rocks. After that we made our way home over Alston moor.

Somewhere along the road, looking out at a wide, bare expanse of harsh heathers and grasses, like the pelt of an old lion, I found that I was talking about my garden. 'I don't know if I can face it, Martin. It's going to look just the same as ever, but I know I've poisoned it. It all seems a bit mad from here.'

'Tell you what,' he said. 'Why not rescue it? Stick a whole lot of those plastic packs I use for posting plants in the back of the Rover. Clone everything you really care about, and send it all up to me by the ordinary post. Just put the packs in one of those Post Office boxes with a bit of bubble-wrap, and they'll be fine. I'll grow it all on for you in a corner of one of the polytunnels, and then when you decide what you want to do with yourself, I can send it all south.'

'Oh, Martin, darling. That's just – oh, it's the most brilliant idea, an absolute lifesaver. But are you sure it's not an imposition? You're overstretched as it is.'

'But you care about them. So of course I'd do it. Don't be silly.'

It is just as well that the Pennines are pretty empty, because the road was swimming before my eyes.

It felt extremely odd getting ready for bed in Martin's spare room. It really was very grotty indeed. The limp, faded curtains hung like grey dishcloths, and there was nothing in it but a bed, a chair, and an awful little Utility bureau with treacly brown varnish. But there were enough blankets on the bed. Possibly too many; I decided to get up and take one off. Then I got back in, but I still wasn't nodding off. Perhaps I should get up and fetch myself a glass of water. I put my dressing-gown on, and tiptoed out. There was a line of light under Martin's door. I dithered for a moment, and went in.

Martin was tucked up in an old-fashioned iron bedstead; the phrase 'snug as a bug in a rug' came to mind. He was propped up on a pile of pillows, wearing a tee-shirt which said 'Saddleworth Folk at t'Mill', and a pair of half-moon, gold-framed glasses, and he was reading *Tales of the City*. There were no photographs and no pictures in this room either, but a whole wall was lined with dog-eared paperbacks, and here and there on the shelves there were interesting stones. Leaning in the corner was a wooden propellor off a wartime plane, scarred paintless by the sea.

'Hello, Alice,' he said.

I walked over to the propellor, and touched it, running my finger down the leading edge.

'It's lovely, isn't it? I found it on the beach near Maryport.'

I sat down on the end of the bed and the springs twangled, a sound I'd forgotten. There were so many things I wanted to say. That I had never, ever, even thought of being unfaithful to Geoff. That none of this was a good idea. That I might make us a cup of tea, and since he wasn't sleeping either, we might talk for a bit.

He tossed the book onto the floor, and took off his glasses. 'You staying?' he asked.

I said nothing at all, and after a moment or two, he put his glasses on the adjacent bookshelf and turned off the light. I sat there in the dark for a little while; then I shrugged out of my dressing-gown and my pyjama top. I could hear Martin's faint grunt as he tugged his tee-shirt off over his head. How right he'd been to turn the light off. I'd have felt awfully shy about showing him my terrible old boobs. I groped forward, reaching out for him, and when my palms met the cushiony, hairy surface of his chest, it came as a shock, quite irrationally. I think I must've been more in love with Martin once than I'd let myself believe, because somehow, in the dark, my mind had gone back in time as if fifty-odd years had been cancelled out – I'd had a sort of mad expectation of encountering a young man's smooth, hard body; Martin's, in fact, and I thought, what a pair of old fools we're being.

He reached for me; I felt his hands closing warmly around my wrists, sliding up towards my shoulders. He pulled me gently towards him, and as I slid down beside him, he kissed me. It was the most peculiar sensation – up to that point, I'd never, ever, been kissed by a man with a beard. All that softish, wooly hair against one's face, and in it, a wet, smooth tongue. His kiss was so much subtler than the way he talked, it surprised me very much. It seemed to be asking delicately, do you like this? and questing for an answer. I began to relax, and stopped feeling self-conscious. The thing is, I'd only ever been made love *to*, if you see what I mean. Geoff tended to use the word 'performance', and I'm sure that was how he thought about the whole business. But Martin seemed to think it was more like a sort of conversation, which was less exciting, perhaps, but nice. I stopped worrying about my breasts, apart from faintly regretting that he'd never seen them when they were still pretty. We were a pair of old wrecks, but what did it matter? I wriggled out of my pyjama bottoms, and kicked them out of the bed.

When we finally got to the crucial point, he pulled me on top of him. I settled myself astride him, sitting upright with the cold night air sliding round my bare torso, his hands warm on my hips. It took me a moment to get comfortable. Then all I had to do was rock.

IV

Pueraria montana kills or degrades other plants, either by smothering them under a solid blanket of leaves, by strangling woody stems and tree trunks, or simply by breaking branches or uprooting entire trees and shrubs through its sheer weight. Once established, the plants grow rapidly, reaching a length of as much as sixty feet in a season, at a rate of approximately one foot per day. The individual vines may be thirty to a hundred feet in length, with stems as much as four inches in diameter. The huge tap roots, seven inches or more in diameter and six feet or more in length, weigh as much as four hundred pounds. As many as thirty vines may grow from a single root crown.

Martin snored, just like Geoff. I wondered if there were men who didn't, but at my time of life I was unlikely to find out. One becomes accustomed, but I was out of the habit of sleeping through it. While on the one hand I was in a position gratefully to acknowledge that his beatnik girlfriends had taught Martin a thing or two, on the other, I was a little jaded come the dawn.

'Martin, I really must go home,' I said over breakfast.

He nodded. 'But come back sometime.' I reached out, and put my hand over his. A snatch of three-a.m. conversation came back to me. We had been lying companionably cuddled up, feeling rather pleased with ourselves.

'Martin, I've just had an important thought.'

'What?'

'I'm not nice. I've spent my life *being* nice, but basically, I'm not.'

'I never used to think you were nice, darling.'

'No?' I had felt a bit injured.

'No. You were a sexy little bitch, and what's worse, you were a part-time *bon copain* with notions of bourgeois respectability which got right up my nose. But I'll say this for you. You could be a good mate. I borrowed my rent off you at least once, and it wasn't every girl you could owe ten shillings to in those days, without them thinking they'd bought the right to tell you what to do.'

'Did you pay me back?' I'd completely forgotten it.

'I did, actually. I got that commission from the *How & Why Wonder Book*, and I was in the money for a while. You got your ten bob all right.'

I had thought about what he had said for a while.

'I don't see what else I could have done,' I said.

There was no answer beyond a deep-drawn, gentle wheeze.

The journey back was entirely without incident. I took the two days: having started late and tired, I thought I had better leave Birmingham till I'd had a good night's sleep. But I got to London much faster than I had expected to, around lunchtime, and I realised that if I was organised about making an early start, now I was getting more confident, I could do the whole trip in a day quite easily, even allowing for little rests.

It seemed very hot in London and rather airless. I walked into my big, beautiful house like a stranger. Bacon and Shakespeare were ecstatically pleased to see me; they came hurtling down the stairs and demanded to be picked up. I can't really manage both of them at once, so I simply had to sit on the floor for a while until they calmed down. I went round to tell Ludmila I was back, with the cats following me in an anxious procession, taking her her thank-you presents, a cake from the Melmerby baker, and a sweet pink-lustre plate from the Alston antique shop. She was pleased, I think.

Absolutely nothing had happened since I left. A sheaf of estate agents' envelopes and the usual flyers were neatly stacked on the hall table: the only personal item was a postcard from an old friend who now lives in the Dordogne and has been conscientious about keeping in touch since I was left on my own. 'The roses are out, I was thinking of you, love, P.'; a postcard like a light touch on the arm, an indication that somebody knew I existed.

I walked round my empty house, just looking at it, and realised that I no longer felt very strongly about it. It was the place where I lived, and if it became the place where I used to live, I began to feel that perhaps I wouldn't mind very much. It seemed rather disloyal to be thinking like that. I sat down on the bed where I had slept with Geoff for so many years – a Vono, very comfortable – and the cats immediately jumped up beside me. They roll in the dust in the summer, the bad boys, and they had made a grubby little two-cat-sized depression in the middle of the white candlewick bedspread; I'd have to take it off and wash it. Mechanically stroking the nearest kitling, I tried to take stock of my position.

It was not a single night of bliss with Martin which had changed me, but the recognition that I was being forced to adapt or die. Geoff's widow faced a future in which she was a problem to be grudgingly solved by the deployment of the minimum possible amount of family assets, unless she simplified everybody's life by building a bonfire in the back garden (strictly forbidden in our part of London, I might add), jumping on top of it, and disappearing in a puff of smoke like those poor girls in India. Alice Wright was, at least potentially, someone else entirely. It could not be disloyal to Geoff to find out who; it had been Geoff, after all, who had made my life impossible. In fact, it was there and then, sitting on our bed, that I left him, if you see what I mean. I finally acknowledged to myself that it wasn't just Karen I was angry with, and David that I felt betrayed by. I'd put in all those years of selfless loyalty, and he'd been a rat; I had to face it.

The garden needed quite a bit of work. Some of my lilies had gone over, and were beginning to go brown round the edges, and one of the camellias had some kind of a virus; on a couple of branches, the leaves were dying back at the tips. I'd have to prune back beyond the point the damage was visible, and destroy all the material with care in case it spread. Gardening is a passionate business, but not sentimental. You can love and cherish a tree for twenty years, but if you detect symptoms of the dreaded honey-fungus, you know that even if it looks just as beautiful as it did yesterday, it's actually dead. Your feelings about it have to change, because you have to get it out of there in order to protect everything else.

That was more or less how I felt about the garden as a whole. The plants from Alston were lying low; like true garden guerrillas, they were flourishing and digging themselves in, but they didn't look like anything out of the way. Only I knew that they were the seeds of future destruction.

But it could all rise again, that was the thought I hung on to, in the utterly wonderful way that plants have. I could start an orderly programme of hardwood and softwood cuttings; root cuttings in one or two cases; saving seed. I knew how to do all that. I could not clone my beloved olive tree, nearly a hundred and fifty years old, which I bought in Columbia Road about ten years ago, but fortunately I had decided that he should live permanently in a beautiful weathered pot from Whichford. Come the day, he could go with me, pot and all.

I rang David that evening, reminding myself that he did not know I had been away. All the same, I needed to speak to him, to tell him I was there.

'Oh, hello, Mum,' he said, sounding rather surprised. 'Have you got any news?' From him, of course, that meant only one thing.

''Fraid not, darling, but there are one or two possibilities.' Guiltily I reminded myself that I must open the estate agents' envelopes and make some more appointments to view.

'Mum, I don't want to nag, but you've got to remember, the market's still rising. The longer you faff about, the less you'll get. I haven't time to go around for you, you're going to have to manage this one by yourself.'

Not long since, I would've felt very hurt and upset by that remark, but I realised that it seemed not to be making much impact. Perhaps I had changed. 'You're going to have to let me do this my own way, David.'

'On your own head be it,' he said, sounding sulky.

I was starting to think about my 'Dou Lou'. I proposed to try taking softwood cuttings now, when the plant was in full growth, but I was rather inclined to suspect that I might do better if I waited a few months, and took hardwood cuttings in the autumn. I had a feeling it was going to be tricky. I knew some of the plantsmen at Kew; I might pop my head round some doors, and ask them what they thought. They do some very high-tech work with cloning plants, but I didn't have that sort of equipment; I was going to have to stick with the old ways. I'd read somewhere they could be propagated by air-layering, it might be worth a try. 'Rome wasn't built in a day,' I said vaguely. 'How are the boys?'

He told me, and we parted on reasonably good terms.

I went into the Gardens on the next day, which was blazing hot. High summer isn't my favourite time for Kew, there are too many people lying about on towels sunbathing; not that I don't think they're entitled to enjoy public space in their own way, but instead of avenues and peaceful vistas, it was looking a bit like a green beach.

I made my way across to Joseph Paxton's Palm House. The white-painted cast-iron door was as familiar to me, as I pulled it open, leaning back against its weight, as the door of my own house. It was about as hot outside as it was inside on a day like that, but the humidity enclosed me like a steam-bath. I could feel the thin skin on my cheekbones relaxing and drinking in the moisture. The Palm House is so big that even if it's full of people, the height and the greenery absorb most of the noise, except for the distinctive clanking of people moving up and down the spiral wrought-iron staircases. I moved absent-mindedly along the path, oblivious of the fact that I was in a shuffling, well-mannered queue. The banana had fruited, I observed; the giant fruiting body made me think of an enormous green laburnum flower, and I remembered that the comparison had occurred to me before. In my mind's eye was a young woman with back-combed hair, T-strapped shoes, a white plastic belt, and a baby.

'Look, darling! Bananas!'

'Glah,' said David. I'd had to leave the pram outside, and he'd reached the stage when they're too heavy to lug about in comfort and too little to walk. I had been in a state approaching despair that day. B.K., as I sometimes thought of it, Before Kew, we had lived rather well. Before the baby came, we'd gone to films and dined out in trattorias, and even after David, I'd sometimes bought us steaks or chops. Meat was absolutely the thing, if you were brought up under rationing. When Karen got snooty about red meat, I wanted to tell her that, and remind her that we were a damned sight healthier than people are now. I don't think I ever met a child with an allergy when David was going through school, but the twins have three or four.

But A.K., we'd had to cut the housekeeping to the bone; I was having to buy dubious stuff like spam and snoek that I'd devoutly hoped never to eat again, and tins the labels had come off, and yesterday's bread. Shopping took forever, because I was going from place to place trying to save a shilling here and a penny there. We were so poor that summer, I was putting cardboard in the soles of my shoes. Someone had just told us the roof was 'nailsick', and we'd have to get it seen to before all the tiles fell off in the first autumn storm, and we couldn't borrow another ha'penny. 'It's all going wrong,' I had thought to myself, clutching my son in my aching arms. 'We've over-extended. Something'll give, and they'll end up putting us in jail, and then what'll happen to David?' And what made it even worse was knowing it was all my fault.

'I should never've listened to your blasted notions,' Geoff had said, with real bitterness and not for the first time, poking at his macaroni cheese with an expression of nausea. He had been working late as usual, and it was pretty dried out, but I had done my best, and there was quite simply nothing else in the house except porridge and the baby's milk. David had had some earlier, and I'd made do with just the macaroni. Geoff had thrown his fork down after a token mouthful, and I had picked up his plate, hurled it at the wall, and burst into tears. When he had gone off to work in the morning, we still weren't speaking. Walking round the empty Palm House with my child, I had asked myself the question, would it make things better if I just put David back in his pram and went and jumped in the lake? I answered myself almost immediately. No, because David needed his mum, and I didn't carry insurance, only Geoff did. Apart from to my baby, I was a person without value, alive or dead.

How passionately I had thought, back in 1963, that if we'd only had enough money to take the edge off that chronic fear, and for us to eat properly again, nothing could really go wrong – I mean, simply nothing except death could be that awful. And how very wrong I had been. I thought of something I had said to Martin in the restaurant at Nenthead, when I dumped the whole saga on him.

'Geoff preferred to forget it was me being so-called arty and impractical that landed us up in a Georgian house in Kew Green and not a bog-standard semi in Ealing,' I said bitterly. 'And David simply assumes it was his dad thinking ahead.'

'Well, what did you expect, darling? Gratitude?'

Yes: when I thought about it, I had expected gratitude, really. It took Martin's simple question to put this into focus. I wandered out of the Palm House and into the Rose Garden, where I could sit down and rest for a while. I'd let myself get angry with my situation, because I felt that the house had cost me so much in one way and another, in humiliation and fear and anger, and Geoff and David ought to have known it. Perhaps I had gone a bit mad; but then, why shouldn't I? Like Martin, I felt inclined to tolerate my own actions, even if I no longer experienced the emotions which had led me into them. The really crucial thing was to think what to do next.

Summer inched along. At one point I got so flustered by David's nagging that I lost my head and put in an offer on a little house in East Sheen; fortunately, it was in a chain and after a lot of to-ing and fro-ing, the whole thing fell through. Meanwhile, a steady procession of carefully packaged plantlets went north to Alston. I went up myself more than once. Martin never came down, because he couldn't leave the nursery; as he frankly told me, he needed to save up local goodwill for bailing him out of his winter bout of bronchitis. He asked me wistfully about jazz gigs at the Pizza Express, which he'd heard about from someone, and I hadn't the heart to tell him I hadn't done that kind of thing in years. Somehow getting up to town from Kew always seems so much of an effort; if you drive there's nowhere to park, and it's actually easier to take the 65 bus to the station, and the District Line, which is slow, into the centre. Frankly, I have lost the habit of doing so; I find the Tube dirty, unreliable, and rather dangerous. Like so many of Martin's questions, it focused a perception for me. That in fact I had come to live in Kew as if it was a small county town. Martin's world in Alston, in real terms, was about the same size.

It was September, and the boys had gone back to school. I had had a couple of time-consuming near misses, and David and Karen seemed to have reconciled themselves to the fact that they were unlikely to winkle me out until spring, though if I were not out by the following summer, I could see that all of Karen's ferocious will would be bent on getting me out. She could see a new life opening up; she wanted to be settled, sorted out and established by the time the boys went to big school. I could even acknowledge that it was in a way legitimate that she should; I'd have done the same in her place.

I had actually nearly bought a house about three weeks before. In my new mellow frame of mind; I had found a place I thought I might just settle for, out towards Perivale. But it attracted a lot of interest and it was near the top of my 'budget'; so I had to get back to David, lawyer had spoken unto lawyer, and by the time they'd all finished, someone else had put in an offer and promptly had it accepted; the vendors weren't unduly greedy, they just wanted something quick, fair and water-tight. It had all been rather hard on David; he was getting nightly curtain lectures from Karen, no doubt. He's been prone to nervous indigestion since his A level days, and he was starting to look pretty yellow round the eyeballs, poor lamb. He was determined that this particular fiasco shouldn't happen again, so we had another round of talks with the men in suits, and my own solicitors were empowered to act on my behalf without further consultation, if we perceived a need to move very swiftly.

Coming back to September – the phone rang about halfway through the month, and it was Martin.

'Darling, I think you should come up when you can,' he said without preamble.

'What is it?'

'I'll show you when you're here,' he said. 'I don't want you thinking about it. You're your own worst enemy with thinking.'

'Chauvinist.'

'Rubbish.'

Whatever I said, he refused to be drawn, but he did tell me that the three baby 'Dou Lou's were being cosseted in Pennine Perennials, and were showing the first signs of new growth. I was absolutely delighted, and told him to thank his friend for me very sincerely. If they survived, I intended to give her one. They come from northern Japan, to the best of my knowledge; I'd seen photos of them flowering in deep snow. I was sure they could cope with a walled garden in Alston. I rang off, and made arrangements with dear Ludmila to go up on the following Tuesday. I'd found by experience that if I left at about quarter to seven in the morning, I could be across the M25 before it actually went solid; after that, it was pretty straightforward. I still took the view that slow and steady does it, but I no longer hid behind lorries: I cruised in the middle lane at just under seventy, humming 'The Little Old Lady from Pasadena'. The fact is, I had discovered, motorway driving's easier than any other kind, just so long as you concentrate, and take breaks, the way you're supposed to.

I reached Alston in the crisp coolness of early evening, about sixish. Martin came out when he heard the Rover, and gave me a kiss.

'Come with me,' he said. We walked down the high street and turned right at the market cross, going towards the Gossipgate Gallery. It was the last road on the south-east side of town, and the high moor rose bleak and bright behind a single row of stone houses. Just a bit along from the gallery, there was a house with a 'for sale' sign, slightly retired from the street by a three-foot hedge of mature box-bushes which had, within living memory, been clipped into the shape of acorns. It was very symmetrical, built of the yellowish-grey local stone, and it had a little pedimented porch, and five windows, one on either side of the door, three above. It was called Crow Ghyll. Martin produced a key from his pocket, and opened the door. A central corridor ran from front to back, with four doors off it; the house was virtually a cube. I followed him straight through to the back door, which he also unlocked.

There were three steps down; the garden was a little lower than the house. It was sheltered, folded into the hillside, with mature trees beyond, whitebeam and ash, then a belt of dark pine. 'Oh,' I said. It had fifteen-foot stone walls, and it was a couple of hundred feet long. It was desperately neglected-looking, though at least someone had mown the grass once in a while; there were the remains of one and a half conventional long borders, currently a romantic tangle of unpruned late roses, nettles and windflowers. The garden proper terminated in tall yew hedges, their darkness alight with skeins of *Tropaeolum speciosum*, the flame-flower, behind which, I supposed, there was some space for vegetables, compost-heaps, and what have you. But what was really engaging my attention was what took up the other half of the second long border, as it were: a gigantic Victorian glasshouse, rising to the full height of the wall, and not looking in bad shape at all. Some panes of glass had got broken, but that was on the whole a mercy, both from the point of view of ventilation and of letting in some rain to the poor plants.

I walked down the steps and opened the greenhouse door, which stuck a bit because of the damp. Most of the interior wall was occupied by a fan-trained 'Brown Turkey' fig tree, slugging it out with an espaliered peach, and the ground was deep in mouldering fruit. A sweet, mildewy smell hung in the air, and both trees desperately needed pruning.

'You didn't bring a pair of secateurs, did you?' I asked.

Martin shook his head. 'Are you going to look at the house?'

'In a minute,' I said. I explored the rest of the greenhouse, and noted that it also had interior steps down from a glass door, so that it could be entered from a room in the house. What fun, and so convenient in bad weather.

'The structure's quite sound,' I observed, squinting up at the roof.

'Yes, it is. Just as well, or you'd be properly in pound-note country, even up here. Basically you'd just want someone to check over the glazing, though you might want to substitute modern conservatory roofing in the fullness of time. I've got a friend who's a glazier.'

I took a good look at the borders to see what else was there, and noticed a nice established clump of *Nerine bowdenii*, its sugar-pink flowers just beginning to come into bud; *Helleborus corsicus*, oh goody;

it's poisonous, so I'd never grown it, but its jade green cups in the early spring are frankly hard to resist. Peonies, they'd be the old red-satin cottage peony, *P. officinalis*, I was pretty sure, and very nice too. Colchicums in quantity, which was super, peeking up through the tangle. They're expensive to buy. Through what remained of the gap in the yew hedge, I found what I had been half expecting: a rank patch of potatoes and collapsed runner-beans, a compost-heap, a place for fires, a galvanised water tank, and a little shed.

'Who lived here?' I asked.

'An old codger called Tom Appleby. I knew him to speak to. He'd pop into the nursery once in a while, and we'd have a word.'

'I don't suppose he bought anything,' I said, looking around. It bore all the hallmarks of a garden which had become self-sufficient, flourishing on its own seedlings and cuttings; I doubted if anything new had come in for a decade.

'No, he didn't.'

We went back to the house. Sitting-room, drawing-room, dining-room, kitchen, which had the door to the greenhouse. It was almost as bad as Martin's, but the cupboards were pre-war wood, and there was a very dirty coal-fired Rayburn Royal. Upstairs, a spartan bathroom with a rolltop bath, and three bedrooms. All the rooms were about fourteen by fourteen, not cramped, but not impossible to heat. The rooms all had variants on the theme of terrible Forties-ish wallpaper with flowers and trellis, scuffed and forlornly marked with clean patches where items of furniture had once stood. The whole place was a little bit dirty and desolate, and all the rooms had soot, twigs and dead birds in them, from them falling down the chimneys. There were wooden shutters on the front windows.

'How much do they want for it?' I asked Martin.

'Ninety-five.'

'*What*! But that's ridiculous. You couldn't buy a garage for that.'

'But this is Alston.'

'Let's go out into the garden again,' I said.

Later, back at the nursery, we sat down together over Burgundy and cabbage soup. 'Well?' he said.

'I can put all the really tender stuff in the greenhouse,' I said. 'It's surprising what you can grow in pots.'

'It's in terrible nick.'

'It doesn't matter. It'll clean up. I'll have to put in central heating, I can't bear the thought of running around slaving over fires, I've done enough of it for one lifetime. But I get the impression it's been quite well maintained. There's nothing sprouting out of the gutters, and I can't see any cracks or damp bits.'

'I'd've thought. You'd want a surveyor over it to make sure, but he was a careful old boy. I'd forgotten all about this place – people tell me nobody ever got inside since his wife died, which was years ago now, before I moved up here. He dropped off the perch about May, there were no kids, and he didn't leave a will. It's taken months for it to get onto the market.'

'It's got a beautiful roof,' I said. One of those roofs you get in the north of England, not slate, but some kind of limestone, about an inch thick. The slabs up near the roof-tree are quite small, and the ones at the bottom about two feet long; it gives a tremendous feeling of strength and stability.

'What'd you do to the house, if you bought it?' he asked.

'Secondary glazing, oil-fired central heating, rewiring, electric cooker, plain fitted carpeting throughout, and paint it cream from top to bottom,' I said at once.

'There's nothing like knowing what you want,' Martin observed. 'Unless the surveyor reckons the place has sprung a major leak, and I don't think it has, £20k should see you through that lot, easily. You might need to spend a bob or two on the greenhouse, which'll need scaffolding, and roughing out the garden'll cost a few thousand. You'll want to renew exterior paintwork, but that'll have to wait till next summer. I'm surprised you're not planning paint schemes. I thought you were into that sort of stuff.'

'I can't be having with interior decoration any more. It's all got far too complicated. As far as I can see, everyone's running around trying to get it just right and then six months later they find it's all gone out of fashion. I put a lot of thought into my house in the early Seventies, only to find that the children are actively sneering at everything I thought was smart, so why bother? Have you ever seen any of those dreadful makeover shows?'

'I don't have a telly, darling. I listen to the radio. Did you notice there's a garden door at the far end beyond the hedge? It must lead to that alley along the side of the churchyard. I think my mate Chris could get his JCB through it – he's got one of those little ones.'

'Oh, I do hope so. It'd simplify the rough-work no end.' I looked across at Martin. Without really thinking about it, I seemed to have committed myself, though I'd no idea what it would be like to live through a winter up there, which any sensible person would doubtless tell me was insane. And I certainly wasn't in love with Martin any more, though I was very much enjoying having a lover . . . I hadn't been giving our relationship much thought, but it struck me then that what had really happened to us was that we'd gone back to being good friends and partners in crime, as we'd been at college, a thought which made me smile.

'Hmmm?' he said.

'I was just thinking, Alston's full of nice people. There's that lovely woman at the antique shop, and all the bods at the whole-food collective. I feel as if I've already got friends.'

'It's true. You're fitting in, all right. If I dropped dead tomorrow, you'd still have reasons to be here.'

'Oh, Martin.'

'Face it, darling. Life is uncertain. That's why it's important to have fun.'

The thought stayed with me when I went back to London. I wasn't expecting the next bit to be any fun at all, which is just as well because it wasn't.

It got hotter and hotter as I drove south. I often find myself thinking that something most peculiar has happened to the weather. We used to get real, baking heat in July and August from time to time, but never these airless Septembers where one still sleeps with the window open and a single blanket on the bed. We don't have proper winters any more, either, which means that summer is a constant battle against aphids and whitefly, to say nothing of snails and slugs.

As I swung the car into the Green, I realised that we were being visited by one of West London's more surreal manifestations; a sizeable flock of feral parakeets which seems to move in some

kind of definite circuit; David and Karen tell me they pass through
Ealing a couple of times a year. The bright little birds were perched
about in trees and bushes, chattering happily, while visitors were
stopping to take photographs. They're attractive, but I am not fond
of them. I think I might like them a bit more were it not the case
that the London house sparrow is just about extinct. It's not that
I blame the budgies, it's just that even in the natural world, the
London I knew is being replaced by something else, and when I
think about it, it makes me sad.

I rang up Reed's, the Cumbrian estate agents, and organised for
a surveyor to go over Crow Ghyll. I got the report about ten days
later, and read it very carefully. In the course of sorting out the house
on the Green, we had found out from bitter experience about more
or less everything that an old house can think of to do. I gave close
attention to everything the report had to say about wood, which was
on the whole encouraging. There were patches of rot in some
window-sills and bottom rails; that's not deadly. Almost none of the
windows still had functioning sash-cords, which was a nuisance but
nothing more; they are very expensive to remake, but one can at a
pinch live with propping them open. The message which was coming
through loud and clear was structural soundness. The roof timbers
were healthy, thank God, and the fireplaces worked; I had become
aware that capping off ours hadn't been in the interests of the long-
term health of the house, though we'd been advised to do it at the
time. I wondered if David and Karen would think of restoring them,
but I suspected that the basic messiness of open fires, birds falling
down the chimneys, sweeps, etcetera, was something they wouldn't
want to make time for. In any case, they would be deaf to any suggestions of mine, though doubtless they'd leap to do it if George and
Harriet told them it was a good idea.

I thought about the report for a while, while I pottered in the
garden and did my shopping. Then I rang my solicitor and
instructed him to put in an offer. After that, I rang David and left
a message saying that I thought I'd found somewhere at last. He
rang the bell at about half past six.

'Mum, that's wonderful news! Show me. Where is it?' He had
the decency not to ask 'How much?'. Bless him.

'It's in Alston,' I said.

He misunderstood me. 'God, Mum. Are you sure? I didn't know you were looking in the East End! Won't you find it a bit rough?'

'Not Dalston, darling. Alston, in Cumbria.'

I've often heard people talk about jaws dropping, but in the course of a long life, I had never actually seen it. David looked as if someone had suddenly hit him between the shoulderblades with something heavy.

'Where the fuck is Alston?' he demanded.

'David!'

'Sorry, Mum.'

I had to some extent anticipated this, so I got out my road atlas, and showed him on the route-planner map.

'But it's the middle of nowhere!'

'No, David. It's the middle of somewhere, and that's quite different.'

'Oh, for crying out loud. Look, if you've somehow got fixated on that part of the world, why not the Lake District? Ambleside, maybe. I'm sure you could get a nice little place which'd hold its value.'

'Well, among other reasons, because I'm tired of being mown down by mobs of tourists every time I set foot outside my door.'

He pinched the bridge of his nose. 'Have you even been there?' he demanded.

'Yes, of course. I've been up there about five times.'

'Without telling me?'

'David, why *should* I tell you? I'm perfectly capable of driving to Alston all by myself. You're a busy man, you don't want to listen to me yattering on about my little week.'

I did feel, at that moment, that I was behaving very badly, because he looked completely betrayed, as if he'd found his wife in bed with another man.

'But you never go anywhere,' he said.

'Now listen, David. I loved your father very much. And when he died, part of me died too. A lot of people were very kind to me at that time, and what you all said was, you have to start thinking of life in a different way, and explore different sides of your person-

223

ality, perhaps aspects that you haven't had a chance to develop before, isn't that right?' I was quoting. Karen is a great one for 'moving on', she'd tried very hard to make me see, even at the funeral, that losing one's husband after forty-three years is potentially a key opportunity for personal growth. I wondered if he remembered that. 'It's taken me a little while, you know, but I have.'

'I think you've gone mad.'

'That's just rude and silly.'

'But you'll never see the boys. Don't you care about them?'

'Aren't you ever going to ask me to stay?' At that, he had the grace to look singularly foolish. There was a subtext here, I suspected, which was, we'd been counting on you for babysitting at a moment's notice.

'You could come up and see me,' I persisted. 'It's very nice up there, and I'll have three bedrooms. I'll put bunk-beds in the second spare room, and there'll be plenty of room for all four of you. No one *makes* you go to Lanzarote.'

'Don't be ridiculous. But Mum, what are you going to *do*? All your friends are here!'

'You weren't thinking about that when you started trying to heave me out,' I said.

'I meant West London.'

'Did you? You know very well it's out of sight, out of mind. The Green'll put me on their Christmas card lists, but how long d'you think they'll really remember I even exist?'

'What about Uncle Bob and Auntie Emily?'

'David, the truth is, they were your father's friends, really. Haven't you noticed that I haven't seen hide or hair of them since the funeral? And Piers is in France, and Tony's dead. Name three other people I know in London, outside the Green. You don't know very much about me, darling. You've just taken my life for granted.'

'I just can't get my head round this,' he said.

'I can see it's been a bit of a shock.'

'Look, I'm going home, before I lose my temper. I'll see you.' He got up, and banged his way out; I heard the door slam. It was quite like old times.

The next thing, of course, was that David and Karen found

themselves a babysitter, and came round in committee the following evening.

'Okay,' said David grimly, 'tell us the worst.'

'I have found my ideal house,' I said.

'But it's in Alston,' said Karen.

'Yes?'

'I looked Alston up on the Net,' she said.

Computers are beyond me. 'What did it say?' I asked with interest.

'Look, the key thing is I checked out property prices, and stuff's worth nothing up there. It's so remote, there's no chance there'll ever be an upturn. It'd be throwing money away, Alice.'

'Hardly that,' I said, 'it's just that you won't make a huge juicy profit.'

'But you've got to think about the investment aspect,' she protested. 'Be sensible. You can't expect us to subsidise you without a decent return.'

'No, Karen, dear. I have to think about having a life. *You* want to think about the investment aspect. But if I'm giving up this house, which is quite possibly hitting the two million mark this very week, I honestly think you can spare me a hundred and fifty.'

'But it's already ours,' she said.

'Cool it, Kay,' said David, who was looking thoroughly uncomfortable. 'You can't look at it like that.'

Karen flushed; it was always a bit difficult to tell what was going on under all that make-up, but you could see the ugly redness on her neck.

'David, we've got the boys to think of,' she said.

'How much thinking about do they need?' I asked. 'In that sense, I mean. If you've got a hugely valuable house, and dear old Granny's stumping up the school fees, the only remaining problem is that when you're having to launch them into the world, you'll have to release a bit of equity. Or is there something I'm missing here? It seems to me that Geoff and I have done a great deal of thinking about them already.'

'Well, so how much is this tip of yours?' she demanded, rather rudely, I thought.

'About a hundred, but it needs doing up. It's got open fires and no proper cooker and the wiring's unsafe, so I'm going to need a hundred and fifty.'

'Christ, that's just throwing good money after bad!' Karen exploded.

I was beginning get to angry myself by then. 'It's less than you're expecting to get from Carlyle Road. I need the extra money to consolidate the place and bring it up to habitable. And I've a very shrewd notion you're planning to spend rather more than that on getting this place to your liking.'

'That's because you wrecked it,' she snarled.

'There's only one bathroom,' David hastily added, in mitigation.

I just looked at him, my child who had never lived in a house where there was a bath rota, and you had your designated weekly hour. He wilted just a little under my stare, confused, angry and miserable.

'I need to put in heating, David, or I'll die. It's not quite the same thing.'

'Alice, we're not going to let you do this,' said Karen. 'You're not being sensible.'

I blew my top at that point. 'Sensible! And just exactly where has being sensible got me? Ignored, and patronised, and treated like an idiot! One. If you try and throw me out of here, I'll fight you every inch of the way. Two. I can force you to buy me this place, because you've given me the power to act. But if you won't make it up to a hundred and fifty, I'll have to cash in the boys' trust fund and use that.'

'You can't.'

'Oh, yes I can. We all know Geoff set it up to pay the boys' school fees, but it's my name on the documents, not yours. I'm the only surviving signatory, so I can break it and recover the capital, and if I have to, I will.'

'For fuck's sake, why are we fighting like this?' David was abruptly in tears, to my astonishment. It's so horrible watching an adult man cry, even if you don't love him; Karen and I both lost the thread and sat there goggling at him while he sobbed. I was completely appalled.

It only went on for a minute or two, but it felt like forever. He scrabbled for a handkerchief, wiped his face and blew his nose. 'I give up,' he said. 'Shut up, Kay,' he added, as she showed signs of speaking. 'You've turned me into some kind of monster in your mind. What's got into you?'

I was very near tears myself. I felt so sorry for him, harried as he was, and I couldn't bring myself to say that his behaviour, viewed from my perspective, really *was* monstrous. 'We all need to calm down,' I said. 'I'm sorry you're not seeing my point of view. But I need to have some kind of a life, and all you can think of is tidying me out of the way.'

'Why are you doing this?' he demanded.

'David, do you know where I come from?' I asked. 'I know I'm going off annoyingly at a tangent, the way I do, but bear with me for this once.'

'Kent,' he answered automatically.

'Actually, no. It was Geoff who was from Kent.'

'So d'you come from Alston?' he asked, bewildered.

I don't actually. My mother was pure London as far back as anyone knew, and my dad was ultimately Scottish, via Peterborough, where he was brought up. I didn't answer David directly.

'Do you know where I went to college?' I asked.

'Of course not. Look, Mum. What're you getting at?'

'Just this. What do you know about me? You don't know where I'm from.' I followed up my advantage. 'You don't know anything about me before I married your father. It wasn't the only life I could have had, you know. The fact of the matter is, I'm picking up some old threads.'

'I can't take much more of this,' David said. 'All right. Have it your own way. We'll get you your hundred and fifty.'

'David!' said Karen, very sharply.

'Kay, Alice is my mother, even if she's trying to divorce me. Just stay out of this.'

I was cut to the heart that he saw it in that light, but I was proud of him. There'd been a tiny moment of compunction, even if there wasn't any sympathy.

'Thank you, David, darling,' I said. 'I don't really expect you to understand.' Which is not quite true. I expected him to understand very well in about thirty years' time, the day his twins turned into cold-eyed strangers, if London hadn't killed him by then.

When they left, I felt absolutely shattered. I went and poured myself a large gin, and the cats zoomed in to comfort me. They hadn't liked the atmosphere, clearly, and had made themselves scarce while the children were still there. I suspected that David and Karen would be arguing all the way home, if not far into the night, and I felt rather sorry for David. I thought he would stick to his guns. He's his father's son in all kinds of ways, good as well as bad. I was sorry I'd caused him so much pain, but there are moments when men's absolute lack of curiosity about their female belongings becomes unbearable. I was hurt, too, by the way I'd discovered that I seemed to be a Mum-shaped blank in his mind. I'd told him the odd story about my early life, of course I had, but it seemed that he'd never troubled to remember any of them. Yet he knew quite a bit about his father's family.

I rang Martin the next day when I was a bit less upset, and sobbed on his shoulder. All he said was, 'It's time you left London.'

Nobody else had made an offer on Crow Ghyll, so things went through fairly quickly. But it still all takes a while, so I actually exchanged at the beginning of January. I didn't want to move then, of course, it wasn't sensible, so with Martin's help, I arranged for the basic work to be done on the house before I actually went up myself. The plan was that the cats and I would finally be moving out of Kew on the twenty-fifth of March, which someone once told me people used to think was the date the world was created. I liked the thought of that, which is just as well, because otherwise, the prospect was anything but pleasing. Bacon and Shakespeare associated the car with the vet's, and habitually howled without drawing breath from the moment they were put in their baskets. I was having a completely miserable time, and barely on speaking terms with my own son. Everything was getting so difficult and nasty that I fervently wished I'd never got myself into this mess.

I went up to Alston again late in February, after Martin had rung to tell me there was a break in the weather. I rang the AA and double-checked the forecast before I set out, but there wasn't a problem. In fact, there wasn't that much snow; I'd thought that the A686 might be much worse than it actually was, given the snow-poles which marked much of its length, but it wasn't a very bad winter, apparently, because it was perfectly drivable. Even so, it was a lot more winter than I'd seen for quite a while.

I stopped the car at the highest point, Hartside Height, where there's a viewing station, and looked out over the long slope of the Eden Valley. It was a landscape of white and grey in February, under a chilly sky, snow lying thinly on the moors, and banked-up on the windward side of the drystone walls; the distance was a heavy, slaty-blue, fading into cloud. Rather frightening, but beautiful. My world, now.

Coming into Alston itself, I finally understood the way the town turned its back to the hills and wound itself into nooks and crannies. One was grateful for shelter. At Crow Ghyll itself, I found the plumber and electrician were packing up to go, reasonably enough since it was just on five. They had been getting on nicely, and the wiring and the heating were just about organised. Of course, it wasn't a very complicated house. They were both charming personalities, with a slightly old-hippie, marijuana-using air, friends of Martin's, inevitably. It was nice to think that I was coming to live somewhere where tradesmen could be trusted. Apart from my old friend Mr Bryce, who'd been doing the building work on my house for decades, there was nobody else that I'd had in for anything who'd do a day's work without being stood over.

I was staying with Martin while the work was in progress, so after I'd talked to Mr Catton and Mr Hesketh, I went up to Garden Gorillas. The nursery made me think of wartime films; very monochrome, the polytunnels, opaque and grey with frost, looked like Nissen huts, and everything was tidy, bleak and bare. Most of the stuff which was overwintering outside was protected from the wind, mysterious sacking bundles like furled sails or flags; one sensed that every plant was dormant, all that rampant energy in temporary suspension, frozen into stillness.

Martin brought my bags in, and made me a cup of tea. The stove was lit, filling the ugly room with warmth, and Jeff the Mutt lay flat on his side in front of it, dozing on a rag rug. He looked a bit like a rug himself, one of those Greek flotaki things, or is it flokati? 'Well, darling,' Martin said, 'How's it looking?'

'Vastly encouraging. I've been bracing myself, of course, but it's miles further on than I'd let myself hope.'

'They're good blokes, and they know what they're doing. Kev Catton plays guitar in a folk-rock outfit called Dolmen, by the way. They're not too bad, actually. We'll catch them at the Blue Bell next summer.'

'That'll be nice,' I said, and found that I was in tears.

'What's up, Alice?'

'I was just wondering if I'd ever see David again, once all this is over.'

'Could be you won't,' observed Martin uncomfortingly.

'He's trying to punish me for upsetting Karen.'

'Alice, I haven't met your son, but I've heard plenty about him. He's a dickhead.'

I was angered at once, and wanted to rush to his defence, but thought better of it. 'I've just realised I was about to open my mouth and try and convince you it's somehow not his fault,' I confessed. 'It's the really appalling thing about being a mother. He did try and see my point of view for a while, but it was so much easier for him not to.'

We sat in silence for a while, and I finished my tea. 'D'you think we could go out and visit my cuttings, while there's still some light?' I asked.

''Course.' I put my coat back on, Martin shrugged into his old donkey-jacket, and we went outside.

'The only person who's really sorry I'm going away, I mean, for myself, is Ludmila,' I told him. 'It makes me so sad.'

'In the end, you've just got to be yourself.'

'Not when you're somebody's Mum.'

'No? Well, you could've gone and lived in Riverside Whatsits and babysat your grandchildren. Why didn't you?'

'To be absolutely honest, Martin, because I didn't think he'd be like this about it. If I'd known he'd stop speaking to me, I'd never have dared to go my own way.'

Martin pushed open the door of the polytunnel where he kept

my stuff, and we went inside. It had a cold, vegetable smell. He flicked on the striplights. 'Well, he has. You've just got to go on from where you've got to. There are such things as mid-life crises, after all. He's not necessarily stuck with being a dickhead for ever. Which reminds me. I've got a present for your daughter-in-law.' He left me, and went back to the house. I looked at my cuttings, which were shaping up into nice little plants, and showed no sign of the dreaded mildew. One thing about icy winds, you don't have to worry too much about air circulation. Nearly everything had taken, and I was going to have more than I could use, especially given that I was planning to bring some stuff with me. If Karen wanted four-foot high box obelisks, she'd have to buy them. 'Shut your eyes and hold out your hands,' he said, when he came back a minute or two later.

I did as I was told, and felt something in my palm. Smooth, rounded and quite heavy, seeds, of course. I looked at them. 'What are they?'

'*Pueraria montana*. It has strongly-scented purple flowers in late summer. Very attractive, and edible, I'm told.'

'I've never heard of it. Has it got another name?'

He gave me an innocent stare. 'Kudzu.'

'Oh, my God. I can't possibly seed the garden with kudzu!'

'But London's practically tropical these days,' he said, affecting not to understand. 'It'll do fine.'

'Look, Martin, there are limits.' I was appalled.

He put his hand out for the seeds. I gave them back to him, and he poured them into a little brown envelope. 'I got in touch with a friend in Louisiana,' he explained.

'I'm sure it can't be legal to export the stuff,' I said, and realised that I must sound idiotic, since when did Martin ever fret about legality?

He shrugged.

'What does it do, anyway?' I asked.

'It produces the aforementioned purple flowers. It was introduced as a decorative, you know, and it is. Only it grows at a rate of a foot a day in optimal conditions, and develops a six-foot tap root. It needs mild winters, hot summers, and plenty of rain, and if it gets them, it's quite capable of climbing the Kew Pagoda.'

'Oh, my goodness. One just can't. How d'you kill it?'

'You need to destroy the tap root.'

'But that'd mean digging up half the garden! Martin, I think you're absolutely awful.'

'This is from a woman who planted a *Rosa filipes* 'Kiftsgate' in a suburban garden? You can cry if you like, darling. It gets a girl out of those awkward moments.'

I'd seldom felt less like crying. 'No wonder I didn't marry you. You're completely irresponsible. You were rotten husband material.'

'I never asked you,' he pointed out. He took the envelope back out of his pocket, and licked the flap carefully. Then he sealed it down, making a careful, thorough job of it. I watched his stubby brown hands, hypnotised. When he was absolutely sure he'd got it completely secured, he tossed it into my lap.

'Put it in your handbag, darling. You don't have to use them.'

I suppose I could've thrown it away, but I found that somehow I'd slipped it into my pocket.

Martin was holding out his hand to me. 'Come on, Alice. Put it all behind you and forget it. Let's go and cultivate your garden.'